The Veiled
Detective

The Veiled Detective

David Stuart Davies

ROBERT HALE · LONDON

© David Stuart Davies 2004
First published in Great Britain 2004

ISBN 0 7090 7579 0

Robert Hale Limited
Clerkenwell House
Clerkenwell Green
London EC1R 0HT

2 4 6 8 10 9 7 5 3

Typeset in 10/14pt New Century Schoolbook
by Derek Doyle & Associates in Liverpool.
Printed in Great Britain by
St Edmundsbury Press Ltd, Bury St Edmunds, Suffolk.
Bound by Woolnough Bookbinding Ltd.

*This book is dedicated to the memory of
my dear friend, Tony Howlett*

'I never get your limits, Watson. There are unexplored possibilities about you.'

Sherlock Holmes in *The Sussex Vampire*

Chapter One

Afghanistan, the evening of 27 June 1880

The full moon hovered like a spectral observer over the British camp. The faint cries of the dying and wounded were carried by the warm night breeze out into the arid wastes beyond. John Walker staggered out of the hospital tent, his face begrimed with dried blood and sweat. For a moment he threw his head back and stared at the wide expanse of starless sky as if seeking an answer, an explanation. He had just lost another of his comrades. There were now at least six wounded men whom he had failed to save. He was losing count. And, by God, what was the point of counting in such small numbers anyway? Hundreds of British soldiers had died that day. Slaughtered by the Afghan warriors. They had been outnumbered, outflanked and routed by the forces of Ayub Khan in that fatal battle at Maiwand. These cunning tribesmen had truly rubbed the Union Jack into the desert dust. Nearly a third of the company had fallen. It was only the reluctance of the Afghans to carry out further carnage that had prevented the British troops from being completely annihilated. Ayub Khan had his victory. He had made his point. Let the survivors report the news of his invincibility.

For the British, a ragged retreat was the only option. They withdrew into the desert, to lick their wounds and then to limp back to Candahar. They had had to leave their dead littering the bloody scrubland, soon to be prey to the vultures and vermin.

Walker was too tired, too sick to his stomach to feel anger, pain or frustration. All he knew was that when he trained to be a doctor, it had been for the purpose of saving lives. It was not to watch young men's pale, bloody faces grimace with pain and their eyes close gradually as life ebbed away from them, while he stood by, helpless, gazing at a gaping wound spilling out intestines.

He needed a drink. Ducking back into the tent, he grabbed his medical bag. There were still three wounded men lying on makeshift beds in there, but no amount of medical treatment could save them from the grim reaper. He felt guilty to be in their presence. He had instructed his orderly to administer large doses of laudanum to help numb the pain until the inevitable overtook them.

As Walker wandered to the edge of the tattered encampment, he encountered no other officer. Of course, there were very few left. Colonel MacDonald, who had been in charge, had been decapitated by an Afghan blade very early in the battle. Captain Alistair Thornton was now in charge of the ragged remnants of the company of the Berkshire regiment, and he was no doubt in his tent nursing his wound. He had been struck in the shoulder by a jezail bullet which had shattered the bone.

Just beyond the perimeter of the camp, Walker slumped down at the base of a skeletal tree, resting his back against the rough bark. Opening his medical bag, he extracted a bottle of brandy. Uncorking it, he sniffed the neck of the bottle, allowing the alcoholic fumes to drift up his nose. And then he hesitated.

Something deep within his conscience made him pause. Little did this tired army surgeon realize that he was facing a decisive moment of Fate. He was about to commit an act that would alter the course of his life for ever. With a frown, he shook the vague dark unformed thoughts from his mind and returned his attention to the bottle.

The tantalizing fumes did their work. They promised comfort and oblivion. He lifted the neck of the bottle to his mouth and took a large gulp. Fire spilled down his throat and raced through his senses. Within moments he felt his body ease and relax, the inner tension melting with the warmth of the brandy. He took another gulp, and the effect increased. He had found an escape from the heat, the blood, the cries of pain and the scenes of slaughter. A blessed escape. He took another drink. Within twenty minutes the bottle was empty and John Walker was floating away on a pleasant, drunken dream. He was also floating away from the life he knew. He had cut himself adrift and was now heading for stormy, unchartered waters.

As consciousness slowly returned to him several hours later, he felt a sudden, sharp stabbing pain in his leg. It came again. And again. He forced his eyes open and bright sunlight seared in. Splinters of yellow light pierced his brain. He clamped his eyes shut, embracing the darkness once more. Again he felt the pain in his leg. This time, it was accompanied by a strident voice: 'Walker! Wake up, damn you!'

He recognized the voice. It belonged to Captain Thornton. With some effort he opened his eyes again, but this time he did it more slowly, allowing the brightness to seep in gently so as not to blind him. He saw three figures standing before him, each silhouetted against the vivid blue sky of an Afghan dawn. One of them was kicking his leg viciously in an effort to rouse him.

'You despicable swine, Walker!' cried the middle figure, whose left arm was held in a blood-splattered sling. It was Thornton, his commanding officer.

Walker tried to get to his feet, but his body, still under the thrall of the alcohol, refused to co-operate.

'Get him up,' said Thornton.

The two soldiers grabbed Walker and hauled him to his feet. With his good hand, Thornton thrust the empty brandy bottle before his face. For a moment, he thought the captain was going to hit him with it.

'Drunk on duty, Walker. No, by God, worse than that. Drunk while your fellow soldiers were in desperate need of your attention. You left them . . . left them to die while you . . . you went to get drunk. I should have you shot for this – but shooting is too good for you. I want you to live . . . to live with your guilt.' Thornton spoke in

11

tortured bursts, so great was his fury.

'There was nothing I could do for them,' Walker tried to explain, but his words escaped in a thick and slurred manner. 'Nothing I could—'

Thornton threw the bottle down into the sand. 'You disgust me, Walker. You realize that this is a court martial offence, and believe me I shall make it my personal duty to see that you are disgraced and kicked out of the army.'

Words failed Walker, but it began to sink in to his foggy mind that he had made a very big mistake – a life-changing mistake.

London, 4 October 1880

'Are you sure he can be trusted?' Arthur Sims sniffed and nodded towards the silhouetted figure at the end of the alleyway, standing under a flickering gas lamp.

Badger Johnson, so called because of the vivid white streak that ran through the centre of his dark thatch of hair, nodded and grinned.

'Yeah. He's a bit simple, but he'll be fine for what we want him for. And if he's any trouble . . .' He paused to retrieve a cut-throat razor from his inside pocket. The blade snapped open, and it swished through the air. 'I'll just have to give him a bloody throat, won't I?'

Arthur Sims was not amused. 'Where d'you find him?'

'Where d'you think? In The Black Swan. Don't you worry. I've seen him in there before – and I seen him do a bit of dipping. Very nifty he was, an' all. And he's done time. In Wandsworth. He's happy to be our crow for just five sovereigns.'

'What did you tell him?'

'Hardly anything. What d'you take me for? Just said we were cracking a little crib in Hanson Lane and we needed a lookout. He's done the work before.'

Sims sniffed again. 'I'm not sure. You know as well as I do he ought to be vetted by the Man himself before we use him. If something goes wrong, we'll *all* have bloody throats . . . or worse.'

Badger gurgled with merriment. 'You scared, are you?'

'Cautious, that's all. This is a big job for us.'

'And the pickin's will be very tasty, an' all, don't you worry. If it's cautious you're being, then you know it's in our best interest that we have a little crow keeping his beady eyes wide open. Never mind how much the Man has planned this little jaunt, *we're* the ones putting our heads in the noose.'

Sims shuddered at the thought. 'All right, you made your point. What's his name?'

'Jordan. Harry Jordan.' Badger slipped his razor back into its special pocket and flipped out his watch. 'Time to make our move.'

Badger giggled as the key slipped neatly into the lock. 'It's hardly criminal work if one can just walk in.'

Arthur Sims gave his partner a shove. 'Come on, get in,' he whispered, and then he turned to the shadowy figure standing nearby. 'OK, Jordan, you know the business.'

Harry Jordan gave a mock salute.

Once inside the building, Badger lit the bull's-eye lantern and consulted the map. 'The safe is in the office on the second floor at the far end, up a spiral staircase.' He muttered the information, which he knew by heart anyway, as if to reassure himself now that theory had turned into practice.

The two men made their way through the silent premises, the thin yellow beam of the lamp carving a way through the darkness ahead of them. As the spidery metal of the staircase flashed into view, they spied an obstacle on the floor directly below it. The inert body of a bald-headed man.

Arthur Sims knelt by him. 'Night-watchman. Out like a light. Very special tea he's drunk tonight.' Delicately, he lifted the man's eyelids to reveal the whites of his eyes. 'He'll not bother us now, Badger. I reckon he'll wake up with a thundering headache around breakfast-time.'

Badger giggled. It was all going according to plan.

Once up the staircase, the two men approached the room containing the safe. Again Badger produced the keyring from his pocket and slipped a key into the lock. The door swung open with ease. The bull's-eye soon located the imposing Smith–Anderson safe, a huge impenetrable iron contraption that stood defiantly in the far corner of the room. It was as tall as a man and weighed somewhere around three tons. The men knew from experience that the only way to get into this peter was by using the key – or rather the keys. There were five in all required. Certainly it would take a small army to move the giant safe, and God knows how much dynamite would be needed to blow it open, an act that would create enough noise to reach Scotland Yard itself.

Badger passed the bull's-eye to his confederate, who held the beam steady, centred on the great iron sarcophagus and the five locks. With another gurgle of pleasure, Badger dug deep into his trouser pocket and pulled out a brass ring containing five keys, all cut in a different manner. Scratched into the head of each key was a number – one that corresponded with the arrangement of locks on the safe.

Kneeling down in the centre of the beam, he slipped in the first key. It turned smoothly, with a decided click. So did the second. And the third. But the fourth refused to budge. Badger cast a worried glance at his confederate, but neither man spoke. Badger withdrew the key and tried again, with the same result. A thin sheen of sweat materialized on his brow. What the hell was wrong here? This certainly wasn't in the plan. The first three keys had been fine. He couldn't believe the Man had made a mistake. It was unheard of.

'Try the fifth key,' whispered Arthur, who was equally perplexed and worried.

In the desperate need to take action of some kind, Badger obeyed. Remarkably, the fifth key slipped in easily and turned smoothly, with the same definite click as the first three. A flicker of hope rallied Badger's dampened spirits and he turned the handle of the safe. Nothing happened. It would not budge. He swore and sat back on his haunches. 'What the hell now?'

'Try the fourth key again,' came his partner's voice from the darkness.

Badger did as he was told and held his breath. The key fitted the

14

aperture without problem. Now his hands were shaking and he paused, fearful of failure again.

'Come on, Badger.'

He turned the key. At first there was some resistance, and then . . . it moved. It revolved. It clicked.

'The bastards,' exclaimed Arthur Sims in a harsh whisper. 'They've altered the arrangement of the locks so they can't be opened in order. His nibs ain't sussed that out.'

Badger was now on his feet and tugging at the large safe door. 'Blimey, it's a weight,' he muttered, as the ponderous portal began to move. 'It's bigger than my old woman,' he observed, his spirits lightening again. The door creaked open with magisterial slowness. It took Badger almost a minute of effort before the safe door was wide open.

At last, Arthur Sims was able to direct the beam of the lantern to illuminate the interior of the safe. When he had done so, his jaw dropped and he let out a strangled gasp.

'What is it?' puffed Badger, sweat now streaming down his face.

'Take a look for yourself,' came the reply.

As Badger pulled himself forward and peered round the corner of the massive safe door, a second lantern beam joined theirs.

'The cupboard is bare, I am afraid.'

The voice, clear, brittle and authoritative, came from behind them, and both felons turned in unison to gaze at the speaker.

The bull's-eye spotlit a tall young man standing in the doorway, a sardonic smile touching his thin lips. It was Harry Jordan. Or was it? He was certainly dressed in the shabby checked suit that Jordan wore – but where was the bulbous nose and large moustache?

'I am afraid the game is no longer afoot, gentlemen. I think the phrase is, "You've been caught red-handed." Now, please do not make any rash attempts to escape. The police are outside the building, awaiting my signal.'

Arthur Sims and Badger Johnson stared in dumbfounded amazement as the young man took a silver whistle from his jacket pocket and blew on it three times. The shrill sound reverberated in their ears.

*

Inspector Giles Lestrade of Scotland Yard cradled a tin mug of hot, sweet tea in his hands and smiled contentedly. 'I reckon that was a pretty good night's work.'

It was an hour later, after the arrest of Badger Johnson and Arthur Sims, and the inspector was ensconced in his cramped office back at the Yard.

The young man sitting opposite him, wearing a disreputable checked suit which had seen better days, did not respond. His silence took the smile from Lestrade's face and replaced it with a furrowed brow.

'You don't agree, Mr Holmes?'

The young man pursed his lips for a moment before replying. 'In a manner of speaking, it has been a successful venture. You have two of the niftiest felons under lock and key, and saved the firm of Meredith and Co. the loss of a considerable amount of cash.'

'Exactly.' The smile returned.

'But there are still questions left unanswered.'

'Such as?'

'How did our two friends come into the possession of the key to the building, to the office where the safe was housed – and the five all-important keys to the safe itself?'

'Does that really matter?'

'Indeed it does. It is vital that these questions are answered in order to clear up this matter fully. There was obviously an accomplice involved who obtained the keys and was responsible for drugging the night-watchman. Badger Johnson intimated as much when he engaged my services as lookout, but when I pressed him for further information, he clammed up like a zealous oyster.'

Lestrade took a drink of the tea. 'Now, you don't bother your head about such inconsequentialities. If there was another bloke involved, he certainly made himself scarce this evening and so it would be nigh on impossible to pin anything on him. No, we are very happy to have caught two of the sharpest petermen in London, thanks to your help, Mr Holmes. From now on, however,

16

it is a job for the professionals.'

The young man gave a gracious nod of the head as though in some vague acquiescence to the wisdom of the Scotland Yarder. In reality he thought that, while Lestrade was not quite a fool, he was blinkered to the ramifications of the attempted robbery, and too easily pleased at landing a couple of medium-size fish in his net, while the really big catch swam free. Crime was never quite as cut and dried as Lestrade and his fellow professionals seemed to think. That was why this young man knew that he could never work within the constraints of the organized force as a detective. While at present he was reasonably content to be a help to the police, his ambitions lay elsewhere.

For his own part, Lestrade was unsure what to make of this lean youth with piercing grey eyes and gaunt, hawk-like features that revealed little of what he was thinking. There was something cold and impenetrable about his personality that made the inspector feel uncomfortable. In the last six months, Holmes had brought several cases to the attention of the Yard which he or his fellow officer, Inspector Gregson, had followed up, and a number of arrests had resulted. What Sherlock Holmes achieved from his activities, apart from the satisfaction every good citizen would feel at either preventing or solving a crime, Lestrade could not fathom. Holmes never spoke of personal matters, and the inspector was never tempted to ask.

At the same time as this conversation was taking place in Scotland Yard, in another part of the city the Professor was being informed of the failure of that night's operation at Meredith and Co. by his number two, Colonel Sebastian Moran.

The Professor rose from his *chaise-longue*, cast aside the mathematical tome he had been studying and walked to the window. Pulling back the curtains, he gazed out on the river below him, its murky surface reflecting the silver of the moon.

'In itself, the matter is of little consequence,' he said, in a dark, even voice. 'Merely a flea-bite on the body of our organization. But there have been rather too many of these flea-bites of late. They are now beginning to irritate me.' He turned sharply, his eyes flashing with anger. 'Where lies the incompetence?'

Moran was initially taken aback by so sudden a change in the Professor's demeanour. 'I am not entirely sure,' he stuttered.

The Professor's cruelly handsome face darkened with rage. 'Well, you should be, Moran. You should be sure. It is your job to know. That is what you are paid for.'

'Well . . . it seems that someone is tipping the police off in advance.'

The Professor gave a derisory laugh. 'Brilliant deduction, Moran. Your public-school education has stood you in good stead. Unfortunately, it does not take a genius to arrive at that rather obvious conclusion. I had a visit from Scoular earlier this evening. Thank goodness there is *one* smart man on whom I can rely.'

At the mention of Scoular's name, Moran blanched. Scoular was cunning, very sharp and very ambitious. This upstart was gradually worming his way into the Professor's confidence, assuming the role of court favourite; consequently, Moran felt his own position in jeopardy. He knew there was no demotion in the organization. If you lost favour, you lost your life also.

'What did he want?'

'He wanted nothing other than to give me information regarding our irritant flea. Apparently, he has been using the persona of Harry Jordan. He's been working out of some of the East End alehouses, The Black Swan in particular, where he latches on to our more gullible agents, like Johnson and Sims, and then narks to the police.'

'What's his angle?'

Moriarty shrugged. 'I don't know – or at least Scoular doesn't know. We need to find out, don't we? Put Hawkins on to the matter. He's a bright spark and will know what to do. Apprise him of the situation and see what he can come up with. I've no doubt Mr Jordan will return to his lucrative nest at The Black Swan within the next few days. I want information only. This Jordan character must not be harmed. I just want to know all about him before I take any action. Do you think you can organize that without any slip-ups?'

Moran clenched his fists with anger and frustration. He should-n't be spoken to in such a manner – like an inefficient corporal with muddy boots. He would dearly have liked to wipe that sarcastic smirk off the Professor's face, but he knew that such a rash action would be the ultimate folly.

'I'll get on to it immediately,' he said briskly, and left the room.

The Professor chuckled to himself and turned back to the window. His own reflection stared back at him from the night-darkened pane. He was a tall man, with luxuriant black hair and angular features that would have been very attractive were it not for the cruel mouth and the cold, merciless grey eyes.

'Mr Jordan,' he said, softly addressing his own reflection, 'I am very intrigued by you. I hope it will not be too long before I welcome you into my parlour.'

Dawn was just breaking as Sherlock Holmes made his weary way past the British Museum and into Montague Street, where he lodged. He was no longer dressed in the cheap suit that he had used in his persona as Harry Jordan, but while his own clothes were less ostentatious, they were no less shabby. Helping the police as he did was certainly broadening his experience of detective work, but it did not put bread and cheese on the table or pay the rent on his two cramped rooms. He longed for his own private investigation – one of real quality. Since coming to London from university to make his way in the world as a consulting detective, he had managed to attract some clients, but they had been few and far between, and the nature of the cases – an absent husband, the theft of a brooch, a disputed will, and such like – had all been mundane. But, tired as he was, and somewhat dismayed at the short-sightedness of his professional colleagues at Scotland Yard, he did not waver in his belief that one day he would reach his goal and have a solvent and successful detective practice. And it needed to be happening soon. He could not keep borrowing money from his brother, Mycroft, in order to fund his activities.

He entered 14 Montague Street and made his way up the three flights of stairs to his humble quarters. Once inside, with some urgency he threw off his jacket and rolled up the sleeve of his shirt. Crossing to the mantelpiece, he retrieved a small bottle and a hypodermic syringe from a morocco leather case. Breathing heavily with anticipation, he adjusted the delicate needle before thrusting the sharp point home into his sinewy forearm, which was already dotted and scarred with innumerable puncture-marks. His long, white, nervous fingers depressed the piston, and he gave a cry of ecstasy as he flopped down in a battered armchair, a broad, vacant smile lighting upon his tired features.

Chapter Two

From the journal of John Walker

Captain Thornton was as good as his word in wanting to make me suffer. Once the remnants of the bloody company limped through the gates of the garrison at Candahar, I was thrown in gaol and, it seemed, forgotten about. I languished there for three months and, despite my daily protests to my native gaolers, no officer came to see me. I was kept in isolation in a cell that measured eight feet by eight feet. Some two feet above my head there was a grilled window which allowed only the faintest glimmers of daylight to filter through. My days were spent in a permanent twilight. I was being punished even before I came to trial.

I cannot tell how many times I relived the experience of that fateful night. It came to me unbidden in vivid scenes, as though I were an observer in my own downfall. There I was, leaving the hospital tent, the smell of blood and death clinging to me like an invisible miasma. The scene then shifted to the leafless tree under which I crouched and took my first taste of the brandy. My dry throat ached to taste that warm liquid again and experience the beauteous oblivion it brought. But I knew now that it brought ignominy and disgrace also. Was I really a coward? Was I really a deserter? Had I really neglected the men under my charge? The questions rattled and repeated in my brain like some awful machine. There is no inquisition more painful than that of your own making. Certainly I had been weak and lost some kind of faith that night. I had seen men, young men with smooth carefree faces, men who had not quite tasted life, mown down. The less fortunate, injured beyond help, were brought to me. And I had tried to mend the horrifically unmendable. Never had the futility of medicine in the face of cruel physical damage been made as clear and as painful to me as on that damnable night.

And then one day in late September, Thornton visited me in my cell. He looked fit and well and, apart from exhibiting a certain stiffness in his left arm, there was no indication that he had been injured at all. However, although he treated me with cold civility, the intervening months had done nothing to lessen his anger towards me. He informed me of the date of my court martial and advised me that my best course of action – 'the gentleman's way' was to offer up no defence. 'That way the matter can be dealt with swiftly, and you can be on your way home – and we in the British Army can be rid of you for good.'

I had no stomach left for a fight, and I was fully aware that whatever plea I put forward, and however convincing my defence, I was already branded guilty. I agreed to all his suggestions. Anything to say goodbye to the grey walls and isolation of the last three months. In my naïvety, I believed that once I had escaped from India, I would be able to pick up the pieces of my shattered life. Little did I realize at the time that the taint and the stench I carried with me because of my offence would follow me all the way to England.

London, October 1880

Sherlock Holmes moved to the window and scrutinized the piece of paper by daylight with his magnifying-glass. His fingers trembled with excitement. Here, he realized, he held in his hand the key to a real mystery at last. It was a terse, emotional cryptogram. And he was the only person capable of dealing with it. I have the genius, he told himself, which, as yet, has not really been put to the test. Maybe the time has come.

He suppressed the grin that was waiting to break through and, turning to face the bearer of the note, he offered his opinion.

'The message was written by a left-handed man – the curl of the "Ls" clearly indicates this – and although the paper is of cheap manufacture, the author was using a fountain pen, which is not usually found in the possession of those from the lower orders. The author wears a large ring on the fourth finger of his left hand: it has made tiny scratches on the surface of the paper.' He held the note to his nose and sniffed. 'There is a strong indication that whoever wrote this was in the habit of taking snuff – Moroccan in origin, I believe. I am afraid my knowledge of the types of snuff is still quite limited.'

With a theatrical flourish, he placed the note on the table by his chair and sat opposite the visitor, who, to his disappointment, did not seem impressed by his analysis.

'That's all very well, Mr Holmes,' came the querulous voice, 'but what about the message itself? What am I to do?' The speaker, who had introduced himself as Jonas Abercrombie, was a plump, middle-aged man, dressed in a smart city suit which boasted a carnation in the lapel. His face was pale with worry, and he continued to turn the brim of his hat around in his hands in a nervous, agitated fashion. He desperately needed *help*, not conjuring tricks. How could his dilemma be eased by the knowledge that the writer of that accursed note enjoyed taking snuff and was left-handed?

While Holmes was aware of the man's obvious distress, he was far more interested in the recherché elements of the case – by the mysteries locked up in the note. He was not conscious of his own naïvety or lack of sympathy in interviewing his client. And even if he had been, he would have regarded them as irrelevant. What was paramount was the thought that, at last, here was a real challenge for his talents.

Holmes picked up the note again and read it aloud: ' "We have your daughter. To ensure her safe return, we require a favour from you. We shall be in touch shortly. Do not go to the police." '

'I'm sure they mean to kill her. Oh, my God!'

'Why would they want to do that, Mr Abercrombie? What possible benefit could they gain from killing her?'

Abercrombie looked bewildered and shook his head. 'I don't know. But why abduct her in the first place?'

Sherlock Holmes gave a sigh of impatience. Could clients really be this dim?

'Because, Mr Abercrombie, you are the manager of the Portland Street branch of the City Bank. Therefore, it seems to me most likely that they intend to use your daughter as a bargaining-tool for something in return – something that will bring them a large amount of money.'

Abercrombie appeared genuinely shocked at this analysis. 'You mean . . . they plan to rob the bank.'

Yes, clients could be this dim.

'In a manner of speaking. At the present time, there is a lack of sufficient data to indicate what method they intend to use to extract the money that lodges in your vaults, but I am convinced they are relying on your assistance.'

The banker mopped his brow. 'What on earth am I to do?'

'Nothing for the time being. You must be patient and wait until they contact you again. As soon as they do, you must inform me immediately.'

'*Nothing*? How can I do nothing when they have my daughter?'

'Because I say so. If you do not trust me or my judgement, then pray seek your solace elsewhere!' It was a passionate response – but an unfeeling one. From the very beginning Holmes had trained himself to seal off all emotions when dealing with crime. He must be an automaton. At night sometimes he would hold a candle close to his face and stare into the mirror. The cold mask would stare back at him, a mask devoid of humanity or emotion. Even when he brought the candle-flame close to his face so that he could feel the fierce yellow tongue begin to singe his flesh. This pleased him. The precision and objectivity that he deemed as essential in solving crime could only be tainted by emotion.

He knew that, in speaking to Abercrombie as he had done, he was taking a risk. He had to keep this client, but it had to be on his terms, or there was no game.

Abercrombie's mouth gaped and he fell into silence.

'You sought my advice,' said Holmes, aware now that his cold bait was attractive, 'and I am giving it. We wait, and let the villains make the next move. Believe me, they are sailing uncharted waters. They will not do anything rash until they believe that their plan has failed. They want the money, rather than your daughter. Let me know as soon as you hear from them again.'

Abercrombie, defeated and bewildered, nodded.

'And should I need to get in touch with *you*?'

The question shook the banker as though he were awaking from some terrible dream. 'Please contact me at my home address. It might be dangerous to come to the bank.' Hurriedly, he extracted a card from his waistcoat pocket and passed it to the detective, who glanced at it, noting the address near Clapham Common.

'My daughter, Mr Holmes…'

'I am sure she will be safe, as long as you do as you're told and do not contact the police. Now, sir, for my benefit, in order for me to clarify the matter very clearly in my mind, I would appreciate it if you would describe once again the series of events that brought you to my door. And pray be precise.'

Abercrombie nodded. 'I will do my best. I received that accursed note this morning. I found it on the desk in my office at the bank. I don't know how it got there. I rushed home immediately to see if my daughter, Amelia, was safe. I am a widower, and she is my only treasure.' He dabbed at his eyes, which had begun to water.

Holmes nodded. 'And on your return you discovered that this treasure was missing.'

'The maid said that Amelia had received a note from me asking her to meet me for lunch, and had gone out straightaway.'

'You do not have that note?'

'No. I suppose she took it with her.'

'Did you often invite her to lunch in this manner?'

'Once or twice a month, yes.'

'So our villains must have been watching you for a while. Where do you take lunch?'

'At Carlo's, a little restaurant on Marylebone High Street. I went there at once, but of course the staff who know her assured me they hadn't seen her today.'

'Give me a description of your daughter, please.'

'She is tall, quite thin, has auburn hair, usually fastened in a bun. She is very short-sighted and wears glasses with powerful lenses. Blue eyes. A lovely girl.' Abercrombie turned away and blew heavily into his handkerchief.

'Do you know what clothes she was wearing?'

The banker shrugged. 'I think it would be a brown two-piece trimmed with fur, and a little hat with a veil. It is her favourite outfit.'

Holmes sat back in his chair and steepled his fingers. 'Well, I think that's all for now. It is imperative that you return to work and act as normally as you can. You must be patient and resolute, Mr Abercrombie. I am convinced that you will be contacted in due course. It is most probable that the villains will make you stew a little in order to weaken your resistance to whatever demands they intend to make on you. But I am confident that we shall bring this matter to a happy conclusion.'

'I hope so. I will do anything to see the safe return of my little girl.' Abercrombie rose, his eyes now red with tears, and grasped Sherlock Holmes by the hand. 'Thank you. Thank you. I don't know what I would have done without your help and assurance.'

Without another word, he left the room.

Sherlock Holmes smiled and rubbed his hands with glee. 'Ah, ah,' he said, in a hoarse whisper. 'At last, at last . . . the game's afoot.'

As Abercrombie emerged on to the pavement, he also gave himself a self-satisfied smile.

'Irving could not have done better,' he told himself.

The following day, there was an unfortunate incident at the Portland Street branch of the City Bank.

A disreputable-looking fellow in ragged clothes and reeking of alcohol claimed that he wished to open an account with a single sovereign. On being told by the teller that he could not do so with such a small sum of money, he became abusive and then violent. He fell into a drunken rage, throwing papers around, shouting and knocking potted palms to the floor. The manager, who was engaged with an important new client, was summoned, and he, in turn, summoned the police. The recalcitrant drunk was handcuffed and taken away. While all this was happening, no one seemed to take particular notice of an old, sunburned gentleman sitting in the corner by the window, smoking a dark cheroot and reading the *Financial Times* as though he were at his club.

That same evening, Abercrombie called once again on Sherlock Holmes. He found the young detective curled up in his chair before the meagre fire, smoking a cherrywood pipe. Although Holmes had been anticipating – indeed, hoping for – this visit, his bored expression gave none of his feelings away.

'I've heard from them again!' cried the banker, sloughing off his overcoat and joining Holmes by the fire.

'Excellent. Show me the note.'

Holmes almost snatched the envelope from Abercrombie's fingers. The note was written in the same fluid hand as before, but this time the message was much darker in tone.

'Bring ten thousand pounds in used bank-notes to Wayland's Wharf, off the India Dock Road, at midnight. Come alone. If we do not receive the money on time, we shall cut off the girl's foot,' he read.

'What am I to do? I don't have ten thousand pounds.'

'No, but your bank has.'

'But it's not my money. If I took that, I would be committing a crime!'

Holmes puffed gently on his pipe, his face partially obliterated for a moment by a thin cloud of smoke. 'On your last visit, you told me that you would do anything to ensure the safe return of your daughter.'

'So I would,' came the sullen reply. 'But I had not counted on robbing my own bank. I put my trust in you to save me from such an escapade.'

Holmes stroked his chin thoughtfully. 'Perhaps I can. Certainly it would be very dangerous for you to go to Wayland's Wharf on your own . . .'

'But if I don't, who knows what harm might come to Amelia?'

'Oh, *someone* should go – but it does not necessarily have to be you.'

Abercrombie shook his head in some bewilderment. 'I don't understand. Who. . . ?'

Holmes gave him a smug grin. 'Me, of course. I could easily go in your place. I am quite adept at disguise. It is one of the necessary talents of the modern detective. A little padding, your overcoat and hat and some judicious make-up, and I am sure that I could pass for you in a darkened street.'

'This is madness. What if they take you somewhere and you are detected? I will have lost my daughter *and* the money.'

Holmes rose from his chair and turned his back on his visitor. 'Either you trust me or not. There is still time to contact Scotland Yard.'

'I am not sure.'

Holmes turned round and leaned on the back of his chair so that the light from the grate threw his features into bas-relief. 'Do you really have an alternative?'

Abercrombie hesitated, his pale face a mask of pained indecision. 'Very well,' he said at length, the words emerging in a hoarse, emotional whisper.

'Then it is settled.'

'But what about the money?'

'No doubt the safe at the bank will hold ten thousand pounds?'

Abercrombie nodded.

'Then I shall have to steal it.'

'*You?*'

'If I am to deliver the cash, I might as well be the one to extract it, don't you think? No doubt you have the appropriate keys that will gain me access to the bank and to the safe?'

'Well, yes, but . . .'

'Good. I suggest you hand those over to me. Then you can draw me a map detailing the layout of the bank. I think you had better book yourself into a hotel for the night. You must not go home, in case the place is being watched.'

Abercrombie shook his head. 'This is all going too fast for me.'

'There is no need for you to understand every turn of the cog. Just draw me the map and then off you go to some hotel for the night. In the morning I shall have both your daughter and the money.'

'It would be a miracle if it were true.'

Holmes grimaced. 'Miracles are the work of God. I function at a more practical level.'

Some hours later, Sherlock Holmes, disguised as Abercrombie, let himself in to the side entrance of the Portland Street branch of the City Bank, using the key provided by his client. It was unusually warm for a late October evening, and in the heavy coat and the padding, Holmes was already beginning to perspire. His nerves tingled with excitement as he made his way noiselessly through the darkened premises towards the bank's strongroom safe. A wicked thought crossed his mind. Why not give up the ambition to be a private detective and just steal the money? Just take it and walk away. Ten thousand pounds could secure a very comfortable way of life for many years. Within twenty-four hours he could easily lose himself on the Continent. Europe was full of nooks and crannies where a man of wealth could live an anonymous and contented life. He grinned at this unbidden fancy. He was pleased with the surprising duality of his nature at times. Certainly, the ability to think like a criminal was an essential facility for a specialist in crime detection.

He paused by the strongroom door and opened the large carpet-bag he had brought with him. He consulted his watch. It was just before eleven o'clock. He had better set to work.

Twenty minutes later, the dark, muffled figure of a man turned the corner of Portland Street carrying a bulging carpet-bag. He seemed in a hurry and rather nervous. It was a misty night, and fragile grey tendrils clung to the figure as he moved swiftly down the street, his footfall like a sharp, rhythmic tattoo on the wet pavement.

On turning into Water Street, he espied a lonely cab meandering its way back to the depot. He hailed it, persuading the driver to take one last fare for the night. With an inarticulate grunt and a nod, the cabbie agreed and the man climbed aboard. But as he did so, two other figures materialized out of the shadows and also leapt into the cab.

'Hello, Mr Holmes,' said one of the men, his voice guttural and ill-educated. 'We believe you have a little bag for us.'

Holmes attempted to struggle, but he felt the barrel of a revolver thrust against his ribs.

'No amount of paddin' will stop one of these little beauties, if yer force me to pull the trigger, Mr Holmes. Now, our orders are not to hurt yer, unless you become uncooperative, like. So, just do as you're told and hand over the bag.'

The detective could not see the face of either of his assailants, but he was convinced the threat was a very real one. He released his grip on the carpet-bag.

'Good boy. And good-night!'

A bright light filled his vision as his brain exploded with a sudden sharp pain. His body turned to jelly and he flopped forward, unconscious, to the floor of the cab.

'Sweet dreams, Mr Holmes,' gurgled one of the assailants as they both pushed the detective's inert body from the cab, where it rolled into the gutter.

'Right, Harry,' one of the men called to the driver, 'mission accomplished. Set sail for the Professor's place!'

Chapter Three

From the journal of John Walker

I was despatched from India on the steamship *Orontes* in the January of 1881. My journey home was wretched. Although by now I was a 'civilian' and supposedly a 'free man', I carried with me the taint of my court martial. There had been reports in the newspapers, and it seemed to me that every face on board averted their gaze from mine. Their expressions told me that they knew who I was and what I had done. No doubt the heinous nature of my crime had grown in the telling and the retelling. I was a pariah dog: an outcast amongst my fellow countrymen.

I spent many long hours alone in my cramped cabin or leaning over the ship's rail staring at the dark turbulent waters below me, feeling wretched and very sorry for myself. More than once I contemplated how easy it would be to let myself slip over the side into that cold watery embrace and thus escape the painful reality of my situation. Soon I would land in London, that great cesspool into which all the idlers and loungers of the empire are irresistibly drained. There would be no friends or family waiting on the quayside waving in welcome. No one to help and cherish me; and with only my meagre savings for financial security, the future looked very bleak indeed. On the occasions when my grip eased on the handrail, as the heaving swell of the water beckoned enticingly, some instinct, some little voice within, pulled me back from acting upon these desperate thoughts.

However, one evening when we were just two days away from England, the prospect of watery oblivion was more than usually attractive. I had been snubbed in the dining-room by a fat northern businessman who told me in a loud, grating voice that he 'was not afraid to be blunt, sir' and that 'we don't want the likes of you attending our table.' This was the first time someone had actually voiced their feelings to me – and it was done in such a cruel and public way that I was speechless. I opened my mouth to respond, but no words came. I found the blood draining from my face as I beat a hasty retreat from the dining-room. Gasping for air, I leaned over the rail, feeling myself close to tears.

'You don't want to take any notice of that pompous windbag.'

I looked up and saw a tall, thin, handsome middle-aged man with a neatly trimmed moustache which was tinged with grey, as was the hair at his temples. He was dressed immaculately in a dinner suit which boasted several medals across the breast. He proffered an open silver cigarette-case.

'Have a smoke, old man, and you'll feel better.'

This time I really had to fight back the tears. My emotions were unfettered on a wild see-saw. After such harsh cruelty from the fat businessman, here now was the first gesture of kindness I had received for many months – and it came from someone who was obviously an officer and a gentleman.

Gingerly, I took a cigarette and gave a nod of thanks.

'That's the ticket. Watson, isn't it?'

'Walker. John Walker.'

'Of course.'

The 'of course' told me instantly that he knew all about me.

'Pleased to meet you.' He shook my limp hand. 'I'm Reed. Alexander Reed. Used to be Captain Reed. Once upon a time.'

I repeated his words. 'Used to be?'

Reed lit his own cigarette and grinned. It was a pleasant grin, which caused his taut sunburned face to splinter with numerous wrinkles. 'Same way as you used to be Assistant Surgeon to the

Fifth Northumberland Fusiliers.' The smile broadened.

So, Reed was a fellow outcast.

He blew out a stream of smoke, which was caught by the wind and disappeared into the darkness.

'Yes, Walker, old chap, my military masters disapproved of my dealings with the mess funds, I'm afraid. They probably would have been more sanguine about the matter if the blessed horse had won.' This time the smile became a laugh – a laugh so charming that it was infectious, and I found myself laughing along with him.

'That's the ticket, old fellow. First time I've seen you without a grimace or that black cloud you've been carrying around with you all the voyage. Oh, yes, I've been watching you. I like to keep an eye on kindred spirits. You see, I know what you're going through and what you're feeling. And that,' he nodded at the water below us, 'is certainly not the answer. I'm living proof that one not only *survives* such ignominy – but, one can prosper, too.'

I was dumbstruck by this stranger's revelations, but, at the same time, his words began to rekindle the spirit of hope and defiance that had been all but extinguished within me. He spoke with warmth and kindness, something I had not experienced for six months or more.

'Come to the bar, Walker. Let me buy you a drink. I think I can help you.'

Like the pied piper, he beckoned me and I followed. As we entered the bar, the fat northern businessman came in with his entourage, which included his equally large wife, who was smothered in a volu-minous velvet gown that made her look more than faintly ridiculous. My spirits had been so lightened by my new companion, that I gave them an irreverent light-hearted wave.

'The *nouveau riche* are always so vulgar, Walker, old feller. Give me old money every time,' Reed announced, loud enough to be over-heard. The fat businessman scowled at us with bulging eyes, and shepherded his wife to the further end of the bar.

'Now then, a brandy and soda?'

I shook my head. I had vowed never to touch the accursed brandy again as long as I lived. 'A seltzer will be fine.'

Reed groaned. 'Nonsense. I'm not going to sit here with a fellow officer while he sips a nursery-time drink. You've got to shake off the past. Defy it, my boy. You can't let it drag you down. This is a time for new beginnings.' He turned to the barman. 'Two large brandies with just a whisper of soda, there's a good chap.'

I shrugged my shoulders in defeat. I felt like a schoolboy in the charge of his forceful yet benevolent headmaster. Having obtained the drinks, my new acquaintance led me to a quiet table. He raised his glass and nodded that I should do the same. Again, I obeyed him. I smelt the brandy, the thick, sweet intoxicating smell, and once more I was back at the camp, sitting under that skeletal tree beneath a pale Afghan moon, my body weary and my mind numb. The night breeze ruffled my hair and my hand gripped the neck of the bottle. I closed my eyes momentarily to lose the vision.

I swirled the brandy round in the glass so that it produced a miniature whirlpool. If I cast it aside now; if I threw the drink away and returned to the medical tent; if . . .

My reverie was broken by Reed whispering in my ear. 'There's no going back, old boy. The only direction left is forward. So, drink up!'

The brandy caught the back of my throat and I spluttered.

Reed laughed. 'You'll soon get used to it again, Watson.'

I wiped my chin awkwardly. 'Walker,' I corrected him gently.

'Yes, I know, but somehow I see you as a Watson. Funny that, isn't it?'

Sherlock Holmes touched the tender lump on his scalp where he had been clubbed, and winced.

Observing him, Inspector Giles Lestrade could not resist a chuckle. 'Big as a quail's egg, and twice as unpleasant.' He laughed again, this time at his own weak conceit.

It was past midnight and the two men were sitting once more in Lestrade's office at Scotland Yard. Holmes had dispensed with his disguise, although his face was still smeared with faint traces of make-up.

'Well, Mr Holmes,' added Lestrade, sitting back in his chair, 'if you will play dodgy games, you must expect to end up with a few bruises.'

'I am not complaining, Inspector, just trying to establish the extent of the damage.'

'You'll live. A large headache for a while and a tender pate for a week, and then I reckon you'll be right as rain.'

'Thank you. I never knew you practised medicine as well as police work.'

Lestrade did not rise to the bait. 'We modern officers have many varied talents.'

Holmes allowed himself a thin smile. 'Well, apart from my quail's egg, as you put it, it has been a fairly successful night.'

'Certainly has – but a strange one. And I'm still not sure I understand this business fully.'

'If it is any consolation, I'm not sure I do either . . . yet. As I have told you before, it is as though someone has been testing me, trying to trick me.'

Lestrade shook his head. He was far from convinced. 'Why should anyone want to do that?'

'I don't know.'

'Rare words from you, if I may say so. Still, I must admit it has been a funny carry-on. All this business with the bogus bank manager – we got him, by the way, as he was leaving your digs. Real name: Ernest Brand, a villain with a theatrical flair.'

'Lot of theatricality, little flair,' observed Holmes as he lit a cigarette. 'He was working under orders, of course, as were the two characters who produced my cranial appendage.' He touched his lump again. 'Whoever planned this business knew a fair bit about me. He knows how my mind works.'

'Blimey,' cried Lestrade in surprise, 'he must be a blooming genius then!'

'He was certain that I would arrange to rob the bank for Abercrombie. That was an essential part of the plan.'

'Brand.'

'Yes. Thus, we have the rather nice arrangement where the detective carries out the work of the thieves for them. A wonderful irony.

35

Or at least that was how it would have been if the plan had worked.'

'Ah, but you got the better of them, Mr Holmes.'

'Did I?'

Lestrade frowned. 'Of course you did.'

Abstractly, Holmes examined the glowing end of his cigarette. 'Some aspects of the scheme were very clever, but there were too many weak elements.'

'Such as?'

'Did they never think I would check if Abercrombie really was the manager of the Portland Street branch of the City Bank, and if he had a daughter called Amelia whom he took to Carlo's restaurant for lunch? Or that I would visit his supposed address in Clapham?'

'*Did* you?'

Holmes gave an irritated sigh. 'Of course I did. One of the elementary rules of detective work is to check your sources of information to make sure that what you are being told is the truth. I had a very pleasant afternoon at the Portland Street branch of the City Bank, disguised as an old colonial. Not only did I manage to observe the real manager, but, as luck would have it, I also saw how the gang worked it so that they were able to get hold of the keys to the bank.'

Lestrade sat up. 'How's that?'

'Another set of performances was involved. One character pretends to be the rich client intent on opening a very large account. He's ushered into the manager's office. It is my experience that bank managers are very obsequious where wealthy men are concerned. The "client" is there long enough to take stock of the chamber and the strongroom. Then there is a commotion in the lobby of the bank, and the manager is called for . . .'

'Leaving our fellow behind in his office.'

'Precisely. Long enough for him to take all the details he needs and maybe even make some wax impressions of keys left behind by the flustered manager. Left alone for a short time, any experienced cracksman could easily acquire all the necessaries to carry out a job.'

'Very clever indeed.'

'Yes, and that's what leads me to my dilemma. What I cannot

understand is how the brain who conceived that part of the plan allowed the other loopholes to exist. They were stupid weaknesses which could easily have been remedied. Of course, such elements also muddied the waters somewhat. So, as I say, it is as though I was being put through some test to see how clever I am.'

'Well, if that is the case, you passed with flying colours.'

'Not quite. Two of the accomplices escaped, and I have a rather nasty trophy.' He indicated his wound.

'Sometimes, Mr Holmes, you appear to me to be more baffling than the crimes you investigate. It seems to me as a humble, practical, professional policeman, you have managed to scupper a very clever bank robbery where you, being used as a dupe, were supposed to do the job for the thieves. The rest is some weird concoction of your own making. I ask you seriously, Mr Holmes, who on earth would want to test you, as you call it, and give you a sort of exam to see how good a 'tec you are?'

'That is what *I* would really like to know.'

Professor James Moriarty stared at the carpet-bag, a faint smile touching his lips.

'I'm disappointed in Mr Sherlock Holmes,' he said softly. 'I never thought he'd let us get our hands on this.'

'He was bright enough to see through Brand's performance,' observed Colonel Sebastian Moran.

Moriarty gave a derisive chuckle. 'So, he has the talents of a second-rate drama critic. No, no, my dear Moran, I expected so much more of Mr Holmes. I expected incandescence. Still, it has been an interesting exercise.'

'Forgive me, Professor, but I cannot understand your interest in this man.'

'Of course not,' he sneered. 'You wouldn't. It's to do with the brain, Moran. There are individuals who, for one reason or another, are trapped in isolation in their lives. The poet, the pauper and the thinker -- the genius, if you like. I am not being immodest when I think of myself as a genius – after all, I am someone who has a supreme talent to conceive and organize a vast criminal establishment. I have the special intellectual abilities for this most refined and specialized of callings. There is no one like me. But it is a lonely position – when there is no one equal to you. No one on the same intellectual plane.' Moriarty turned to face Moran. 'That is no insult to you, my dear fellow. Insults are emotional barbs. What I am talking about here are cold facts. Imagine, then, when I perceived in this fellow Sherlock Holmes not only someone who was potentially on the same intellectual level as myself, but also someone whose pursuit was diametrically opposed to mine. How delicious! He was an opponent on a grand chessboard of law and order. What stimulating times I could have, working out plans and stratagems to challenge, confuse and beat this man. It would raise the game and give me that much-needed frisson that so often seems lacking in my life.'

'But he failed your first test.'

Moriarty threw his arm out towards the carpet-bag. 'Indeed, he did. He let us have the spoils.'

'Well, at least all your efforts were not in vain. We have ten thousand pounds.'

The Professor did not respond. Moran would never understand. What was a paltry ten thousand pounds against the opportunity to indulge in a battle of wits with an equal?

Moran opened the bag and dug his hand inside. 'Wait a minute!' he cried, his voice full of alarm and apprehension.

The Professor's eyes sparked with interest. 'What is it?'

Quickly, without a word, Moran turned the bag upside-down, tipping the contents on to the Professor's desk. Sheets of blank white paper spilled out – blank, that is, except for a single sheet that appeared to have writing on it. Deftly, Moriarty extracted this from the pile. Holding it close to the lamp on his desk, he read the sheet out loud: 'Sorry. SH.'

The Professor folded the sheet neatly and burst out laughing.

Chapter Four

From the journal of John Walker

Alexander Reed was the most charming and persuasive of companions, and by the time we were on to our third brandy I had not only told him the story of my life, but also had described in detail the battle of Maiwand and the terrible aftermath which had not only ended my military career, but, as I saw it, had blighted the rest of my life as well. He made little comment as I talked, merely nodding his head sympathetically from time to time and sometimes repeating facts so that he was sure that he understood them. Why he was so interested in my story I had no idea – then – but it was a wonderful tonic for me to be able to unburden myself, to unleash the misery and despair I had kept within me. In medical terms, I suppose it was a kind of therapy. Whatever it was, I felt somehow better when I had finished.

Reed remained silent for a while when I reached the end of my narrative, and stared meditatively into his drink. I wondered if I had made a fool of myself, and was on the brink of excusing myself in order to go to my cabin, when he turned to me with a sigh.

'You've certainly had a rough time, and I reckon you have been treated very unfairly. It can be a tough old world at times. Still, *nil desperandum,* as my old pater used to say when my school was being thrashed at cricket. You see, I think I can help you – or, to put it more precisely, I have friends who may be of assistance to you. Help you get on your feet again.'

'That's awfully kind, Reed, but I couldn't possibly accept any hand-outs.'

Reed laughed. 'My, what a noble fellow you are! Your principles would not allow it, eh?'

I nodded sheepishly. 'Something like that.'

'Well, then, you'll be pleased to hear that I was suggesting nothing of the sort. These friends . . . they may be able to offer you some kind of work.'

'What kind of work? As a doctor?'

My companion shrugged. 'I'm not sure. I can't be certain of anything exactly, but I expect that if I put a good word in for you, they could fix you up with something that would suit the both of you. It's a probability rather than a possibility, anyway. I do a little recruiting for them from time to time. Are you interested?'

It sounded very mysterious, and under normal circumstances I would have had strong reservations about accepting such a vague offer, but these were not normal circumstances. I had long forgotten what normal circumstances were. I was a drowning man and here was the proverbial straw. I clutched at it.

'I should be delighted if they could help.'

Reed beamed. 'Splendid. I'm being met off the boat by one of the friends I have just mentioned, a gentleman named Scoular. I shall introduce you to him and act as your sponsor. Then we shall take it from there, eh?'

'I don't know how I can thank you enough.'

Reed winked and raised his empty glass. 'Well, for a start, you could fill this little blighter up, eh?'

I slept well that night. The first time in many months. I convinced myself that it wasn't just the alcohol that lulled me into deep, untroubled sleep, but rather a new feeling of hope that had been engendered within me by meeting Alexander Reed. In a few short hours he had convinced me that my life was not at an end – that somehow I could have a successful and happy future. And not only that, he had held out his hand in friendship in order to help me achieve what previously I had thought was impossible – to seal the past behind me and create a new life. *A new life* – that phrase bobbed like flotsam on the sea of sleep before it finally engulfed me.

Grey morning brought with it doubts. On reviewing my conversation with Reed in the cold light of day, I felt certain that my revived spirits had more to do with the effects of the brandy than any vague offer that my new acquaintance had made. My doubts increased when I failed to see Reed anywhere on board the ship. I searched all the decks, dining-rooms and bars, but to no avail. I even enquired of the purser for his cabin number, but was told there was no one of that name on board the *Orontes*. I was dumbfounded. Thinking back to the previous evening, I began to see the occasion as possessing a dreamlike quality. Maybe I had imagined it. The whole episode had an element of wish-fulfilment about it: I had been given a kind sympathetic ear, friendship and the offer of employment. Perhaps I was going mad.

By early evening we were sailing up the Thames and I was packing my scant possessions in readiness to disembark. The pendulum of my spirits had swung back into the dark zone and I felt thoroughly depressed. Disconsolately, I joined the throng of passengers on deck to view some of the familiar landmarks of London, all silhouettes now, merging into the darkening sky.

'Ah, there you are. Been looking for you,' said a voice at my side. I turned, and to my surprise I saw Reed's smiling face. He was dressed in an expensive black coat with an astrakhan collar and was wearing an opera hat.

'And I've been looking for *you*.' My response was automatic and unreasonably indignant.

Reed ignored my rudeness. 'Looks like we've both been playing hide-and-seek, then. Well, journey's end in lovers' meeting, eh? Now, you're to leave the boat with me. My friend Scoular will be waiting, and then the three of us can repair to my club for a pork chop or two and discuss the future. What do you say?'

His charm and easy manner quickly dispelled my anger, frustration and despair within seconds. I grinned. 'I should be delighted to go along with your plans.'

'Good man.'

Out across the city, the melancholy chimes of Big Ben could be heard signalling the hour as though in welcome to the weary travellers about to set foot once more on their native soil.

Accompanied by a raucous cheer from the crowd waiting on the dockside, the gangplanks were lowered. People waved and cried, babies and infants were held aloft, and the air seemed to crackle with the heightened excitement of anticipated reunion. As I gazed down on those eager, smiling faces, I felt a pang of jealousy. There were no hugs, kisses or firm handshakes waiting for me. There was no one waiting to greet and welcome me back home.

'Stick close, old boy,' said Reed, grabbing my sleeve. 'There'll be an almighty rush once they lift the barriers.'

He was right. The crush of passengers desperate to escape the confines of the ship surged forward, squeezing down the narrow lanes of the gangways. It was like being caught up with a fierce river current and being swept away against one's will. Reed and I were carried along, tossed and buffeted like driftwood.

'I rate myself a lover of my fellow man,' whispered my companion in my ear as we were jostled nearer the gangway, 'but I ain't so sure I like them *this* close.'

Within five minutes, somewhat breathless and dishevelled, we found ourselves standing on the dockside.

'Well, here we are, Walker. The old country. Breathe in that damp, tainted air. Grand, eh?'

I smiled. Reed seemed to find amusement and enjoyment in most things. Nothing seemed to ruffle his even temperament or throw a cloud across his sanguine outlook on life. I found myself liking and admiring my new acquaintance more and more. I did take in a lungful of air. Tainted as it was with myriad vapours and smells, so different from the dry, dusty air of Afghanistan, it tasted good to me.

We stood for some time on the dockside as passengers scurried passed us and porters conveyed large trunks to waiting conveyances. It was dark now, and the area was illuminated by a series of gas lamps that bathed us in a soft yellow glow. Neither of us felt the need to talk: we were just taking time to acknowledge our new reality. After weeks bobbing on the waters in an artificial, enclosed environment, we were now back in England, our home. Back where we belonged. And I felt in my heart that, whatever unknown problems I now had to face, I would much prefer to face them here than anywhere else.

As the crowd dissipated, a tall, imposing figure emerged from the gloom and stood for a moment under one of the gas lamps, watching us. He was well over six feet in height, a height that was exaggerated by the top hat he was wearing. Reed observed him and raised his hand in greeting. This prompted the stranger to approach us. He moved like a cat, with soft sinewy movements, his feet making no sound on the damp paving stones. As he drew closer, I saw that he was a black man, with a remarkably handsome face. He stopped some little distance from where we were standing and touched the brim of his hat with his silver-topped cane, acknowledging Reed's greeting.

Reed beamed. 'Scoular, my old friend, how good to see you.' He stepped forward, grabbed the man's hand and gave it a vigorous shake. There was no obvious response: no reciprocal smile or warm words. The fellow's expression hardly altered. He looked beyond Reed at me, his eyes registering some interest at my presence. Reed noticed this, and his whole body stiffened awkwardly. He threw a nervous smile in my direction.

'Excuse me, Walker, for a moment, while I have some private words with my old chum.'

I nodded, feeling rather like a child left outside the headmaster's study while one of the masters and the head decide on what punishment to administer.

The two men moved some distance away, whereupon Reed spoke rapidly in an animated fashion. I could not hear what he was saying, but it was clear that he was telling the impassive stranger all about me. From time to time, both men glanced in my direction as though I were some item at an auction which was under discussion by two potential bidders. Obviously Reed had overestimated the welcome and help I would receive from his friends, and he was having to persuade the icy Scoular of my worth. I felt very uncomfortable and was tempted to leave, to walk away. What stopped me was the knowledge that I had nowhere to walk away to. In essence, I was trapped.

When Reed had finished his recital, he waited nervously for Scoular to respond. The gentleman stood impassively for some time, and then he asked a few questions. In the growing quiet, I heard the dark, silky tone of his voice on the night air.

And then suddenly, Scoular moved with the speed of a leopard and before I knew it, he was by my side, his gloved hand extended and a broad grin on that dark, handsome face of his. 'Doctor Walker, I am so pleased to meet you. I am Lincoln Scoular.'

Dumbly I took his hand and shook it. Like a gas mantle being turned down, the smile faded quickly.

'I have a carriage waiting. We shall repair to Reed's club for drink and refreshment, and to provide you with a night's accommodation. Over our meal we shall discuss your future. I trust that these arrangements are in accordance with your wishes?'

I nodded. 'Indeed,' I said, unsure whether they were or not. I knew that in reality I had no other option. Once again, it was a decision that was to change my life for ever.

'Where is he now?' Professor Moriarty handed his two visitors a glass of brandy each before seating himself behind his large desk.

'At my club, snoring his head off no doubt,' grinned Reed, cradling the brandy glass in both hands. 'We made sure he had plenty to eat and drink.'

Moriarty nodded and turned to his other visitor. 'Impressions?'

Scoular pursed his lips. 'There is steel and fire in his nature, I am sure. At present he is demoralized, but, given time, the phoenix will rise.'

'With our help, eh, Professor?' Reed raised his glass in a mock toast.

The Professor did not seem amused. 'You are rarely wrong in finding the organization effective recruits, Reed, but this time I must be absolutely certain about this man. I have a particular project in mind for him – if he is the right man.'

'There is no doubt that all the biographical details are true. I read all about his case in the local press in Candahar and thought then that he might make a suitable candidate for recruitment. When I learned that he would be sailing on the same boat back here, I made it my business to find out all about him.'

Now Moriarty did smile. 'Your thoroughness is commendable – but facts do not always reveal the man.'

'Ah,' said Reed, warming with the compliment, 'but I watched him closely on the voyage and I spent several hours in conversation with him. He has all the qualities we look for in a recruit: nobility, courage, but a life damaged and a nature simmering with bitterness. He is ready, I am sure.'

'I believe Reed is right,' agreed Scoular softly. 'In his present state of mind, Walker is rather like a dog that has been rescued from being destroyed. He will give obedience and loyalty to anyone who shows him any form of kindness and generosity.'

Moriarty sipped his brandy, trapping the mouthful until it began to burn his tongue before releasing it. 'I am encouraged by your words, gentlemen. If what you say is accurate, it is so very opportune that this remarkable individual has been washed up on our beach at this particular time. He seems to have all the qualities needed for the job I have in mind.'

'May I ask what job that is?' enquired Reed.

Moriarty grinned. 'Of course you may. However, you should not expect an answer. Not yet, at least.'

Reed looked nervously away and took a large gulp of brandy.

The room fell into silence, a silence both visitors knew it would be inappropriate to break. The Professor was thinking, and he would be the one to speak first. Scoular and Reed sat impassively as the silence settled on the room, accentuating the crackle of the coals in the grate and the soft tick of the clock on the mantel. At length the Professor began tapping his fingers in a staccato rhythm on the desk, and then at last he spoke.

'You are excellent lieutenants, and I trust your word and your judgement implicitly. However, on this occasion, I need to judge for myself before we go any further with this matter. Reed, I shall call round to your club tomorrow at noon. Make sure there is a private room available where I may have a meeting with Doctor John H. Walker.'

'It shall be done.'

'Very good. Now, gentlemen, I do not think I need keep you any more from your beds or what other pursuits you have in mind at this late hour. Therefore, I bid you good-night.'

After the two men had gone, Moriarty picked up a copy of the *Temple Bar* magazine, which Reed had brought him that evening. It was dated 1878. He flipped it open to the page that Reed had marked: *'The Missing Dagger* – a mystery story by John H. Walker.' Professor James Moriarty settled down in his chair and began to read.

Chapter Five

From the journal of John Walker

I only met Professor James Moriarty twice. The first time was in a small dark room at Reed's club, the morning following my arrival back in England.

The previous evening I had dined with Reed and Scoular, who, although maintaining a veneer of affability, spent the whole time quizzing me about my life, my politics, my family and my views on a whole range of subjects. I realized that they were, in fact, assembling my autobiography as a kind of screening process. I didn't mind. It was good to feel free to talk about myself again without the fear of censure, and I knew that every firm or organization of quality has its own method of gauging the worth of a prospective employee. The only aspect of the matter that puzzled me was the exact nature of the position they had in mind for me. But I was prepared to be patient. There were no other demands upon my time or company.

The following morning, I discovered a letter on the breakfast tray that was brought to my room. I had spent the night at the club and slept late, enjoying the luxury of a proper bed after months on straw and sacking in the army prison, and weeks in a cramped bed on board ship, and was surprised to find that it was after ten o'clock.

47

The letter was from Reed.

> My dear Walker,
>
> I trust you slept well. I have to be about my business. Being out of the country for a few months, there is now much for me to attend to. I am not sure when we shall meet again. However, the principal of the establishment that I represent will be calling on you at the club at noon, and I believe he will be offering you a lucrative role in our organization. Your appointment is in the Red Room on the second floor. I advise you to be prompt.
>
> Allow me to take this opportunity to wish you the best of luck.
>
> In all sincerity,
A. Reed, Capt. (Retd.)

The tone of the letter suggested that I should not be seeing my newly made acquaintance again. It was as though his part in the strange process of recruitment was over and it was time for him to step out of the picture. Where all this was leading, I could not begin to discern, but I comforted myself that by the time noon had arrived, along with my important visitor, I should be much the wiser.

At the appointed hour, a lackey showed me in to the Red Room, a small book-lined apartment with scarlet furnishings. Two large armchairs were placed on either side of the fireplace, which contained a meagre fire that had only recently been lit and was still struggling for life. On being left alone, I began perusing the shelves. Then a voice addressed me.

'I suspect you will find little to interest you, Doctor. It is just a second-rate collection of outdated tomes. No adventure stories at all.'

I whipped around and found that the voice belonged to a saturnine young man who was sitting in one of the chairs, which had its back to me. He rose and we shook hands.

'I know of your penchant for adventure stories,' he continued, his lips spreading into a wide smile. 'I spent an enjoyable hour reading your *Mystery of the Missing Dagger* last night.'

'Really?' I stuttered, in some amazement. 'I wrote that some time ago when I was in general medical practice. The long intervals between patients—'

The smile broadened. 'I am Professor James Moriarty and I am very pleased to meet you, Doctor John H. Walker. Do sit down.'

I did as I was bid.

'I know all about you. Well, perhaps that is an exaggeration, for who can know *everything* about anyone? There are always dark, private quarters of the mind and soul that we never reveal to anyone. So, allow me to rephrase that statement. I know a great deal about you. On the other hand, you know nothing about me.'

'Apart from your name and that you are acquainted with Alexander Reed and Lincoln Scoular.'

Moriarty's eyes twinkled with amusement. 'True, but that is very little and of no consequence. If you should seek out the aforementioned gentlemen to verify your assertion regarding our acquaintance, I am sure you would not find them.' The smile vanished and the eyes grew icy.

'I'm sorry, I don't quite understand . . .' I said, shaking my head.

'Of course you don't, my dear doctor. Let me help you a little. I am the head of a vast criminal organization. It is an efficient structure, which carries out robberies, forgeries and even the occasional murder.'

He paused and raised an eyebrow, awaiting my reaction to this startling revelation. I did not know whether this was some monstrous joke or whether the fellow was mad. My expression must have revealed my thoughts.

'I speak nothing but the truth. At least half of the crimes committed in this great grey city are perpetrated by my employees. And I am the organizing power in charge of this most profitable of enterprises.'

'Either this is some rather bizarre test or a jest in bad taste—'

Moriarty shook his head. 'It is no jest. Despite my calling, I believe in telling the truth. When necessary. Honesty is a fine virtue, even if it should be exercised sparingly. I assure you, I have no intention of misleading you.'

I rose from my chair, anger boiling within me. 'I thank you for that, sir,' I snapped, 'but why on earth you feel the need to convey this information to me, I do not know, and furthermore, I do not *want* to know. However, let me state clearly lest there should be some misunderstanding in the matter, if you hold any notions of involving me in your . . . *activities*, let me disabuse you of such ideas now.'

Moriarty did not reply; his features remained passive, but I detected a trace of amusement in his eyes.

'So,' I continued, 'having established that, I believe there is no further purpose to this interview, and therefore if you will excuse me . . .'

I moved towards the door.

'Stop where you are, Doctor.' His voice was brittle and harsh, like the crack of a whip. 'You will appreciate that the knowledge you now possess concerning me and my "activities", as you referred to them so decorously, places you in rather a privileged and, I am afraid, very precarious position. You have now become a threat to my anonymity and safety. I assure you, Doctor, if you leave this room now, you will be dead within the hour. Another fatality floating in the Thames.'

'*What?*' My blood ran cold at these words. Whatever nightmarish charade I had found myself party to, I was convinced by Moriarty's demeanour that he meant every word of his warning.

'Trust me. It is not an idle threat. Now, do please sit down, Doctor, and try not to look quite so outraged. You have made the mistake of not listening to the full story – a mistake I had not expected either a doctor or a writer to make.'

I felt trapped, caught in some diabolical web of intrigue which I could not explain. Numbed by fear and with my mind reeling, I slumped down into the chair. What on earth had I let myself in for? There was something about this man – his presence, and the fierce aura that seemed to surround him – that convinced me that all he told me was true, and that indeed my life was in his hands.

'It is not to any stranger that I divulge the secrets of my calling, but of course in one sense you are not quite any stranger. Thanks to my colleagues, Captain Reed and Mr Scoular, I know a great deal about you.'

Until Reed's name was mentioned, my befuddled mind had not connected him with the creature before me, but then suddenly so many little pieces seemed to float together in my mind to create a very disturbing picture. Reed and the mess funds. Once a thief, always a thief, keeping the company of thieves. And he saw me as being bitter and demoralized enough to turn my hand to crime and join his filthy band. Anger rose within me again. If Reed had been present, I would have knocked the scoundrel to the ground.

'Rest assured, Doctor,' Moriarty continued, breaking into my thoughts, 'I have no intention of placing a jemmy in your hand, slipping a black mask over your face and asking you to carry out a burglary. I have something far more sophisticated and essentially law-abiding in mind for you. Something more suited to your talents than cracking a crib.' He laughed.

I opened my mouth to respond, but he held up his gloved hand to silence me.

'The full story, Walker, the full story before you make any more rash statements. Allow me to furnish you with all the facts, and then we can discuss the matter like gentlemen.'

Ambrose Jones was thirsty. And, he thought, so he should be, after traversing the city all morning visiting the various establishments he owned to collect the rent. 'Establishments' is how Jones thought of them, but in reality most of them were ramshackle doss-houses in the poorest parts of the city – Houndsditch, Whitechapel and Bethnal Green. Rats, mice and other vermin shared the premises with the poorest families in these damp and depressing dwellings. To Ambrose Jones's mind, it was a pity that he could not charge the rats and mice rent in addition to his wretched tenants.

There was one property which was in reasonable condition, in the heart of the metropolis, the one where Jones dwelt himself, letting out the two upper floors to 'his young gentlemen', as he referred to them. That was to be his last port of call, but, consulting his watch and noting that it was just past midday, he decided, as he'd had a good morning – no defaulters and only one threatened eviction – that he would treat himself to a glass of ale and some vittals at his favourite inn, The Sparrow's Nest in Holborn. The inn was situated down a narrow lane off the main thoroughfare. As Jones turned down the lane, a hansom cab drew up beside him at the kerb and the passenger leaned out to address him. He was well made, of muscular build, and dressed as far as Jones could see like so many of the City businessmen that scurry around like ants near St Paul's.

'Excuse me, sir,' said the stranger. 'I wonder if you could help me.'

Jones's eagle eye noted that the man held a coin in his hand. Grinning, and raising his greasy Homburg, Jones stepped forward. 'I should be happy to, if I can, sir.'

The stout man returned the grin and opened the door of the cab. 'My query is of a rather delicate nature,' he said, lowering his voice. He beckoned Jones to come near, which the greedy landlord duly did. He now observed that there was another passenger in the cab, his features veiled by shadow.

'What is the query, then?' Jones asked.

Before he knew what was happening, the stranger whipped his arm out and grasped Jones by the neck and pulled him forward. It was an expert move, for not only did it take the landlord by surprise, but also the pressure on his windpipe prevented him from calling out.

'Come gently now,' murmured his assailant, and with a further tug he lifted Jones off the ground and hauled him inside the cab.

The door shut. The blind came down and the cab set off. Jones lay sprawled on the floor of the vehicle, panting for breath and wondering if his world was coming to an end. He was conscious of the cash stowed in his money-belt, his takings from the morning, but in a rare moment he thought more about the possibility of losing his life to these ruffians than losing his ill-gotten gains.

'Take the money,' he croaked, 'but don't hurt me. Please don't hurt me.'

'It's not your money we are after, Mr Jones,' came a voice from the darkness. It was not the voice of his assailant. It had a strange dark timbre to it and sounded somehow foreign.

Rather than calming him, this statement made him panic. If they didn't want his money, then they wanted to kill him. He tried to struggle to his feet while at the same time crying out at the top of his voice, 'Help! Murder!'

He felt a blow to the side of the head. Something heavy, like the butt of a revolver, connected with his temple. Further cries for help died in his throat and he slumped back to the floor, dazed and gasping for breath.

Briefly, light flared in the cab as one of the men lit a cigarette, and through bleary eyes Jones saw his abductors. There was the stout man who had first approached him and who had just hit him, judging by the gun he held in his hand. The other man, who reclined in the corner of the cab with his cigarette, was a good-looking black man.

'Relax, Mr Jones, we mean you no harm.'

'Like the devil, you do! You've just nearly knocked my brains out!'

'A simple matter of restraint. We have a favour to ask of you, one for which we will gladly pay you.'

At the mention of money, Ambrose Jones's pulse quickened all the more.

'Favour? What favour? Why not come to see me in my office in Montague Street? Why abduct me, if all you want to do is ask me a favour?'

'We have our methods, Mr Jones,' the voice purred in the darkness. 'This way, you know what to expect if you do not agree to our offer.'

'What to expect. . . ?'

'I think you know what we mean.'

Jones felt the barrel of the cold revolver press hard against his forehead. His mouth was now so parched with fear that he could hardly croak a response.

'What do you want of me?'

'It concerns a lodger of yours. In Montague Street.'

'A lodger?'

'Yes, a certain Mr Sherlock Holmes.'

Chapter Six

From the journal of John Walker

'I am easily bored, Doctor Walker. You see, I am very successful at what I do, and with success comes a certain security, which is tedious. I abhor the dull routine of existence. Sometimes I long for the excitement and frustration of failure, so that I can rise to the challenge of overcoming it. For a man of my intellectual capacity, I am in constant need of such challenges, something to stimulate me, to strive for. Give me danger, give me risks, give me a puzzle, and I am in my element.'

Professor Moriarty leaned back in his chair and stared into the fire. Although he was talking to me, his expression and demeanour indicated that he was in essence merely using my presence to express thoughts that had been bound up within him for some time. Much of what he was telling me was a kind of confession, and who better to confess to than a stranger whose very existence you hold in your power? Strangely, I began to feel sorry for this man, trapped, as he seemed to believe, atop his own unique, rarefied ivory tower.

'Please do not think me arrogant when I refer to my intellectual capacity. I speak merely the truth. As I mentioned earlier, I am a strong advocate of the truth in the appropriate circumstances. That I have a refined intelligence is not a brag or boast; it is fact. I am not one of those who rate modesty amongst the virtues.'

He paused again and then suddenly his eyes narrowed, focused, and lost their dreamlike quality. He took a cigarette-case from his pocket and offered it to me. I declined with a shake of the head.

'Pity. They are a special Ukrainian blend. An excellent smoke.' He lit the cigarette and took a deep breath, and then allowed the grey tendrils to drift slowly from his mouth.

'So, you see, Walker,' he said at length, 'my life is a continual search for stimulation, that sense of danger, that unique entertainment. Something to keep me from going mad. After all, madness is akin to genius. That lack of fear for the consequences that allows one to dare – and then do. Certainly, that is part of my genius.'

Moriarty drew on the cigarette again and smiled a secret smile to himself. 'Something to keep me from going mad,' he repeated softly. 'And do you know, I think I have found that stimulation. You will not have heard of a young man called Sherlock Holmes?'

I shook my head again.

'No, of course not. Very few people have – yet. But they will, I am sure, with your help.'

'With my help?' I parroted the words back at him.

'The full story, please, Walker. Questions later. Sherlock Holmes is a private detective. He is also a brilliant fellow. He is the greatest mind fighting on behalf of law and order in London today. His intellectual capacity is as great as mine. We are twins, he and I, and we stand like two colossi facing each other across the great divide. He solves crimes, and I commit them. He is younger than I – by some five years – and so I have a march on him at present, but his greatness will come. This delights and also concerns me. His activities, so beautifully crafted and shrewdly conceived, are a delight to perceive, but at the same time he causes me problems. Already, he has "interfered" in a number of my schemes, causing them to fail. The nature of this paradox fascinates me. I could easily dispose of this thorn in my flesh, of course. A word from me and he would soon be shuffling off this mortal coil. However, not only would that be too easy, but it would also remove the challenge and the problem. And they are so stimulating. A nice dilemma, eh, Walker? I have thought long and hard about this situation. I felt sure that I could come to some delicious compromise regarding myself and Mr Sherlock Holmes, who, by the way, I am sure, at present at least, has no notion of my existence or my role whatsoever.

'Well, I have decided to conduct an experiment that will give me both the pleasure of seeing Mr Holmes's talents develop and his career progress, while at the same time reduce the real danger he poses to me and my organization. I intend to place him under the microscope, to use a metaphor a writer like yourself will readily appreciate. And this is where *you* come in. In simple terms, you are to be my spy in his camp. You are to befriend him, share lodgings with him, become his associate, and then report on his dealings to me. You will, while delighting me with tales of his brilliant work, be able to alert me if he is sniffing too close to my territory.'

'You are mad!' I cried. 'This is a preposterous scheme.'

Moriarty frowned, and when he responded to my outburst, his voice was full of anger. 'I had hoped that, by now, whatever view you have of my moral nature, you would be aware of the thoroughness of my planning, the efficiency of my scheming and the reliability of my visions. Otherwise, sir, you would not be trapped here with me now. A man I have watched and waited for since learning of your disgrace in Afghanistan. A man I have lured into my web by means of my operatives. A man who is now completely at my mercy. Do you call that preposterous?'

As he spoke, he leaned forward, his face thrusting into mine, his roaring voice filling the room. Not for the first time in his company I was lost for words.

'My plan is audacious, it is dangerous, it is unique,' and now he lowered his voice to a harsh whisper, 'but it is not preposterous. Even as we speak, action is being taken to bring about all I have conceived.'

'How on earth can this work? If the man is as brilliant as you say, he will discover the trick.'

'Ah, yes, that is part of the fun, the entertainment. There is always a danger. What is life without there being "always a danger"? But it will be your job to minimalize that danger. You will be his true friend in all things except your allegiance to me. When the crime has nothing to do with me, you will do all you can to help Holmes bring the perpetrator to justice. When the crime involves my organization, you will inform me of Holmes's progress and do all in your power to hinder him. Think of it, my dear Watson – oh, and *Watson* it will be, near enough to your own name, but not traceable to the scoundrel who got drunk on duty, eh? Reed's idea. Think of it, Watson, as a wonderful charade.'

'And what if I refuse?'

'The Thames is very cold at this time of year.'

'I see,' I said softly, my eyes misting with fear and frustration. I wanted to rush at the man and knock his brains out, but I was fully aware how futile such a gesture would be.

'My dear Watson, you were not chosen at random. I know you are the man for the job. You have many sterling qualities that are unique. And, of course, you will be rewarded handsomely for your services. Never again will you have to count your small change to ensure that you can pay for a meal or a room for the night. For the first time in your life, you will be self-sufficient.'

'What is there stopping me from telling this Sherlock Holmes or the police about your plan?'

'I doubt if the police would believe you. They lack the mental capacity to conceive of a criminal organization almost as big as they are. As for Holmes, well, as soon as he finds out, he will be joining you in the morgue. His life is now in your hands.'

'You bastard.'

'Possibly, Doctor Watson – but a very clever and powerful bastard, all the same. I am sure you would agree.'

'Of course, as you well know, I have done little jobs for the Professor in the past – walk-on parts, as I like to think of them – but this seems like a major role.'

'One of the biggest, Kitty, and it is destined to be a long run,' agreed Reed, flashing one of his warm, friendly smiles.

Kitty Hudson matched it. 'And here's me thinking I'd said goodbye to the theatre. You know, the last time I was on a stage must have been over five years ago. They just don't want scrawny widow-women, especially when they hit the fifty mark.'

'Well, you're perfect for the part the Professor's chosen for you to play – and no auditions.'

'Bliss.' Kitty Hudson closed her eyes to emphasize the emotion. Since she had been a child she had been fascinated by the theatre, by the whole process of dressing-up, putting on a performance and becoming someone else. It was an escape route, to leave drab reality behind. As a young girl, Kitty had joined the chorus in the music hall in her native Edinburgh and then progressed to being a member of a travelling troupe, Harry Saville's Revels, which put on sketches and melodramas in the small provincial theatres around the country. It was while she was appearing in Liverpool that she met Frank Hudson, a burly good-looking sailor who was a steward on the Liverpool–Dublin Steam Packet Company. For a while the magic of romance and marriage lured her away from the stage, but after her baby was stillborn, and Frank took to drinking and knocking her about, she escaped once more to the fantasy life behind the footlights. She left Liverpool and Frank Hudson, and eventually found herself in London acting as comic feed to Stanley Dawkins, 'The Lambeth Layabout', at the Craven Street Theatre. She was quite a success. Her comic timing was natural, and she became a favourite with the regulars. When in a good mood, Dawkins would let her have her own solo spot where she would sing a novelty song, 'I'm Looking for the Vital Spark'.

It was at the Craven Street Theatre, a time that Kitty now remembered as being the best in her life, that romance and tragedy struck again. She formed a relationship with Ted Baldwin, the assistant stage manager, a kind and sensitive man, the exact opposite of her brutish husband, and they set up home together. As Kitty observed at the time, 'all seemed pretty in our own little backyard'. Then one night Ted was set about by a gang of drunken roughs, who stole what little money he had about his person and left him with a cracked skull. He died two days later.

For a time Kitty was inconsolable, and eventually she left the Craven. The theatre reminded her too much of her kind and loving Ted. For many years she drifted, taking any kind of job just to keep a roof above her head. When theatrical work was scarce, she drifted into petty crime, which is when she came under the Professor's purview. He used her in many roles, especially as a lookout, or someone used to detain the foil from returning to his premises which were being robbed. She was very skilful in not letting the foil realize that he was being detained. Kitty relished these jobs because they were 'proper acting parts', and never really considered her activities as unlawful. And so here she was, rattling through the streets of west London in a hansom cab, in the company of Captain Reed, on the brink of being offered her biggest job, her biggest acting role yet.

'Bliss,' she repeated, as the cab drew up outside a three-storey terraced house in a smart residential street.

'Here we are, Kitty. Let's take a look at your new home.' Reed skipped out of the cab and helped her down from the vehicle. Kitty liked Reed because he always treated her like a lady, as though she was a dowager duchess or someone of that ilk. That, according to Kitty, is what a gentleman does: whether you are a real lady or a fishwife. Pulling a set of keys from his frock coat, he approached the door. Kitty looked up at the building. It was a bit of all right. Never had she seen such nice quarters. She even liked the address: 221B Baker Street.

Chapter Seven

From the journal of John Walker

'I cannot understand how you can believe that this wild scheme of yours will ever work. Even if I threw myself into the enterprise with great enthusiasm, I am not an actor. I cannot dissemble to order. If this Sherlock Holmes is such a great detective, as you say he is, he will easily spot me for the impostor that I am. Through my own behaviour, I would give the game away.'

I believed every word I said to Professor Moriarty, but I gave them extra emphasis, hoping that I could persuade him to drop this crazy charade by convincing him of the impractical nature of it. Thus, I would be able to slip from his noose and walk from the room a free man. However, I could see from his unruffled demeanour that my argument had fallen on stony ground. His confidence did not falter for an instant.

'But, my dear doctor, you will *not* be an impostor,' he replied easily. 'Apart from a slight change of name and a certain adjustment to your recent history, you will be the same man who is sitting in front of me now: a penurious ex-army surgeon recently arrived from Afghanistan and looking for cheap lodgings.'

'What "adjustment" to my recent history?'

'Rather than being cashiered, you were badly wounded in the Battle of Maiwand, and while recovering you contracted enteric fever, the curse of our Afghan possessions. As a result, you were invalided out of the army and sent home to England.'

'That is crazy.'

'Fact. A little news item to that effect was inserted into several of the London newspapers this morning, including *The Times*. My influence reaches into many areas. And as every Englishman knows, whatever appears in *The Times* must be the absolute truth. And Sherlock Holmes is an avid reader of the press.'

'But it's a lie.'

He shrugged his shoulders. 'Colouring the truth. You believe that you were unfairly treated in Afghanistan, do you not?'

I nodded.

'And so I have redressed the balance.'

I threw my head in my hands and groaned. 'Oh, my God, I wish I could wake up now. This must be some terrible dream.'

'No dream, Watson, but for you a kind of salvation. It is a wonderful opportunity, and it is about time you opened your mind to the vast possibilities that this arrangement offers to you. And, of course, there is your writing, your adventure stories. What scope there will be for penning mystery yarns while accompanying London's most brilliant detective on his investigations. You'll not only make him famous by recording his cases, but also create a name for yourself into the bargain.'

'Not my *own* name,' I pointed out tersely.

'A minor matter. You quibble too much. I think your brain is now crowded with details, and the newness and audacity of this enterprise is dulling your thoughts. You need time to think things through.'

'What is the point? There is no choice.'

Moriarty grinned. 'There *is* choice, although I grant you, it is rather limited.'

'How am I supposed to meet this man? You say I am to share rooms with him – what if he doesn't agree to it? There are so many uncertainties.'

'These are not things you need worry your head about. It has all been planned for and arranged. I can assure you that nothing has been left to chance. That is my way.'

What was I to do? Even in my current startled state I realized that, for the time being, I had to accept the situation and throw my hand in with the Professor, otherwise it was unlikely that I would see another sunrise. In surviving for the moment, it was possible that I could then begin to plot my own escape. Maybe I could enlist the help of this Sherlock Holmes to carry out a coup on my new master? I also realized that I must convince Moriarty that I wasn't entering into the game with any great reluctance, otherwise it would be much harder for me to persuade him that he could trust me and therefore relax his gaze upon me.

'You mentioned remuneration,' I said, sitting forward.

'I did. A very healthy sum of money will be paid in to your new bank account, one in the name of Watson, on the first of every month.'

'A healthy sum. . . ?'

'One hundred pounds every month.'

At this, my mouth really did drop open in surprise. To me, in my impoverished state, that was a king's ransom. For an unguarded moment, I bathed in the glow of my new-found wealth until a small voice inside reminded me from whence the money came.

'I pay my trusted employees very well, Watson. And in your new position you will be one of the most important and one of the most trusted.' He raised his finger in warning. 'So, do make sure that you deserve my trust.'

'I . . . I will do my best.' The words stuck in my throat and I felt an overwhelming sense of unease take hold of my senses.

'I feel sure your best will be good enough. I am rarely wrong in my judgement of character. So, then, have we an arrangement?'

With as much conviction as possible, I mustered a smile – a dead smile. 'Yes,' I said, 'we have an arrangement.'

'Excellent!' cried the Professor, grasping my hand.

It was early evening when Sherlock Holmes made his way back to his diggings in Montague Street. His mind was whirling with figures and formulae. He had spent the day working in one of the laboratories at St Bart's Hospital, attempting to develop a solution which would indicate the presence of bloodstains, however infinitesimal they might be. He wished to create a reagent that was precipitated solely by haemoglobin and thus could provide incontrovertible proof that human blood had been spilt. The old guaiacum test was clumsy and uncertain and therefore could not be relied upon in criminal matters. If he could create an infallible test, one that would work no matter how old the bloodstains were, it would be the most important medico-legal discovery for years, and would certainly boost his reputation in the world of crime detection. He had read of the case of Von Bischoff in Frankfurt the previous year, and was convinced that if such a test had been available then, the fellow would have mounted the gallows. As it was, he was set free.

Holmes believed that he was nearly there. A few more days, further experiments with the various combinations of powders, crystals and quantities. He was confident he would reach his goal, but, as always, he was impatient. These ideas jostled around his brain as he climbed the stairs to his quarters.

On entering his sitting-room, he noticed an envelope on the floor which had obviously been slipped under the door. His name was on the envelope, written in the crabbed spidery writing he recognized as belonging to his landlord, Ambrose Jones. Throwing off his coat and turning on the gas lamps, he dropped into a chair and tore open the envelope. The note inside was terse and to the point.

Dear Mr Holmes,
Please take this communication as notice to vacate your quarters within seven days of today's date.
Ambrose Jones

Holmes stroked his chin and frowned. What on earth was this all about?

Ambrose Jones was just heating some soup for his evening meal when there was a tap on his door. He moved the soup from the heat of the gas ring, and with some irritation he pulled his ragged old dressing-gown around him and answered the door, opening it a few inches. In the hallway he saw Sherlock Holmes. He was holding his note.

'Yes?' snapped the landlord.

'About this note—'

'What about it? Can't you read it?'

'Indeed I can, despite your execrable handwriting. The words and the message are clear. You used an HB pencil, and as you wrote just a few words at a time when composing it, you were probably travelling on a horse-bus, as is your wont, and scribbled the words between the stops to avoid being shaken too much by the movement of the vehicle.'

'You saw me!'

Holmes shook his head. 'I deduced it.'

Jones was not quite sure what 'deduced' meant, so his response was an angry but strangely non-committal 'Hah!'

He started to close the door, but Holmes placed his hand against it and held it firmly.

'So, what is your problem?' snapped Jones.

'I want to know why you want me to leave. As far as I am aware, I have caused you no problems and I have paid my rent on time.'

'I don't have to answer any of your questions. You're my tenant, and I am within my rights to chuck you out with a week's notice. And that, Mr Deducer, is what I'm doing.'

Holmes could see that Jones was now very angry, but he was also aware that the anger was a thin veneer covering another more powerful emotion: fear.

'This is all very sudden, Mr Jones. Maybe this action is being forced upon you.'

Jones's face flushed with frustration. 'I do not have to answer to you, or anyone, concerning what I do with my properties. I want you out. There are those who can and will pay more for those rooms.'

'Really? Who?'

Jones stepped back and flung the door open wide while at the same time producing a jack-knife from the pocket of his dressing-gown. He thrust the knife before Holmes's face, the blade glinting in the dim gaslight.

'Listen, you've had your marching orders, Holmes. Don't test my patience any more or . . .'

Holmes smiled. 'Or?'

Jones brought the knife close to Holmes's face. 'Or your next place of residence will be six feet under.'

Nimbly, Holmes snaked his arm up, taking hold of Jones's wrist in a powerful grip, and squeezed hard. Jones gave a sharp cry of pain and, dropping the knife, he staggered backwards, clutching his wrist.

'I will leave,' said Holmes smoothly, retrieving the knife from the floor, 'in seven days. But do not be sure that you have seen the last of me. In the mean time, I'll keep this knife as a souvenir of our encounter.' With these words he left and returned to his room upstairs.

Jones closed the door and slumped against it. His face was awash with perspiration and his body was shaking. At length he staggered to a cupboard. Producing from it a gin bottle, he took a long, good gulp. His eye caught sight of a small canvas bag slipped in between the bottles. After another slurp of gin, he took the bag and examined its contents: a dozen sovereigns. He smiled. Despite the recent unpleasantness, it had not been a bad day's work after all.

Buffeted by the blustery March wind, Henry Stamford trudged up the steps to the entrance of St Bart's Hospital. His eyes ached and his head thumped. Souvenirs of another late-night card game. Always in the bright light of the morning he wondered why on earth he indulged in such a foolish pursuit: he rarely won, and his tiredness was beginning to affect his work. Last night had been disastrous. He had lost over twenty pounds, an amount a junior surgeon could ill afford to lose. How he would survive before his next pay date, he dreaded to think.

He flinched again as the pounding grew louder. He would have to mix a sedative before going on the wards. As he reached the portals of the great hospital, a tall black man stepped from the shadows and approached him.

'If I may have a word, Mr Stamford,' he said softly, the voice silky and persuasive. 'It could be to our mutual advantage.'

Stamford noticed that the man held a white bank-note in his gloved hand.

Some hours later, Stamford, now twenty pounds richer, traversed the lower corridors of the hospital *en route* to the dissecting-room. He was in search of Sherlock Holmes. He knew Holmes in a casual manner. He had seen him about the hospital, and had indulged in a few desultory conversations with the man. He was unsure what to make of him. Holmes was not on the staff of the hospital, and yet he was able to use their facilities. In all likelihood he was engaged in postgraduate studies. Stamford had gleaned that Holmes was well up in anatomy and appeared to be a first-class chemist, but he had no notion of the purpose of his studies. He found Holmes something of a cold fish, approaching his experiments with such extreme objectivity that he failed to take account of the human quotient in such matters. God help us all, thought Stamford, if the man was thinking of taking up medicine as a career. Holmes would quite easily test out the latest serum on a patient in the pursuit of scientific knowledge, without any consideration of the effects it might have on the poor devil who was acting as guinea-pig. Stamford gave a wry grin at the thought and was prompted to admit to himself that, to give Holmes some credit, he would probably take the serum himself if he thought the experiment would aid his findings.

As he approached the dissecting-room, Stamford heard strange sounds emanating from within. He stood by the door and listened. There was what sounded like the violent clapping of hands, followed by a gruff cry of exertion.

Swinging the door open, a most bizarre sight met his eyes. There, lying on the table, was a naked cadaver which Sherlock Holmes, jacket off and sleeves rolled up, was beating with a walking-cane.

'What the devil!' cried Stamford. 'Have you gone mad?'

Sherlock Holmes paused, the stick raised in the air, and turned to Stamford. His face was flushed and bathed in sweat.

'Stamford,' he said, 'I didn't hear you.' He dropped the stick on the table by the corpse, and mopped his brow with his shirtsleeve.

'What on earth do you think you're doing? Have you taken leave of your senses?'

Holmes chuckled. 'Far from it. I have to admit that it must look that way, but I assure you I am carrying out a scientific experiment.'

'Scientific experiment? Beating a corpse with a cane?'

Holmes nodded. 'In an attempt to verify how far bruises may be produced after death. Such information can be vital in the cases of murder; and this old fellow,' – he slapped the chest of the corpse – 'made no objection to assisting me in my studies.'

Stamford shook his head. 'Well, it is bizarre in the extreme.'

'Truth rarely comes simply or by normal channels. I am sorry if I disturbed you by my actions.'

'Well, I must admit I was somewhat shaken, but now that you have explained . . .'

'You still think I'm demented.'

Both men laughed, and the atmosphere eased between them.

'Were you wanting to use the room, Stamford?'

'No, I was looking for you actually.'

'For me?'

'Yes, I've heard that you are in search of new digs.'

'How did you know that?'

'One of the registrars told me, I think. Isn't it true?'

'Oh, yes, it's true. I have to be out of my current quarters by the weekend.'

'Ah, well, I might be able to help you. I've got wind of a nice suite of rooms going begging in Baker Street.'

'Suite of rooms? That sounds rather too expensive for my meagre purse.'

'Still worth a visit, eh? Especially if you are getting desperate.'

'Desperate? Yes, I suppose I am. I really should be trudging the streets now, looking for a new place to lay my head at night, rather than be here, but I was so keen to work out a hypothesis on bruises.'

'Well, why don't you trudge round to Baker Street now and maybe all your worries will be over? Here, I've got the address on a piece of paper: 221B Baker Street. Landlady by the name of Mrs Hudson.'

Chapter Eight

From the journal of John Walker

My memory of what occurred immediately following my interview
with Professor James Moriarty in the Red Room is somewhat hazy.
That is not because I have forgotten, but rather because my mind
was in such a ferocious whirl at the time and not really registering
details. It was as though I had passed from reality into some dark,
fantastic dream and I was unable to wake up.

As I recall, I was given some cash, put up in a private hotel in the
Strand and told to wait for a summons. Although I was only ever to
see Professor Moriarty once more, many years later, his shadow had
now fallen across my life and was destined to remain there for ever.

For the next two days I took very long walks around London,
familiarizing myself once again with the great city. I did feel pleased
to be back on British soil and to be able to wander the streets,
anonymous and unnoticed. I had not realized how much I had
missed the sights and sounds of England. The rattle of the horse-
buses, the bleat of the Cockney costermongers around Covent
Garden, the crowds squeezing themselves down the Strand. I was
entranced by the grey hubbub of it all, and the simple pleasures
such as buying a cup of tea in a small café, or watching children feed
the pigeons in Trafalgar Square. In the evening, I went to Wilton's
Music Hall and lost myself in the warm, garish glamour of the show,

singing lustily when encouraged by the chairman to join in the chorus of some familiar ditty.

It was on the third day after my meeting with Moriarty that I received my instructions. By then I was really beginning to enjoy myself, having pushed my dark secret to the back of my mind, hoping, I suppose, in some kind of childish way, that if I did not acknowledge it, it would go away. But, of course, that was not to be the case.

On returning from a long walk in St James's Park, I discovered an envelope waiting for me on my bedside table. It was addressed to John H. Watson. That was the new me. The name in the hotel register. The name on my new bank book. The name by which Moriarty would call me. This is who I had to be for sanity and survival's sake. As I tore open the envelope, I bid John Walker a final goodbye.

The message inside read simply: 'This hotel is but a temporary measure. Remember you are in need of permanent diggings. Help will be forthcoming. Take a lunchtime drink in the Criterion Bar tomorrow. M.'

'How were the rooms?'

Sherlock Holmes was sitting in the cavernous staff canteen of Bart's Hospital finishing off his breakfast while perusing a copy of *The Times*, when the voice broke in to his thoughts. He looked up to see the eager face of Henry Stamford looming over him. He had broad, plump features, with large vacant blue eyes seated beneath a dark tumble of unruly, curly hair.

Before Holmes had time to respond, Stamford drew up a chair and joined him at the table.

'I trust you went along to see Mrs Hudson's place in Baker Street?'

Holmes smiled and folded the newspaper. 'Yes, I did, thank you. The place is ideal in many ways, but unfortunately I'm not able to take it.'

'Oh, that's a shame. What is the problem?'

'The quarters are somewhat large for one person. Despite my books and my chemical equipment, I think I would be rattling

71

around a little in there. However, that is something I could cope with quite easily, but I am afraid Mrs Hudson is looking for two tenants to share, a fact that is reflected in the rent.'

'Too high.'

'For this man's pocket.'

'Then you'll just have to find some chap to go halves with you.'

Holmes's brow furrowed gently. He had not considered that possibility. 'Share the rooms, you mean?'

'Yes. It seems to me an ideal situation. You go halves with the rent and there's company for you, should you require it.'

'I am not one of those who thrives on company. I am rather a solitary creature. Besides, it would be a hardy soul indeed who could put up with my unusual habits and untidiness.'

Stamford laughed, almost too heartily. 'You mean you are a bachelor! Great heavens, man, you would have great difficulty in pointing out any unmarried fellow who does not have what you describe as "unusual" habits and is excessively untidy.'

Holmes gave Stamford a bleak, condescending smile. 'You might be right.'

'Too damn sure I am right. What you need is a decent fellow to share with you, and Mrs Hudson's gaff is yours. By Jove, I'd join you myself if I wasn't so uncommonly comfortable at my place in Chiswick!'

Holmes thanked some deity for small mercies. He knew little of Stamford, but what little he did know convinced him that he was the last person with whom he would wish to share rooms. It was obvious to Holmes that the man was a hopeless gambler. His clothes clearly indicated the state of his fluctuating wealth: an expensive jacket contrasting with shoes that were in desperate need of repair. Also the bitten fingernails and dark shadows under the eyes told of late nights and desperation. However, Stamford had a point. If he could find someone reasonably compatible with whom to share the very pleasant suite of rooms in Baker Street, it would solve his most pressing of problems. He admitted the fact to Stamford.

'Have you any friends who might be prepared to come in with you?' asked Stamford.

Holmes shook his head. If he were to tell the truth, he would have to confess that he had no friends at all. Friendship was so unscientific, involving as it did emotions and illogical actions, and he shunned it. However, it was also true that at times Sherlock Holmes longed for someone to talk to, to discuss his experiments with or his investigations, someone with whom he could share his thoughts, theories and beliefs.

'Well, I'll keep an eye out for you. You never know.'

'Indeed,' said Holmes quietly, picking up the newspaper again to indicate that the conversation was over.

Stamford needed no further prompting. He rose, smiling. '*Nil desperandum*, Holmes, old chap,' he cried, as he turned and made his way to the exit.

As Stamford disappeared from sight, Holmes lowered his newspaper again and stared off into the middle distance, his sharp penetrating eyes lost in thought.

The Criterion Bar, situated in Piccadilly, was throbbing with noise as Henry Stamford entered just after noon that day. He was later than he intended to be, but his hansom had been caught in the thick flow of traffic around Oxford Circus and so he had decided to walk the rest of the way. He stood by the door, mopping his brow and catching his breath as he peered through the fug of smoke towards the bar. It wasn't long before he spied the man he was there to see.

'Hello, Doctor!' he cried heartily, approaching one of the men leaning indolently on the bar.

The man he addressed turned abruptly to face him. At first he looked puzzled and then recognition dawned.

'Bless my soul, it's Stamford!'

'It is indeed, Doctor . . .'

'Watson,' he came in quickly. 'John Watson.' The two men shook hands. 'I haven't seen you in some four years, I should think, since you were a dresser at Bart's.'

'Still there. Junior doctor now.'

'Congratulations. Let me get you a drink. It's so good to see a friendly face in this great metropolitan wilderness.'

'A glass of claret would suit.'

While Watson caught the attention of one of the barmen, Stamford scrutinized his old acquaintance. He was certainly thinner than he used to be, and although his skin was tanned, his face was drawn and unhealthy-looking. He looked much older; already grey tints were in evidence at the temples of his black, wiry hair. He thought of the Walker of old – he was Walker then, not Watson – and remembered a robust fellow with a cheery smile and a determined spring in his step. This fellow passing him a glass of red wine was a pale ghost of his past self.

Stamford raised his glass. 'To the future.'

Watson nodded shyly, repeated the toast, and then drained his glass. 'Look, Stamford, it's too crowded and noisy in here for a decent conversation. Let's take lunch at The Holborn; my treat. What d'you say?'

'Oh, I couldn't . . .'

'Nonsense. It would be a great pleasure to me to chat about the good old days at Bart's. You're the first genuinely friendly face I've seen in a long while.'

'Well, I must admit, that would suit me, too. Give me a second to dispose of this undistinguished claret, and The Holborn it is.'

Once ensconced in a cab, Stamford touched Watson on the arm. 'I hope you don't think me rather blunt, old man, but you look as though you've been ill. You're as thin as a lath and appear rather the worse for wear. Whatever have you been doing with yourself?'

'I'll tell you over lunch.'

Stamford received the amended account of Watson's experiences in Afghanistan. Watson went into great detail concerning the Battle of Maiwand, but dealt swiftly and sketchily with his injury and his despatch to England after contracting enteric fever. Despite his belief that he had no talent for dissembling, once he had commenced his recital, Watson warmed to the role of story-telling and found himself relishing the task of blending fact with a soupçon of fiction to create an engaging narrative.

'Poor devil,' said Stamford, after he had listened to his friend's misfortunes. 'No wonder you look a little under the weather. Still, that's all behind you. So, tell me, what are you up to now?'

'Very little! One is somewhat hampered on an army pension of eleven shillings and sixpence a day. My main occupation at present is looking for lodgings. Trying to solve the problem as to whether it is possible to get comfortable rooms at a comfortable price.'

Stamford felt as though he were taking part in some stage play and had just been given his cue. 'That's a strange thing,' he said with enthusiasm. 'You are the second man today to use that very same expression to me.'

'And who was the first?'

'A fellow who is working at the chemical laboratory up at the hospital. He was bemoaning himself this morning because he could not get someone to go halves with him in some nice rooms which he had found, and which were too much for his purse. A chap called Sherlock Holmes.'

At the mention of the name, Watson felt the hair on the back of his neck bristle. He was immediately reminded that he was still part of a charade and was being moved like a puppet with great finesse inexorably nearer the goal. It had not struck him until the name of Sherlock Holmes was mentioned that Stamford was in on the game also. Watson had been naïve enough to think that their chance meeting had been just that, and not an arranged rendezvous. He wondered how much Stamford knew of the grand scheme. Very little, he concluded. He was a small pawn, acting merely as a catalyst. But he must have been bribed to play the role. No one, it seemed, could be entirely trusted. With a sigh, Watson played on.

'By Jove!' he cried. 'If he really wants someone to share the rooms and the expense, I am the very man for him. I should prefer a partner to living alone.'

'You don't know Sherlock Holmes?'

'Watson shook his head. 'Is there anything against him?'

'As far as I know, he is a decent enough fellow. But he is a little strange in his ideas – an enthusiast in some branches of science.'

'A medical student, I suppose?'

'No – to be honest, I have no idea what his calling is. He is well up on anatomy, and he is a first-class chemist; but as far as I am aware he has never taken out any systematic medical classes. His studies are very desultory and eccentric, but he has amassed a great deal of out-of-the-way knowledge which would astonish the professors.'

'Did you never ask him what he was going in for?'

'No; he is not an easy man to draw out, though he can be communicative enough when the fancy seizes him.'

'He sounds fascinating. If I am to lodge with anyone, I would prefer it to be with a fellow who was interesting, rather than a dullard. How can I meet this friend of yours?'

'He is sure to be at the laboratory now. He either avoids the place for weeks or else he works there from morning till night. If you like we could drive round together after luncheon.'

'Admirable,' beamed Watson.

Following their meal at The Holborn, the two men hailed a cab and made their way to Bart's Hospital. Fuelled by the wine he had consumed over lunch, Stamford suddenly felt the need to tell Watson more about Sherlock Holmes. He felt a sentimental kinship to this troubled and rather weary doctor, and in giving him sufficient warning about Holmes, he believed that he wasn't breaking faith with the black man who had engaged him to bring about a meeting between the two men. He hadn't been told to ensure that they *liked* each other – just to make sure they met over the matter of lodgings in Baker Street.

Stamford lolled back in the cab and said, 'You mustn't blame me if you don't get on with him – this Holmes character. I know nothing more of him than I have learned from meeting him occasionally about the hospital. Remember, you proposed this arrangement, so don't hold me responsible.'

'If we don't get on, it will be easy to part company. But tell me, it seems to me, Stamford, that you have some reason for washing your hands of the matter. Is this fellow's temper so formidable, or what is it? Don't be mealy-mouthed about it.'

'It's not all that easy to express the inexpressible.' Stamford's

speech was now slightly slurred, and his eyelids flickered errati-
cally. He gave a little laugh before continuing. 'It's just that Holmes
is a little too scientific for my tastes. Cold-blooded . . . like a lizard.
I could imagine him giving a friend a little pinch of the latest
vegetable alkaloid, not out of malevolence, you understand – oh, no
– but simply out of a spirit of enquiry in order to have an accurate
idea of the effects. However, to do Holmes justice, I believe that he
would take the stuff himself with the same readiness.'

'He appears to have a passion for definite and exact knowledge.'

'Quite right, Watson, but. . . .' Stamford pulled himself forward,
and leaning close to Watson's face, lowered his voice to a whisper
'. . . but it may be pushed to excess. When it comes to beating the
subjects in the dissecting-room with a stick, his thirst for knowledge
takes a rather bizarre route.'

'Beating the subjects?'

'Yes. Supposedly, to verify how far bruises may be produced after
death. I saw it with my own eyes.'

'Very strange.'

'Still, you must make up your own mind, Watson. I just thought
you should know . . . Ah, here we are: good old Bart's.'

Stamford led Watson through the labyrinthine passageways of the
great hospital to the chemical laboratory where he felt sure Holmes
would be working. It was familiar ground to Watson, and he really
needed no guiding, but nevertheless he dutifully walked several
paces behind his companion.

At last they came upon a long corridor with a vista of white-
washed walls and dun-coloured doors. Near the far end, a
low-arched passageway branched away from it and led to the chemical laboratory. This was a lofty chamber, lined and littered with
countless bottles, each containing a rainbow hue of coloured liquids.
Broad, low tables were scattered about, which bristled with retorts,
test tubes and little Bunsen lamps with their blue flickering flames.

There was only one occupant of the room, a tall young man who
was bending over a bench, absorbed in his work. At the sound of
their steps, he glanced round, and recognizing Stamford he sprang

to his feet with a cry of pleasure.

'I've found it!' he cried, his high-pitched reedy voice filling the chamber. He ran towards us with a test tube in his hand. 'I've found, it, Stamford. I have discovered a reagent that is precipitated by haemoglobin and nothing else.'

Undeterred by this news, Stamford set about the business of his visit. He took a step back and held his arms out to each of us.

'Gentlemen,' he said, with comic formality, 'Doctor Watson, Mr Sherlock Holmes.'

Somewhere across the city, Professor James Moriarty was sitting, staring at a large chessboard. With a smile, he reached forward and made his move, lifting one of the pieces in the process.

'Rook takes knight,' he said. 'My game.'

Chapter Nine

From the journal of John Walker

'Doctor Watson, Mr Sherlock Holmes.'

And so, at last, I came face to face with Sherlock Holmes, the man with whom my own destiny was now entwined. He was very tall, a little over six feet, and excessively lean. His black hair was swept back from his face, which was pale and gaunt, with high cheekbones and the most startling grey eyes, which shone out either side of a thin hooked nose.

He gave me a quick glance, almost distractedly, I thought, as though I was of little consequence and he was impatient to explain about his chemical discovery. But then he took my hand and gave it a firm shake with a strength that belied his slender physique.

'How are you?' he said cordially. 'You have been in Afghanistan, I perceive.'

My blood ran cold. Was the game up before it had even started?

'You know me?' I gasped.

Holmes chuckled. 'Of course not. I deduced it from your appearance. But that is of no consequence. The question now is about haemoglobin. No doubt you see the significance of my discovery?'

My mind did not register fully his question. I was too concerned as to how this man knew I had been in Afghanistan. Someone must have told him, but who? I glanced at Stamford, but his pasty face gave no clues.

'Come now,' Holmes was saying. 'As medical men you should be able to see the potential of this reagent.'

'Well,' I said awkwardly, 'it is interesting, chemically, no doubt, but as to its practical uses . . .'

The grin on Sherlock Holmes's face informed me that I had responded to his query in exactly the manner he had wished. It gave him the opportunity to explain the potential of his discovery in detail.

'Why, man,' he cried enthusiastically, 'it is the most practical medico-legal discovery for years! It gives an absolutely infallible test for bloodstains. Come over here now!' Seizing my coat-sleeve in his eagerness, he drew me over to the table at which he had been working. 'Let us have some fresh blood,' he said, and without flinching he dug a long bodkin into his finger and drew off the resulting drop of blood into a chemical pipette. 'Now, take note, I add this small quantity of blood to a litre of water. The proportion of blood cannot be more than one in a million. I have no doubt, however, that we shall be able to obtain the characteristic reaction.'

As he spoke, he threw a few white crystals into the vessel and then added some drops of a transparent fluid. The effect was instantaneous. Immediately the contents assumed a dull mahogany colour and a brownish dust precipitated at the bottom of the glass jar.

Holmes's face flushed with pleasure. 'There! What do you think of that, gentlemen?' he cried in triumph.

'It seems to be a very delicate test,' I remarked, 'but effective.'

'Effective? It is *beautiful*! Beautiful! The old guaiacum resin test is so clumsy and unreliable. So is the microscopic examination for blood corpuscles. The latter is valueless if the stains are a few hours old. Now, this test appears to work whether the blood is old or new. Had my discovery been available earlier, there are hundreds of men now walking the earth who would long ago have paid the penalty for their crimes.'

'Yes, I see,' I murmured, somewhat overwhelmed by his enthusiasm.

'*Do* you, Watson? I tell you, criminal cases are continually hinging on that one point. A man is suspected of a crime perhaps months after it has been committed. His linen or his clothes are examined, and brownish stains are discovered upon them. Are they blood-stains, or mud stains, or rust stains, or fruit stains, or what are they? That is a question which has puzzled many a criminal expert, and why? Because there was no reliable test to determine the presence of blood. Now we have the Sherlock Holmes test, and there will no longer be any difficulty.'

His eyes glittered as he spoke, and he placed his hand over his heart and bowed as if to some applauding crowd conjured by his imagination.

I could not help but be moved by the verve and enthusiasm of the man, and I felt myself sharing in his delight at his discovery. 'You are to be congratulated,' I remarked.

'When I think of the cases where this test would have been invaluable. There was Von Bischoff in Frankfurt last year. Then there was Mason of Bradford, and the notorious Muller, and Lefevre of Montpellier, and Samson of New Orleans. Oh, I could name a number of cases in which it would have been decisive.'

'You seem to be a walking calendar of crime,' said Stamford glibly, with a laugh. 'You ought to start up a paper on those lines. Call it *Police News of the Past.*'

'Very interesting reading it would make, too,' replied Sherlock Holmes, sticking a small plaster over the wound on his finger. 'I have to be careful,' he explained, turning to me with a smile, 'for I dabble with poisons a good deal.' He held out his hand as he spoke, and I observed that it was mottled over with similar pieces of plaster, and discoloured with strong acids. His sleeves were rolled up to the elbow, and I also noticed the evidence of pinpricks and small scars on the insides of his white arms. These were the tell-tale marks of a hypodermic needle. I glanced again at those animated features and vibrant eyes, and realized that at least part of his exuberance came from artificial stimulants.

'We came here on business,' said Stamford, perching on a high three-legged stool and pushing another one in my direction with his foot. 'As I intimated this morning, I said I would keep my eye out for you in the matter of living-quarters.'

Sherlock Holmes raised a quizzical brow.

'My friend Watson here is in need of digs, and is very amenable to the notion of sharing, so I thought that I had better bring you two together.'

Sherlock Holmes seemed delighted at the thought of my sharing rooms with him, which surprised me. Perhaps his all-seeing eye, which had told him that I had recently come from Afghanistan, had gleaned sufficient information about me to allow him to be at ease with such a situation.

'I have my eye on a suite of rooms in Baker Street,' he said, washing his hands, 'which would suit us down to the ground. You don't mind the smell of strong tobacco, I hope?'

'I always smoke ship's myself,' I answered.

He nodded approvingly. 'That's good. I usually have chemicals about, and occasionally do experiments. Would that annoy you?'

'By no means.'

'Let me see – what are my other shortcomings . . . ?'

As Holmes confessed his bouts of moodiness and his sulks, I hardly heard him for I was tingling with the realization that it really was going to happen. It had come to pass as Moriarty had planned and promised. I would be sharing rooms with this strange and brilliant young man with the piercing eyes and strange enthusiasms – and I would begin my life as a spy. The enormity of this reality almost took my breath away.

'What have you to confess, Watson?' Holmes was saying. 'It's just as well for two fellows to know the worst of one another before they begin to live together.'

I laughed at this cross-examination. It seemed to have a farcical aspect in relation to the truth of the situation. I noticed also that in Holmes's catalogue of his supposed failings, he did not mention that he was a user of drugs, possibly an addict.

'I am fairly easygoing, I would say,' I responded, 'but I do object to rows, because my nerves are still somewhat shaken. I get up at ungodly hours and I am extremely lazy. I have another set of vices when I'm well, but those are the principal ones at present.'

'Do you include violin-playing in your category of rows?' he asked, with some concern.

'It depends on the player,' I answered. 'A well-played violin is a treat for the gods – a badly played one. . . .'

'Oh, that's all right then,' he murmured smugly. 'I think, my dear doctor, that we may consider the thing settled – that is, if the rooms are acceptable to you.'

I realized that I must not appear too eager. I knew that from now on all my actions must be guarded and calculated. 'When can we see them?'

'Call for me here at noon tomorrow, and we'll go together and settle things up.'

'All right – noon exactly,' said I, shaking his hand.

Stamford and I left him scribbling his findings in a large notebook. On leaving the hospital, we walked for some time in the direction of my hotel.

'By the way,' I said suddenly, stopping and turning to Stamford, 'you didn't tell him that I had just returned from Afghanistan, did you?'

'Of course not. How could I?'

'Then how the deuce did he know?'

My companion smiled an enigmatic smile. 'That's just his little peculiarity,' he said. 'A good many people have wanted to know how he finds things out.'

'Oh, it's a mystery, is it?'

'If you want to unravel it, Watson, you must study the man. You'll find him a knotty problem. I'll wager he learns more about you than you about him.'

'I sincerely hope not. I wish my skeletons to remain firmly in their cupboard.' I spoke jokingly, but I was deadly serious.

Stamford and I parted company at Piccadilly, and I strolled back to my hotel, replaying in my mind my first encounter with Sherlock Holmes in a desperate attempt to learn more about the man. It wasn't a particularly fruitful exercise.

Sherlock Holmes and I met the following day as arranged and we inspected the rooms. It really was a perfunctory exercise on both our parts. He was very keen to seal the arrangement, and I had no choice in the matter anyway.

However, I found the lodgings at 221B Baker Street ideal. They consisted of a couple of comfortable bedrooms, a bathroom and a single large, airy sitting-room, cheerfully furnished and illuminated by two broad windows.

Our landlady, Mrs Kitty Hudson, a widow, a small tidy woman with tightly curled blonde hair rapidly fading to grey, seemed pleasant and gracious, and was delighted at the prospect of 'two young gentlemen of respectable character' coming to live under her roof. Her terms were moderate when divided between the two of us, and so the bargain was concluded upon the spot.

That very evening I moved what few things I had from the hotel, and on the following morning Sherlock Holmes followed me with several boxes and a portmanteaux. For a day, he unpacked and we spent the time laying out our property to the best advantage. That done, we gradually began to settle down and to accustom ourselves to our new surroundings.

The seeming normality of this arrangement, compared with the past six months of my life, was so welcoming to me, that I actually began to enjoy living at 221B. Sherlock Holmes was certainly not a difficult man to share with. He was quiet in his ways, and his habits were regular. Frequently he would have breakfasted and gone out before I rose, and he was very often in bed by ten at night, while I regularly stayed up until after midnight, reading, smoking and enjoying a brandy nightcap.

It was about a week after I had taken up residence in Baker Street that I received my first summons. It came through the post. The message just gave a date and time and location: 'Today, 12 March. 11.30 a.m., the corner of Wigmore Street and Duke Street.' Making a mental note of the details, I threw the note on the fire and watched it burn until it turned into fine black ash.

At the appointed hour, I stood at the corner of Wigmore Street, when a hansom drew up and a voice from within beckoned me to join him.

'It is good to meet you, Doctor Watson,' said the shadowy figure, once I was seated. 'I am Colonel Sebastian Moran, the chief of staff for Professor Moriarty.'

He took my limp hand and shook it. 'Shall we go for a little ride?' He tapped the roof of the cab with his cane, and we set off at a steady trot.

'The purpose of this meeting, as I am sure you are aware, is merely to receive a progress report on the arrangements regarding Mr Sherlock Holmes. How are things between you? Have you settled in quite amicably? And more importantly, do you think that Mr Holmes has any idea of your . . . how shall I put this . . . your ulterior motives?'

These questions did not surprise me. I had been expecting some kind of inquisition, and so I was prepared. Naturally, I had taken great pains to observe Holmes in the few days that we had been living together, and already I was building up a picture of the man. In all fairness, because of my natural curiosity and my penchant for writing from life, I believe I would have done this anyway had I not a reason to do so. There were many aspects of Holmes's character and behaviour that puzzled me, but one thing I was sure of was that he had no suspicions concerning me. For all his reported brilliance as a detective, I was – and remained – his one blind spot.

There had been three callers at our new address enquiring for Mr Holmes: a young girl, fashionably dressed, who arrived in an agitated fashion and stayed about half an hour; a white-haired gentleman with the air of the cleric about him; and a sallow, rat-faced man who was introduced to me as Mr Lestrade. The latter fellow called twice, and behaved in quite a shifty manner on encountering me on both occasions. When these visitors arrived, Holmes requested the use of the sitting-room for privacy. I agreed and took myself off to my bedroom.

I was intrigued by all these comings and goings, but I knew I had to be patient. Despite some desultory conversations over dinner, Sherlock Holmes had not yet divulged to me what his profession was, and I thought it politic, at this early stage, not to appear too inquisitive. I was sure that in his own good time he would reveal all.

I conveyed all this information to Colonel Moran, who listened in silence until I had finished.

'Capital,' he said at last. 'I think you are quite right to stalk your prey at a distance for the time being. A bond of trust and reliance must be established between you, and this can only occur when Holmes feels at complete ease with you. I am a practised hand at tracking tigers in India, Watson. I'm an old shikari, and I know the value of patience and allowing your prey to feel relaxed and confident in its safety.

'You ought to know that Lestrade, the fellow you described as "rat-faced", is a Scotland Yard inspector who has been using Holmes for some months. When he gets stuck – which is often – he goes running to our friend for help. I can tell you that the Professor's organization would not be half as successful as it is, if there was anyone at Scotland Yard with half a brain. That's why your fellow lodger is such a threat.'

There followed an uncomfortable pause during which I felt I was expected to comment on Moran's claim, but I did not know what to say or, rather, what I was expected to say. At length I said awkwardly, 'Is that all for now?' I desperately wanted to escape from the dark confines of the cab and the company of this unpleasant man. Such a conversation only reminded me in bleak terms of the reality of my situation, the lie I was living. For the past week I had relaxed and been content, observing my fellow lodger out of a spirit of curiosity rather than with such a degrading ulterior motive as spying on him.

'In essence, Watson. But please do not be so petulant. You are being paid well for your labours. Remember that.'

I leaned forward, anger welling up inside me. I wanted to say that I had been given no choice in the matter. The whole scenario was forced upon me, but as the words came to my lips, they died away. I knew it was useless to complain. I was the proverbial fly caught in the web, and the spider was certainly not going to let me go.

Moran handed me a piece of paper. Glancing at it in the dim light, I noticed that it contained an address in West London. 'The Professor would like you to compile regular reports on your activities with Sherlock Holmes. They are to be posted to this address on the first of the month. If there is some urgent business you think the Professor should know about, you are to send a telegram to that same address. Do you understand?'

'Yes.'

'Good. Now memorize the address and hand the paper back to me.'

I did as he asked.

Moran tapped the roof of the cab with his cane again and the vehicle drew to a halt.

'This is where you leave us, Watson. We are not far from your lodgings.'

As I rose, Moran offered his hand again. With some reluctance, I took it. 'It's been good to meet you. We expect great things of you, Doctor. Be sure that you do not disappoint us.'

Without responding, I quickly departed the cab, glad to be out in the cold, fresh air once more.

Chapter Ten

Revenge was a flame which had burnt with a steady and fierce intensity in the heart of Jefferson Hope for twenty years. Never in all that time had his determination to murder the two men who had ruined his life and brought about the death of his beloved Lucy wavered for one instant. He had dedicated the rest of his days to the task, and once it was complete, he would be happy to meet his maker with a clear conscience. As he looked out of the grimy window of his lodgings at the gathering dusk and the hurrying silhouettes of the passers-by below, he felt good. He knew, at long last, that he was near to reaching his goal. He had finally tracked Drebber and Stangerson to London. He had always believed that it was just a matter of time before he got his hands on them, but now that time was very short. He prayed that his failing health would not let him down at the last moment. Fate could be cruel; indeed, it had been cruel to him, but surely it could not be *that* cruel – after all this time.

He held up the key against the glow of the gas mantle and examined it as though it were a precious stone, and smiled. It had chanced that, some days before, a passenger in his cab had been engaged in looking over some empty houses in the Brixton Road and had dropped the key to one of them on the floor of the cab. It was claimed the same evening and returned, but not before Hope had arranged for a duplicate to be made. Now he had access to one spot in the whole city where he knew he would be free from interruption to carry out his grisly plan. However, the problem remained of how he could get Drebber there.

That night the dream came again to Jefferson Hope. He was escaping to Carson City with his beloved Lucy and her father. They were fleeing the clutches of the Mormons, crossing the great mountain range that isolated Salt Lake City from the civilized world. In the dream he could feel the scorching power of the sun, and the raging thirst that dries the throat and causes the tongue to swell; and then, as they rose higher in the mountains, reaching nearly five thousand feet, the air grew bitter and keen, cutting through their clothing with the viciousness of sharp knives. But his concerns were for Lucy, his beloved Lucy. In the dream, as in life, he cursed himself for leaving her. It was their second day of flight and they had run out of provisions. As an experienced hunter, Hope knew there was game to be had in the mountains, and so, choosing a sheltered nook for his loved one and her ailing father, he built a fire for them with a few dried branches, and set off in search of food.

As Hope tossed and turned in his troubled sleep, the vivid dream unfolded steadily, as it had done countless times. After two or three hours' fruitless search, he began to despair, and then he spied a lone sheep – a bighorn. It did not take him long to despatch the creature, but it was too unwieldy to lift, so with the practised skill of an old hunter, he cut away one haunch and part of the flank. Flinging these over his shoulder, he hastened back to the makeshift camp.

As the climax of his dream grew closer, Jefferson Hope began to moan aloud in his tormented slumbers. Scrabbling over the cold dry rocks and slithering down narrow ravines, he eventually reached the spot where he had left Lucy and her father. All he saw was the glowing pile of ashes that had once been the fire. There was no living creature nearby: Lucy, her father and the horses were gone. He stood there in horror as the fierce silence of the mountains pressed in on him.

As he approached the camp, he saw signs of numerous hoofprints, indicating that a large party of men had overtaken the fugitives. No doubt this gang had been led by Drebber and Stangerson, eager to capture the girl, eager to get their greedy hands on her father's property. A little way off, on the far side of the camp, Hope observed a low mound of reddish earth. There was no mistaking it for anything but a newly dug grave. With faltering steps he walked towards it, his body shuddering with apprehension. He saw a sheet of paper nailed to a crudely made cross placed at the head of the grave. The inscription on the paper was brief:

JOHN FERRIER

FORMERLY OF SALT LAKE CITY

Died August 4th, 1860

They had killed the old man. What creed, what religion would allow such an act? Hope felt a prickle of tears – tears of frustration and despair. He looked around wildly to see if there was a second grave. He half hoped that there would be one. One containing his darling Lucy. At least then her pain and torment would be over. He searched in vain. There was no other grave.

It was clear then: Drebber and Stangerson had snatched the girl, and when her father attempted to stop them, they had killed him. Lucy would be well on her way back to Salt Lake City now, to fulfil her original destiny: to become a bride of either Drebber or Stangerson – whomever of the two the Elder favoured – and forced to join one of the accursed Mormon harems. He knew now that he was powerless to prevent this from happening. He had lost the love of his life. Jefferson Hope sank to his knees and wept.

He woke with a start – as he always did when he reached that part of the dream – his body bathed in sweat and his hands clenched tightly by his side. He lay there, taking large gulps of air, desperately trying to calm his rapidly beating heart. The doctor had warned him that any abnormal strain could be the end of him. The aortic aneurysm from which he had suffered since the loss of Lucy had worsened drastically in the last few months, to such an extent that he knew he had little time left. Indeed, the doctor had warned him only the week before that he was living on borrowed time.

At length, he rose and stared out of his window, gazing at the rooftops which were slowly taking form and detail in the early morning light. He could not wait any longer. Another night, another dream, and he might not survive. He had to act now. He had to act that very day. Leaning his damp forehead against the cold window-pane, he smiled. His torment was nearly at an end.

Chapter Eleven

From the journal of John Walker

As is sometimes the way, Fate stepped in to help break down Sherlock Holmes's reserve regarding his chosen profession. It was last Tuesday. As usual, Holmes had left our lodgings before I breakfasted, and so, having nothing better to do, I took myself to Regent's Park to observe the effects of the burgeoning spring upon the gardens there. Seeing such new life budding forth was such a contrast to the hot and arid wastes of Afghanistan. However, halfway through the morning, the skies clouded over and I was caught in a heavy shower. I sheltered for some time under a large oak tree, but when the dark grey clouds had completely obliterated any trace of blue, I realized that the rain was set in for some time. I ran to the street, hailed a cab and returned to Baker Street, arriving shortly before noon.

The sight that met me as I entered our shared sitting-room made me gasp. Sherlock Holmes was slumped in the basket-chair, his feet sprawled out across the hearth rug. His left sleeve was rolled up, and a hypodermic syringe dangled precariously from his limp hand. At the sound of my entrance, his eyes opened slowly and his head lolled in my direction.

'The good doctor has returned somewhat early,' he mumbled, attempting to sit up, but not succeeding.

I strode over to him and took the syringe from his hand before it fell to the floor.

'You did not confess to me that you ill used yourself in this fashion, when we were in the business of discussing our failings.'

'Confess. Ill use. Failings. Such emotional language, Watson.'

'What is it?' I asked. 'Cocaine? Morphine?'

He screwed up his face. 'Morphine. Pah! It is cocaine, my dear Watson. A wonderfully soothing preparation – a seven per cent solution. Just enough to stimulate the imagination and relieve the boredom, without deadening the faculties.'

'I would have thought you required neither,' said I, shaking my wet raincoat and hanging it on the stand.

Holmes gave a cry of annoyance and this time managed to pull himself up into a sitting position.

'What on earth do *you* know about such things? My life is devoted to the avoidance of boredom and, oh, how easily I am bored.'

I sat opposite him, realizing that in this state he might well reveal more about himself than he would do under normal circumstances.

'Why is that? Why are you so easily bored?'

He smiled dreamily. 'Because I rarely get the brain food I need. My mind rebels at stagnation. Give me problems, give me the most abstruse cryptogram or the most cunning murder, and then I am alive and have no need for artificial stimulants.'

'Murder?'

'Yes, murder or robbery or forgery. You see, Watson, I am a detective. That is my profession. I am the only unofficial consulting detective in London. Here in London there are lots of government detectives, and a fair number of private ones, and when these fellows go astray, they come to me for advice.'

'They come in their droves,' I observed sarcastically.

'No, they do not come in their droves. Not yet. That is my problem. But they *will* when I have established myself. At present, I have no cases on hand and my brain is lying idle. But when I am famous, I will be able to take my pick of the cases.'

The lethargic Holmes had now disappeared: here again was the bright-eyed enthusiast, engaged upon his favourite topic.

'You see,' he continued, 'I possess a great deal of special know-ledge, and I have trained myself to see and deduce from what I observe. This is what makes me unique. You do not seem convinced.'

'It is an audacious statement.'

'Proof, eh? You need a demonstration of my powers. That is easy. I remember that you appeared surprised when I told you on our first meeting that you had just recently come from Afghanistan.'

'You were told, no doubt.'

'Holmes dismissed my comment with an irritated wave of his hand. 'Nothing of the sort. I knew, *I knew* you came from Afghanistan. From a long habit, the train of thoughts ran so swiftly through my mind that I arrived at the conclusion without being conscious of the process. To me it is akin to tying one's bootlaces in the morning. The procedure is carried out automatically, without any thought as to what one is doing. It is second nature.'

'So, how *did* you know about Afghanistan?'

'My train of reasoning ran thus: here is a gentleman of a medical type, but with the air of a military man. Clearly an army doctor, then. He has just come from the tropics, for his face is dark, but that is not the natural tint of his skin, for his wrists are fair. He has undergone great hardship and probably sickness. Where, currently, in the tropics would an English army doctor be pressed into service that would cause such hardship? Why, Afghanistan, of course. The whole train of reasoning did not take a second.'

I listened with amazement to this analysis.

'Why, that is brilliant!' I said, with genuine admiration.

'Elementary.'

'As explained by you, the process seems simple enough, but I doubt if I or anyone I know could perform such a diagnosis.'

'That is because I have trained myself to perform such a diagno-sis, as you put it. I perhaps ought to add that I had read in *The Times* of an army officer called Watson who had been invalided out of the army and had just arrived back from Afghanistan. Information that merely confirmed my deductions.'

Such a revelation removed much of the magic from his previous claim, and it was the first hint I was to obtain that sometimes Sherlock Holmes pretended to be more brilliant than he actually was. My expression must have revealed my thoughts.

'The end result is the same. In solving crime, one must use every facility at one's command to reach a satisfactory conclusion. The press is a valuable source of information. I scour the papers every day. Luckily I am blessed with a photographic memory, and I can remember the most obscure and *outré* pieces of information and store them in my brain attic until I should require them. I am sure that in the days to come there will be ample opportunity for me to demonstrate my detective powers in order to convince you of my abilities and to prove that I am no charlatan. However, for now, let me add that this morning you visited Regent's Park, sheltered under a tree when it came on to rain and then caught a cab back here.'

I opened my mouth in astonishment.

'Adhering to the soles of your shoes are traces of mud and grass which indicate that you have been walking in one of the parks. As Regent's Park is the nearest, it is fairly safe to assume that to be the one. Also, there is a fragment of an oak leaf caught in the left turn up of your trousers. As it came on to rain heavily and suddenly, it is most likely that you took shelter under one of the giant oaks in the park. It is still raining heavily, but your raincoat is damp rather than soaking wet, so you obviously did not walk back to Baker Street. Observation and deduction, Doctor Watson.'

With these words, he slumped back down in his chair and closed his eyes, shutting me and the real world out of his drug-induced slumbers.

Working as a cab-driver in London, Jefferson Hope had been able to trail Stangerson and Drebber wherever they went. He took satisfaction in dogging their heels, knowing that they were ignorant of his presence. On some occasions, he had even driven the men in his cab. With his full beard and hat pulled low over his brow, he had no fear of being recognized. It was twenty years since they had set eyes upon him, and, he reckoned, no one really looks at cab-drivers in any case. In a strange perverted way, he wished they *had* recognized him. He could not wait to see the look of shock and horror on their faces when they realized that their nemesis was at hand. That day would come, but it would come when he had planned for it – not before.

Hope had traced Drebber and Stangerson half-way across the world, from St Petersburg, to Paris and then on to Copenhagen. Somehow, they sensed that they were being followed, and their restless sojourning was a clear sign of their guilt. Finally catching up with them in London, Hope had discovered them living in a boarding house in Camberwell. The two men never went out alone, and rarely after dark. This was a stumbling-block for Hope. He knew that he could not tackle both of them at once. He had to wait to catch each one on his own.

However, now he knew he could wait no longer. He could not risk his heart giving out on him – not now that he was so close to his dream. He resolved that today had to be the day. Desperate measures were needed. But then luck was on his side. It was late afternoon as he drove down Torquay Terrace, the street in which the two men were living, when he saw a cab draw up to their door. Presently, luggage was brought out, and after a time Drebber and Stangerson appeared. They stood on the pavement, engaged in a heated conversation. As always, on seeing the two men, Hope's pulse quickened. They were the devils responsible for the death of John Ferrier and his darling Lucy, and twenty years had done nothing to dispel the deep hatred he felt for them.

Drebber was the taller of the two. He walked with a swagger, and his slicked-back hair and thin moustache enhanced his air of arrogance. In contrast, Stangerson was short, with stooped shoulders, and bore a constant furtive expression.

As they talked, a red-faced young man in shirtsleeves rushed down the path towards them. He was shouting in a threatening manner at Drebber, who responded by shaking his fist at him. Further angry words were exchanged, and within seconds the two men were locked in a vicious embrace. Hope was too far away to catch the nature of the argument, but both men were hot in temper and threw punches at each other in a wild fashion.

With some effort, Stangerson dragged the two of them apart and pushed his colleague into the cab. With further harsh words hurled at Drebber, the young man returned reluctantly to the boarding-house.

It looked to Hope as though the pair had been evicted from their lodgings for some misdemeanour perpetrated by the arrogant Drebber, and now they were on their travels again. He gave a groan of dismay when he heard Drebber give the driver instructions to take them to Euston Station. No doubt that meant they were planning to take the boat train and leave for the Continent. Once there, he might easily lose them again. With a gnawing feeling of despair in the pit of his stomach, Hope followed them at a safe distance.

At Euston, he tethered his cab and caught up with the two fugitives on the crowded platform. Here, another argument broke out between the men. Hope moved as close as he could in the bustling throng so that he could overhear their conversation. Drebber was castigating Stangerson for having misread the timetable. They had just missed one boat-train, and the next was not to be for nearly two hours.

'You damned idiot,' Drebber was saying, and, from his blotchy face and slightly slurred speech, it was clear that he had been drinking.

'It's only a few hours,' responded Stangerson lamely. 'We can take a seat in the waiting-room. The time will soon pass.'

'The hell it will! You take a seat in the waiting-room and look after the luggage. I have a little business to attend to.'

'What business? You're not going back to the boarding-house?'

'Never you mind. You tend to the luggage.'

'I don't like us splitting up like this. It might not be safe.'

'Stop fussing. You're like a goddamned mother hen at times.'

'What if you're not back in time for the train? It's the last one tonight.'

'I'll be back. But if there is a problem, I'll meet you at Halliday's Private Hotel. You know the place.'

Stangerson nodded.

Without another word, Enoch Drebber turned and walked unsteadily out of the station.

At last, thought Hope, the moment I have waited for: they are on their own and it is after dark. But the game had been a long and strenuous one, and Hope was not about to spoil things by acting with undue precipitation. He followed Drebber in his cab, and the nature of the business that he wished to attend to soon became clear. Within a five-minute stroll of Euston Station, Drebber went in to an alehouse and stayed there for about an hour. On leaving, he was much the worse for drink.

Another call at another alehouse secured Drebber's fate. He was ejected some thirty minutes later by an irate landlord.

'I didn't know the girl was your daughter!' he growled, as he landed on the pavement.

'I don't want scum like you in my place,' bellowed the landlord. 'If I see you in here again, I'll break your bleedin' neck.'

Drebber lay for a moment on the ground as though he was unable to move, and then, with some effort, he gradually pulled himself to his feet and dusted himself down.

'Bastard,' he muttered to himself. 'Merely trying to be friendly to the girl.'

Once standing, albeit in an unsteady fashion, he consulted his watch. 'Blast! Missed the train.'

'Need a cab, sir?'

Drebber looked up and saw a hansom cab at the kerb. The driver, a broad fellow with a florid face and large grey beard, stared down at him.

Drebber thought for a moment. His brain was sluggish with alcohol, and he had to concentrate hard to formulate any simple plan of action.

'Dammit,' he said at length, 'might as well. Do you know Halliday's Private Hotel on Little George Street?'

'Yes, sir.'

'Good. That's for me.' With some effort, Stangerson clambered into the cab and collapsed in the seat. Within seconds of the cab moving off, he had fallen into a drunken slumber.

The cab headed away from Euston. Away from Little George Street. The cab headed for Brixton. Jefferson Hope smiled with a warmth that had not been in evidence for over twenty years.

Enoch Drebber was roused from his sleep by being roughly shaken. As he opened his bleary eyes, he saw the face of the cabbie looming over him.

'It's time to get out.'

'All right, Cabbie.' The voice was thick and virtually unintelligible.

With assistance from the cabbie, Drebber stepped on to the pavement, but then his legs seemed to give way.

'Need so' assistance,' he murmured, leaning heavily on the driver.

'Certainly, sir,' came the reply.

Hope hooked his arm under Drebber's and shepherded him up the path towards the empty house. Unlocking the door, he helped the man inside.

'It's infernally dark in here. Halliday's Private Hotel?' said Drebber, a note of uncertainty introduced into his inebriate tones.

'We'll soon have a light,' said Hope, striking a match and lighting the candle that he had brought with him. The room filled with a gloomy ochre light, revealing it to be empty and derelict. At first, Drebber gazed in wonderment, and then fear caught hold of him.

'What . . . what the hell's going on here? Where are we?'

Hope held the candle to his face and threw off his wide-brimmed hat.

'Never mind where we are, Enoch Drebber, you answer my question. Who am I?'

Open-mouthed, Drebber gazed at him with bleary, drunken eyes, and then they widened in horror and convulsed his whole features. He staggered back, his hand to his mouth, gagging the scream.

'You know me, then?' said Hope steadily.

For Drebber, it was the bleakest and most fearful of nightmares. Of course he knew the man. It was the man in all the world he most feared meeting. The terror that rippled through his body brought about a remarkably quick sobering effect. Suddenly his brain began to function with icy clarity. He had been abducted and brought to this godforsaken dwelling by his greatest enemy.

'I have money, lots of money,' he said feebly. 'I can give you money.'

Jefferson Hope laughed in response.

'What is it that you want?'

'Vengeance,' replied Hope simply. 'I want vengeance.'

Chapter Twelve

From the journal of John Walker

The morning following Holmes's emotional revelation concerning his detective aspirations, I found him in a far more cheerful and bright-eyed mood. I came down to breakfast as usual, and to my surprise discovered my fellow lodger swathed in an enormous purple dressing-gown at our dining-table, lingering over a plate of buttered toast. He was already grinning about something as I entered, and on seeing me his smile broadened.

'Ah, Watson, the very man. I have good news for us both.'

'Really?' I said, with some apprehension, joining him at the table and pouring a cup of coffee.

He scooped up a sheet of paper and waved it triumphantly before his face. 'Brain food, at last. You remember yesterday how down in the dumps I was because I had no criminal investigation to challenge my mind. . . ?'

I nodded.

'Well, here is the answer to my prayers.' He passed the sheet of paper over to me. 'Go on, man, read it!' he cried eagerly.

I did so. The letter ran:

Dear Mr Sherlock Holmes,
There has been a bad business during the night at 3 Lauriston

Gardens, off the Brixton Road. Our man on the beat saw a light there at about two in the morning, and, as the house was an empty one, he suspected something was amiss. He found the door open, and in the front room, which is bare of furniture, discovered the body of a gentleman, well dressed and having cards in his pocket bearing the name Enoch J. Drebber of Cleveland, Ohio, USA.

There had been no robbery, nor is there evidence as to how the man met his death. There are marks of blood in the room, but there is no wound on the person. We are at a loss as to how he came into the empty house; indeed the whole affair is a puzzler. If you can come round to the house at any time before twelve today, you will find me there.

I have left everything in *status quo* until I hear from you. If you are unable to come, I will call upon you this evening to present you with fuller details of the affair, when I hope you will favour me with your opinion.

Yours sincerely,
Tobias Gregson.

I handed the letter back to Holmes. 'It sounds most puzzling,' I said.

'Yes. No robbery; no obvious cause of death; no wounds on the body, but marks of blood in the room. A fine concoction.'

'This Gregson . . .'

'A policeman. Inspector. Along with Lestrade he is the smartest of the Scotland Yarders.' Holmes wrinkled his nose. 'That says little, however. They are the pick of a bad lot. They are quick and energetic – but conventional and limited in their outlook.'

It seemed a bitter irony that Holmes shared the same view of the official police as Professor Moriarty.

'This Gregson is most earnest in his desire that you help them,' I said.

'He knows I am his superior and acknowledges it to me, but he would bite his tongue off rather than confess it to another soul.'

Holmes gave a high-pitched giggle.

'You intend to help him?'

'Of course. I wouldn't miss it for the world. This has all the makings of a splendid case. We shall take a cab immediately to Lauriston Gardens.'

'*We?*'

'Oh, yes, you too, Doctor. I insist!' he cried, rising from the table and flapping off his dressing-gown. 'I want you to witness my brilliance at first hand. I cannot have you thinking that I am merely capable of party tricks, simple deductions concerning where someone comes from or where they have been. You should see for yourself the very practical nature of my skills. I trust you don't object to accompanying me?'

I could not help but grin at his suggestion. It was, of course, just the scenario I had hoped for.

Within five minutes we were in a cab on our way to Lauriston Gardens, off the Brixton Road, and my first adventure with Sherlock Holmes had begun.

It was a cold and misty morning, and a grey veil hung over the house-tops. My companion was in an excited mood and was forever leaning forward to spy out of the window of the cab to check the progress of our journey, so eager was he to reach our destination.

'Have you formulated any theories about this strange business?' I asked.

Holmes shook his head vigorously. 'No data yet. It is a capital mistake to theorize before you have all the evidence. It biases the judgement. That is why it is essential that I visit the scene to investigate it for myself; no doubt Gregson will have missed numerous clues which could point the way to the truth. Ah, here were are at last: Lauriston Gardens.'

Holmes leapt up and instructed the driver to stop immediately. We were some hundred yards from the house in question, and we completed our journey on foot.

Number 3 Lauriston Gardens wore an ill-omened and minatory look. It was one of four crumbling dwellings, all unoccupied and each containing a crooked 'To Let' sign by the front door. Dark, begrimed windows stared with an air of vacant melancholy out on to the empty street. The garden of Number 3 was bounded by a three-foot brick wall with a fringe of wooden rails upon the top, and against this wall was leaning a stalwart policeman, surrounded by a little knot of loafers who craned their necks and strained their eyes in the vain hope of catching a glimpse of the proceedings within.

I had fully expected Sherlock Holmes to bound up the garden path and enter the house in order to study the scene of the crime. This was not the case. With an air of affected nonchalance, he strolled along the pavement, gazing vacantly at the ground, the sky, the houses opposite and the line of railings. I followed some distance behind, feeling uncomfortable and slightly ludicrous.

After having a brief word with the constable, he beckoned me and we proceeded slowly down the path. Holmes kept his eyes riveted to the ground. There were very many marks of footsteps upon the wet clay soil, a great number no doubt belonging to the policemen who had been coming and going. In my opinion there was nothing that my companion could learn from his scrutiny. And yet he gave this performance – and a performance it was, with his facial tics and mutterings. Twice he stopped and I saw him smile, and I heard him utter an exclamation of satisfaction. I felt sure that such actions were self-conscious ones designed to impress and intrigue me.

At the door we were met by a flaxen-haired man with a notebook in his hand who, on seeing my friend, rushed forward and shook his hand effusively.

'It is indeed kind of you to come,' he said, in a rasping voice. 'I have left everything untouched.'

'Except *that*!' Holmes responded, with some heat, indicating the pathway. 'If a herd of buffaloes had passed along there, there could be no greater mess. No doubt, however, you had drawn your own conclusions, Gregson, before you permitted this.'

The policeman flushed. 'I have had so much to do in the house . . . It is in there that the heart of the mystery lies. My colleague, Mr

Lestrade, is here also. I had relied on him to look after this.'

Holmes glanced at me and raised his eyebrows sardonically. 'Well, with two such fellows as yourself and Lestrade upon the case, there will not be much for a third party to find out,' he said smoothly.

'We have done all we can, but I am not sure we have uncovered all that is possible. It's a queer case, and I know of your taste for such things.'

Holmes leaned close to me and whispered in my ear, 'What did I tell you? They are stumped.'

'Would you care to look at the room?' said Lestrade.

'Yes, but first – you did not come in a cab?'

Gregson shook his head.

'Nor Lestrade?'

Another shake of the head.

'You arrived together in a police wagon?'

'Why, yes.'

'I thought so. I recognized the wide spread of the wheels, so much broader than those of a hansom. Good, that's one thing settled. Very well, lay on, Macduff.'

With these words he strode into the house, followed by Gregson, whose features expressed his blank astonishment.

A short passage, bare-planked and dusty, led to the kitchen and other downstairs rooms. Two doors opened out of it, to the left and to the right. One of these had obviously been closed for many weeks. The other belonged to the dining-room, where the body had been found. Holmes walked in, and I followed him with that subdued feeling in my heart which the presence of death inspires.

It was a large square room, looking all the larger for the absence of any furniture. A vulgar flaring-paper adorned the walls, but it was blotched in places with mildew, and here and there great strips had become detached and hung down, exposing the crumbling plaster beneath. Opposite the door was the fireplace, surmounted by a mantelpiece of imitation white marble. On one corner of this was the stump of a red candle.

The solitary window was so thick with dirt that the light which filtered into the room touched everything with a grey bloom that was intensified by the layer of dust which coated the whole apartment.

All these details I noted down afterwards. On entering the room, my immediate attention was captured by the motionless figure that lay stretched out upon the floorboards, with vacant sightless eyes staring at the discoloured ceiling. The figure was that of a man in his early forties, middle-sized, with dark shiny hair which was swept back from his face, and a neatly clipped moustache. He was dressed in a heavy broadcloth frock-coat and waistcoat, with light-coloured trousers, and immaculate collar and cuffs. A top hat was placed on the floor beside him. His hands were clenched, but his arms were spread wide as though the death struggle had been a fierce one. His rigid face bore an expression of horror.

On seeing the man, I felt faint. A sudden searing light flashed before my eyes, blinding me, and for a brief moment I was back in Afghanistan in the heat of the infirmary tent, looking down at a dead colleague. His eyes held the same terror and disbelief, and the body was contorted with agony in a similar fashion.

I stumbled and reached for the wall to steady myself. I shook my head and took a deep intake of breath in an effort to banish this vision from my mind. Thankfully, the others in the room were too absorbed in their preoccupations to notice me.

The man I recognized as Lestrade was standing by the corpse, jotting things down in a notebook. He was lean and ferret-like, with bright beady restless eyes.

'This case will cause us problems, I am sure,' he remarked, addressing Holmes. 'It beats anything I have seen.'

'There are no clues,' said Gregson.

'None at all,' agreed Lestrade.

'We shall see, we shall see,' said Holmes, with no attempt to disguise the arrogance of the remark. He approached the body and, kneeling down, examined it intently. 'You are sure there is no wound?' he asked, pointing to the numerous splashes of blood on the floor around the corpse.

'Positive!' cried the two detectives in unison, as though they were part of a music hall sketch.

'Then this blood belongs to a second individual – presumably the murderer, if indeed murder has been committed. It reminds me of the circumstances attendant on the death of Van Jansen, in Utrecht, in the year '34. Do you remember the case, Gregson?'

'No, Mr Holmes.'

'Read it up – you really should. There is nothing new under the sun. It has all been done before.'

As he spoke, his nimble fingers were flying here, there and everywhere, feeling, pressing, unbuttoning, examining. Despite the swiftness of the examination, it was clear to me that it was carried out with an enviable thoroughness. Finally Holmes leaned over the dead man and sniffed his lips, and then glanced at the soles of his patent leather boots.

As he rose to face us, his expression gave away nothing of his thoughts or conclusions.

'You can take him to the mortuary now. There is nothing more to be learned.'

Gregson had a stretcher and four men at hand. At his call they entered the room, scooped up the body, covered it with a dark blanket and carried it away. As they did so, a ring tinkled down and rolled across the floor.

Lestrade grabbed it and held it up to the light.

'There has been a woman here!' he cried. 'It's a woman's wedding-ring.'

He held it out as he spoke, and we all gathered round and gazed at it. There could be no doubt that this plain gold band had once adorned the finger of a bride.

Gregson frowned and scratched his head. 'This complicates matters,' he said. 'Heaven knows they were complicated enough before.'

'My dear Gregson, there is nothing very complicated about this affair. Come, come, you will not find the key to the mystery by staring at the damned ring,' snapped Holmes, with a swagger, which I felt was manufactured deliberately to impress me as to the way he dealt with the Scotland Yard dunderheads. 'What did you find in his pockets?'

'We have it all here,' said Gregson, leading us into the hallway and pointing to a litter of objects upon one of the bottom steps of the stairway. 'A gold watch, No. 97163 by Barraud of London. Gold Albert chain, very heavy and solid. Gold ring with masonic device. Gold pin – bulldog's head, with rubies as eyes. Russian leather-clad case with cards of Enoch Drebber of Cleveland corresponding with the E.J.D. upon the linen. No purse, but loose money to the extent of seven pounds and thirteen shillings. Pocket edition of Boccaccio's *Decameron,* with the name Joseph Stangerson on the flyleaf. Two letters – one addressed to E.J. Drebber and one to Joseph Stangerson.'

'At what address?' asked Holmes, giving the objects a cursory glance.

'American Exchange, Strand – to be left until called for. The letters are from the Guion Steamship Company and refer to the sailing of their boats from Liverpool. It is clear that the poor blighter was about to return to New York.'

'Have you made enquiries about this other man – Stangerson?'

'I did it at once,' said Gregson, beaming. 'I have had advertisements sent to all newspapers, and one of my men has gone to the American Exchange, but he has not returned yet. '

'Have you sent to Cleveland?'

'We telegraphed this morning.'

'How did you word your enquiries?'

'We simply detailed the circumstances and said that we should be glad of any information which could help us.'

'You did not ask for particulars on any point you considered crucial?'

Gregson seemed somewhat abashed by this query. 'Well, I asked about Stangerson,' he said.

Sherlock Holmes rolled his eyes in despair. 'I have not yet had time to examine the room, but if you will allow me, I shall do so now.'

He strode back into the room, the atmosphere of which felt clearer since the removal of its ghastly inmate. Whipping out a tape-measure and a large magnifying-glass from his pocket, he proceeded to trot around the room, sometimes stopping and sometimes kneeling, and once lying flat upon his face. So engrossed was he with his occupation, he appeared to have forgotten our presence, for he chattered away to himself in a nervous undertone the whole time, sometimes presenting himself with a question and then answering it. As I watched him I was irresistibly reminded of a pure-blooded, well-trained foxhound as it dashes backwards and forwards through the covert, whining in its eagerness, until it comes across the lost scent. Sherlock Holmes was now truly in his element. No drug or stimulant could have so energized and enthused the man as this frantic search for clues. So, for what seemed like fifteen minutes, we stood and watched this remarkable performance as he measured the distance between marks which were entirely invisible to me, and occasionally applied his tape to the walls in an equally incomprehensible manner. In one place he gathered up very carefully a little pile of grey dust from the floor, and dropped it into an envelope. Finally, he examined the fireplace and then gave a cry of delight. Snatching the candlestick which had been placed on the end, he lit it and held it up into the nearby corner.

'What do you think of this, gentlemen?' he cried, with the flourish of a showman introducing his latest exhibit. The flickering light illuminated a portion of the wall where a large piece of the wallpaper had peeled away, leaving a large discoloured oblong of coarse plastering. Across this bare space there was scrawled in blood-red letters a single word:

RACHE

We rushed forward to examine the writing.

'The other visitor to this room – and it is clear that there were two men here last night – has written it with his own blood. See the smear where it has trickled down the wall?'

'Why was it written there?' I asked.

'The candle on the mantelpiece was lit at the time, and this would have been the brightest corner of the room,' explained Holmes.

'And what does it mean, now that you have found it?' asked Gregson, in a deprecating manner.

'Oh, I can answer that,' crowed Lestrade. 'It means that the writer was going to put the female name Rachel, but something prevented him from finishing it. You mark my words, when the case comes to be cleared you will find that a woman by the name of Rachel will feature in the business. It's all very well for you to laugh, Mr Sherlock Holmes; you may think you are very smart and clever, but I think you will discover that in the end the old hound is the best.'

Holmes, who had exploded with rude laughter at Lestrade's assertions, attempted to curb his natural amusement.

'I am sure you are correct,' he beamed, his voice heavily tinged with sarcasm. 'Please let me know how your investigations go. I shall be happy to give you any help I can. In the mean time, I should like to have words with the constable who discovered the body.'

'He's off duty now,' said Lestrade.

'Can you give me his name and address?'

Lestrade glanced at his notebook. 'John Rance. You will find him at 46 Audley Court, Kennington Park Gate.'

Holmes took note of the address.

'Come along, Doctor,' he said, taking my arm. 'We shall go and look him up.'

Gregson stepped forward. 'Before you go, Mr Holmes, have you learned anything from your investigations here that would help us?'

'Oh, certainly.'

The two police officers looked at each other and then back at Holmes, waiting for his words of enlightenment.

'I can tell you that a murder has been done, and the murderer was a man. He was more than six feet in height, was in the prime of life, had small feet for his size, wore coarse square-toed boots and smoked a Trichinopoly cigar. He came here with his victim in a four-wheeled cab, which was drawn by a horse with three old shoes and one new one on his off foreleg. In all probability the murderer had a florid face, and the fingernails of his right hand were remarkably long. These are only a few indications, but they may assist you.'

For a moment, the two policemen were rendered speechless by this authoritative recital, and then Gregson roused himself.

'If this man was murdered, how was it done?' he asked.

'Poison,' said Sherlock Holmes curtly, and strode off. 'One thing more,' he added, turning round at the door. ' *"Rache"* is German for revenge, so don't waste your time looking for a lady by the name of Rachel. Goodbye, gentlemen.'

Chapter Thirteen

From the journal of John Walker

Not only did I share Sherlock Holmes's great amusement at confounding Lestrade and Gregson as we left Number 3 Lauriston Gardens, but also I was excited at the great possibilities which had been bubbling away in my brain as I had watched and listened to my new friend demonstrate his remarkable powers. Despite his pomposity and his unabashed love of the limelight, Sherlock Holmes was not only a unique individual, but also he had fascinating personal qualities which, if presented in a dramatized form in an exciting narrative, would make him a heroic figure. With some felicitous alterations to his character traits, I believed that I could portray Sherlock Holmes as a dynamic detective hero. Indeed, this case in which he was engaged would make an excellent introduction for the reading public. Creating a semi-fictional account of the investigation would both add zest to my time with him and provide me with a more legitimate reason to observe him and his methods.

I felt a warm glow of satisfaction at this revelation. While Moriarty would receive the unadulterated accounts of the doings of Mr Sherlock Holmes, at the same time I would be turning them into dramatic stories. Here was an honest and reasonably noble purpose to my miserable existence. From now on, I reasoned, I had to memorize conversations and incidents, and keep copious notes. I was about to become the biographer of London's greatest private detective.

Holmes interpreted my beaming smile as amusement at his deductive *tour de force* in front of the open-mouthed police inspectors.

'I take it from your expression, Watson, that you do not believe all I told Gregson and Lestrade back there,' he observed, as we settled back in a cab.

'I suspect you embellished the truth a little, and indulged in some guesswork for effect,' I responded honestly.

'Not a bit of it. Everything I said was true. My conclusions were based firmly on all that I observed. The very first thing that caught my eye on arriving at Lauriston Gardens was that a cab had made two ruts with its wheels close to the kerb. Now, up to last night we'd had no rain for a week, so those wheels which left such a deep impression must have been there during the night. There were marks of the horse's hoofs, too, the outline of one of which was far more clearly cut than the other three, indicating that it was a new shoe. Since the cab was there after the rain began, and was not there in the morning – we have Gregson's word for that – it follows that it must have been there during the night, and, therefore, it brought both the murderer and his victim to the house.'

'Well, that seems straightforward enough,' said I, 'but what about the other man's height?'

'Why, the height of a man, in nine cases out of ten, can be determined by the length of his stride. I was able to gauge this fellow's stride on the clay outside and on the dusty floorboards within. To strengthen this deduction, we had the writing on the wall. When a man writes in such a fashion, his instinct leads him to write at about the level of his own eyes. Now, that writing was at just over six feet.'

'And his age?' I asked, determined to follow through all the statements he made, storing them in my memory bank as Holmes explained.

'Well, if a man can stride four and a half feet without the smallest effort, he can't be quite in the sere and yellow. That was the breadth of the puddle on the garden path. Patent leather boots, our victim, had gone round it, and square-toes had hopped over. There really is no mystery to this. I was merely making observations and drawing logical conclusions from them. Is there anything else that puzzles you?'

'Yes, yes. The length of the fingernails and the Trichinopoly cigar, for instance.'

'The writing on the wall was done with a man's forefinger dipped in blood. My magnifying-glass revealed that the plaster was slightly scratched by the lettering – because the fellow had long nails. You no doubt saw me collect some scattered ash from the floor. It was dark in colour and flaky – such an ash is made only by a Trichinopoly cigar.'

'Oh, come now!' I cried. 'How can you be so precise? The ash could be from *any* type of cigar.'

Holmes gave me an indulgent grin. 'I flatter myself that I can distinguish at a glance the ash of any well-known brand of cigar or tobacco. It is in just such details that the skilled detective differs from the Gregson and Lestrade type.'

'And the florid face?'

'Ah, well that was a more daring shot – although I am in no doubt that I was right. I'll keep that to myself for the moment.'

'All these facts are interesting, of course, but they do not take us further down the road of explaining the mystery. How came these two men to the empty house? If one was the murderer, how did he persuade his intended victim to enter? You saw no signs of force.'

Holmes shook his head.

'And,' I continued, 'what has become of the cabman who delivered them? How could one man compel another to take poison? Where did the blood come from? What was the object of the murder? What significance does the woman's wedding-ring have? And, above all, why should the second man scrawl the word RACHE on the wall?'

'Bravo, Watson. You have a sharp mind. You sum up the difficulties admirably. I agree that there is much that is still obscure, though I have quite made up my mind on the main facts.'

'You have?' I was astounded by this arrogant boast.

'Oh, certainly. But do not ask me to divulge them to you just yet. There are certain pieces of the puzzle I wish to see in place before I reveal all. You know that the conjuror receives no credit once he has explained his trick, and if I show too much to you of my method of working, you will come to the conclusion that I am a very ordinary individual.'

This trick of tantalizing me with some details of a case, but withholding the vital ones, was one that Sherlock Holmes was to perform with annoying regularity through our association together. It was appropriate that he referred to himself as a conjuror, for certainly there was a strong streak of the theatrical artiste running through his vain personality. He wished always to be centre-stage, to be in charge, and to mystify and astound. I gradually learned to tolerate his performance.

'However, I will tell you one more thing,' he added, warming to his act of titillation, 'the word RACHE is simply a blind intended to put the police upon the wrong track, by suggesting Socialism and secret societies. It was not done by a German. The "A", if you noticed, was printed somewhat after the German fashion, but a real German invariably prints in the Latin character. Therefore, I suggest that we can safely say that this was written by a clumsy imitator as a ruse to divert inquiry into a wrong channel. No doubt he has been successful with Lestrade and Gregson.'

Joseph Stangerson was frightened. When Drebber failed to turn up at the station, he had not been surprised or unduly worried. It would be a woman. It always was with Drebber. Wherever they went, he couldn't keep his eyes or his hands off a pretty woman. Stangerson had lost count of the number of scrapes they'd landed themselves in because of Drebber's sexual urges. It was his unwanted attentions towards Mrs Charpentier's daughter that had caused them to be evicted from their last place of residence. The brother of the girl had threatened to kill Drebber if he ever set eyes on him again.

No doubt, he mused, Drebber had found some tart in a drinking-saloon somewhere and was indulging in the pleasures of the flesh once again. But when his partner failed to turn up as dawn broke, the chill hand of fear started to take hold of Stangerson. In his coward's heart he always knew that some day retribution would catch up with them for their rash deeds out on that blazing hot desert twenty years ago – when they had shot old man Ferrier in the back and dragged Lucy back to Salt Lake City. He couldn't block the guilt out with alcohol as Drebber could. They never spoke of that time to each other, but they both knew that the cursed memories of those events were never far from their thoughts.

Stangerson always seemed conscious that someone was following them. They could never rest for long for fear that the avenging force caught up with them. And now Drebber had disappeared.

Stangerson pulled back the lace curtain of his room in Halliday's Private Hotel and looked out on the grey street. It was empty, save for a lone hansom cab some ten yards away from the entrance. There was no sign of his companion. He knew that he had to wait. Wait for another day at least, sitting in his room, hoping and praying that Drebber would turn up with an innocent explanation for his delay. If only his faith had not left him, he could have prayed. But even in this desperate state he knew that it would be a futile gesture. Hugging himself for comfort, he threw himself down on the bed and stared blankly at the ceiling.

Outside in the street, Jefferson Hope sat hunched up in the driver's seat of his cab, watching the hotel, a thin cruel smile fixed upon his features. After all these years he was now very close to avenging the death of his beloved. One of the bastards was dead. Now there was just Stangerson. He knew the coward would not dare leave the hotel during the daylight hours. Stangerson would wait to see if his partner returned and then attempt his escape under the cover of darkness.

Hope threw the butt of his cigarette into the street, and with a gentle slap of the reins he set the cab in motion. He would come back at dusk to complete his task.

Chapter Fourteen

From the journal of John Walker

On leaving Lauriston Gardens, we first called at the nearest telegraph office, where Holmes despatched a long telegram. We then continued our journey to Audley Court to interview John Rance, the constable who had discovered the body.

'I doubt if we'll learn anything from this cove,' Holmes said, as we alighted from the cab. 'The intelligence of the average man on the beat is not terribly high.'

Audley Court was not an attractive locality. The narrow passage led us into a quadrangle paved with flags and lined with sordid dwellings. We picked our way among groups of dirty children, and through lines of grey and discoloured linen, until we came to Number 46, the door of which was decorated with a small tarnished slip of brass engraved with the name of Rance. From a small, emaciated-looking woman, whom I assumed was Rance's wife, we learned that the constable was still in bed, and we were shown into a cramped and dowdy front parlour while she went off to rouse him.

He appeared presently, looking a little irritable at having been disturbed in his slumbers.

'I made my report at the office,' he said sharply, as though that were the end of the matter.

Holmes took a half-sovereign from his pocket and played with it pensively.

'We thought that we should like to hear it from your own lips,' he said, flipping the coin in the air.

For a moment an avaricious light flamed in the disgruntled constable's eyes. 'I shall be most happy to tell you anything I can,' he said.

'Just let us hear it all in your own way, as it occurred.'

Rance sat on the horsehair sofa, and knitted his brows, as though determined not to omit any detail in his narrative.

'I'll tell it ye from the beginning,' he said, with enthusiasm.

He was as good as his word; for some five minutes he took us through the course of his evening, from when he came on duty at around ten o'clock. He even rambled on about clearing some roughs away from outside a pawnshop and helping to deal with a fight at The White Hart.

Holmes waited patiently through this irrelevant recital until he reached the part of his narrative we had come to hear: 'It had come on to rain just after two, and I thought I'd take a look round and see that all was right down the Brixton Road. It was precious dirty and lonely. Not a soul did I meet all the way down, though a cab or two went past me. I was wet and miserable, gents, and as I was strollin', between ourselves, I was thinkin' how uncommon handy a four of gin-hot would be, when suddenly the glint of a light caught my eye in the window of that same house. Now, I knows that those dwellings in Lauriston Gardens are empty, on account of him that owns them won't have the drains seen to, though the last tenant died of typhoid fever. I was knocked all in a heap, therefore, at seeing a light in the window, and I suspected something was wrong.'

'There was no one else in the street at the time?'

'Not a soul, sir, nor as much as a dog.'

'Pray continue.'

'I went up the path and pushed the door open. I can tell you, my heart was fair bumpin' inside my uniform. All seemed quiet inside, so I went into the room where the light was a-burnin'.' There was a candle flickering on the mantelpiece – a red wax one – and by its light I saw. . . .'

'Yes, yes, I know what you saw. You walked round the room several times, and you knelt by the body, and then you walked through and tried the kitchen door and then—'

John Rance shifted uneasily. 'Where was you hid to see all this? It seems you know a great deal more of this matter than you should!'

Holmes smiled. 'I am a detective, assisting Mr Gregson and Mr Lestrade. I am one of the hounds, not the fox.' He leaned forward, and lowered his voice for emphasis. 'I detected your actions. Now, please continue.'

Rance resumed his narrative, but retained his suspicious expression. 'I went back to the gate and sounded my whistle. That brought three other constables to the spot.'

'Was the street still empty?'

'Well, it was, as far as anybody that could be of any good goes.'

'What do you mean?'

The constable's features broadened into a grin. 'I've seen many a drunk chap in my time,' he said, 'but never anyone so cryin' drunk as that blighter. He was at the gate when I came out, a-leanin' up ag'in the railings, and a-singin' at the pitch o' his lungs about Columbine's New-fangled Banner, or some such stuff. He couldn't stand, far less help.'

'What sort of a man was he?' asked Sherlock Holmes.

John Rance appeared to be somewhat irritated at this digression. 'He was an uncommon drunk sort o' man,' he said. 'He'd have found himself in the station if we hadn't been so took up.'

'His face – his dress – didn't you notice them?' Holmes broke in impatiently.

'I should think I *did* notice them, seeing that I had to prop him up. He was a long chap, with a red face, the lower part was muffled round—'

'That will do!' cried Holmes. 'What became of him?'

'We'd enough to do without looking after *him*,' the policeman said, in an aggrieved voice. 'I'll wager he found his way home eventually.'

'How was he dressed?'

'A brown overcoat.'

'Had he a whip in his hand?'

'A whip – no.'

'He must have left it behind,' muttered my companion. 'You didn't happen to see or hear a cab after that?'

'No.'

'There's half a sovereign for you,' said Holmes with a sigh, standing up and taking his hat. 'I am afraid, Rance, that you will never rise in the force. That head of yours should be for use as well as ornament. You might have gained your sergeant's stripes last night, if you'd had your wits about you. The man you dismissed as an innocent drunkard is the man who holds the key to this mystery. The man we are seeking.'

'You mean the murderer?'

'The same. Come along, Doctor.'

We started off for the cab together, leaving our informant incredulous, but obviously uncomfortable.

'The blundering fool!' Holmes exclaimed bitterly, as we drove back to our lodgings.

I was still a little puzzled. I knew that the drunken man tallied with Holmes's description of the murderer, but why had he returned to the house after committing his crime? My companion read my thoughts.

'It was to get the ring, of course. That was why our man came back. It obviously has great significance for him. So much so that he was prepared to risk capture to regain it. And it is by the ring we shall catch him.'

'How?'

'By using it as bait. You shall see.' And then he laughed at my mystified expression. 'But, Doctor,' he added, patting my arm, a smile lighting his gaunt features, 'I am so glad you came with me to share this business. It's the finest study I ever came across: a study in scarlet, eh? Why not use a little art jargon? There's a scarlet thread of murder running through the colourless skein of life, and our duty is to unravel it, and isolate it, and expose every inch of it.'

*

Late that afternoon, Jefferson Hope rested his weary bones in The Turk's Head while he sipped a tankard of ale and perused the newspaper in a lazy fashion. He was waiting for the night, the thick darkness when he could complete his mission. As his eyes ran over the small print, one advertisement in the 'Found' column sent his pulse racing:

In Brixton Road this morning, a plain gold wedding-ring, found in the roadway between the White Hart Tavern and Holland Grove. Apply Doctor Watson, 221B, Baker Street between seven and eight this evening.

Hope took a gulp of beer. This was his ring. Without a doubt. The one he risked all to retrieve the previous night. His grin faded a little as he considered the times stated. By eight o'clock it would be dark and Stangerson might well be making a move. Could he risk going to Baker Street before returning to Halliday's Hotel? If he didn't, he might lose the ring. Some chancer might convince this Doctor Watson that it was his. Surely Stangerson would wait until the streets were quiet before making his escape? He glanced once more at the advertisement. It was a risk he would have to take.

Chapter Fifteen

From the journal of John Walker

As we approached the city, after leaving Rance's house, Holmes halted the cab.

'Enough brainwork for the moment, Watson,' he beamed, pulling on his gloves. 'I feel the need to be soothed. Norman-Neruda is giving a concert this afternoon, and I promised myself I would see her again. Her attack and bowing are splendid. I will see you back at our rooms around six o'clock.' So saying, he gave me a cheery wave, hopped on to the pavement and was gone.

I welcomed the opportunity for some time on my own. It would afford me the opportunity to write up my notes of the morning's events. And after a light lunch, this is what I did. However, when it came to describing that gruesome dead body in the derelict house in Brixton, I was surprised to find that my hand was shaking as I wrote. The vision of that pale, contorted face triggered off unwelcome memories in my subconscious. Unbidden thoughts and vivid images of my dead and dying comrades at Maiwand seeped into my mind. I was suddenly aware that my eyes were misting with tears. However strong the conscious will is, it cannot quell the powerful forces that lie within the psyche. I knew then that, try as I might, I would never succeed in blotting out that dreadful experience. With some effort and, God help me, a tot of brandy, I completed a rough draft of my notes, a version that I could present to Moriarty. I knew that my 'romanticized version' would need a little extra effort, to gild both the prose and the detective in order to make both more attractive.

Holmes returned at the hour he stated, but I knew that the concert could not have detained him all that time. He had been at work again. And I needed to know all about it, but I was fairly certain that a direct question would not provide me with an answer. I would have to bide my time. He bustled in, flinging his coat over a chair, humming a snatch of Chopin.

'The concert was magnificent,' he cried. 'What an artist! Do you remember what Darwin says about music? The power of producing and appreciating it existed among the human race long before it acquired the power of speech. It speaks to our simple, primitive nature. There are vague memories in our souls of those misty centuries when the world was in its childhood.'

'Well, that's a rather broad idea,' I remarked.

'One's ideas must be broad as Nature, if we are to interpret Nature.' He sat opposite me and suddenly scrutinized my face. 'But, Watson, how pale you look. Ah, I see. This Brixton Road affair has upset you.'

I shook my head, but I did not convince my companion, who smiled at my deceit.

'I should have thought of that before I dragged you along to see a dead body. It must have brought back memories of Afghanistan. I apologize.'

'No apologies needed. I ought to be case-hardened now. I was just caught off my guard, that's all.'

Holmes gave me a cool smile to indicate that he was closing the subject. 'Did you get a chance to see the evening paper?'

'No.'

'It gives a fairly good account of the Brixton affair. However, fortunately for us it does not mention the fact that a wedding-ring was found at the scene of the crime. Those dunderheads, Lestrade and Gregson, no doubt haven't realized how important it is.'

'Why is that fortunate for us?'

'Look at this advertisement. I had one sent to every paper this morning.'

He threw the paper across to me and I glanced at the place indicated. It was the first announcement in the 'Found' column.

'In Brixton Road this morning,' I read aloud, 'a plain gold wedding-ring, found in the roadway between the White Hart Tavern and Holland Grove. Apply Doctor Watson, 221B, Baker Street between seven and eight this evening.'

'Excuse me using your name,' said Holmes casually. 'If I used my own, Lestrade or Gregson would come blundering in here and want to meddle with my plans.'

'That is all right,' I answered, 'but what if someone actually applies? I have no ring.'

'Oh yes you have,' he said, grinning as he handed me a shiny gold ring. 'This will do as well. It is almost a facsimile.'

'And who do you think will answer this advertisement?'

Holmes held a finger up in admonishment. 'You must avoid the habit of asking superfluous questions. Why, the murderer, of course, our florid-faced fellow with square toes. That ring meant a great deal to him. He was prepared to risk capture by returning for it last night. According to my notion, he dropped it while stooping over Drebber's body, and did not miss it at the time. After leaving the house, he discovered his loss and retraced his steps in the desperate hope of finding the ring. When he reached the empty house, he discovered that the police were already there due to his own folly of leaving the candle burning. He had to pretend to be drunk in order to allay suspicions. Luckily for him he encountered the brilliant Constable Rance.' Holmes chuckled.

'And you think that he will look in the paper this evening in the hope that someone has advertised its find.'

'Indeed I do. He will be so overjoyed that the fellow will never suspect a trap.'

'A trap,' I repeated, with some alarm.

'Why, yes. We'll have him cornered and have the truth out of him in a jiffy.' He opened a drawer and withdrew a pistol. 'Have you arms?'

'I have my old service revolver and a few cartridges.'

'You had better clean it and load it. He will be a desperate man; and though I shall take him unawares, it is as well to be ready for anything.'

I went to my bedroom and followed his advice, although I dreaded the idea of having to use the weapon. I had thought that I had left those days behind. But, I reasoned, if I was to be a close companion of a private detective, there would no doubt be moments of danger, and it was necessary that I should be prepared. With that thought in mind, I carried out my task with alacrity.

When I returned with my pistol, I found Holmes scraping upon his violin. He ignored me for some moments and then put his instrument aside.

'My fiddle would be much better for new strings,' he remarked. 'Put the pistol in your pocket. When the fellow comes, speak to him in a normal fashion. Don't frighten him by staring at him too much or acting oddly. Then leave the rest to me.'

'It is seven o'clock now,' I said, glancing at my watch.

'Yes. He will probably be here in a few minutes. He will want to be certain to be the first to make the claim. Open the door slightly. That will do. Now put the key on the inside. Thank you.'

Holmes had begun speaking in a hushed staccato fashion and his face was slightly flushed. His cool reserve was evaporating as the excitement and potential danger we were about to face began to take hold. Nervously, he snatched a book up from the mantelpiece. 'This is a queer old tome I picked up at a stall yesterday – *De Jure inter Gentes* – published in Latin at Liege in the Lowlands in 1642. Charles's head was still firm on his shoulders when this little brown-backed volume was struck off.'

I nodded politely. I knew he was attempting to divert his mind with idle intellectual conversation, but the tone of his voice clearly indicated that he was failing.

'On the flyleaf, in very faded ink, is written "*ex libris Gulielmi Whyte*". See?'

He held the book out for me to see, and his hand was shaking.

'I wonder who William Whyte was,' he continued, returning the book to the mantelpiece. 'Some pragmatical seventeenth-century lawyer, I suppose. His writing has a legal twist about it.'

He was interrupted by a sudden jangling of our doorbell downstairs.

'I've instructed Mrs Hudson to send all callers up,' he whispered, moving to the door.

'Does Doctor Watson live here?' asked a clear voice from below.

We heard Mrs Hudson's injunction to the stranger to come up to our rooms, and then heard his heavy tread upon the stair. Shortly after, there was a knock at our door.

'Come in,' I called.

At my summons, our visitor entered. I had to steel myself from giving a cry of surprise, for here standing before us was the man whom Sherlock Holmes had described to us in detail that morning in Lauriston Gardens. Dressed in the shabby garb of a cab-driver, our visitor was over six feet tall, with a florid visage and wearing scuffed and muddy square-toed boots.

Holmes flashed me a look of triumph.

The stranger glanced between the two of us.

'Which one of you is Watson – the one who found the ring?'

I stepped forward. 'I am Doctor Watson.'

The man stepped towards me and shook my hand warmly. 'I can't thank you enough, sir. That ring means the world to me.'

I was somewhat taken aback by his effusion, and momentarily felt lost for words, but Holmes intervened.

'My name is Holmes and I am acting in conjunction with my friend here. And you are. . . ?'

'Hawkins . . . Edward Hawkins.'

'Really?' said Holmes. 'Well, Mr Hawkins, you must realize that we cannot just hand the ring over to any Tom, Dick or Hawkins who comes along to claim that it is his. We must have some proof of ownership.'

Hawkins eyes narrowed. 'Proof? And how may I provide that?'

Holmes smiled. 'Come, come. We do not doubt you, Mr . . . Hawkins, but perhaps you could describe the circumstances concerning the loss and to whom the ring really belongs?'

'*Really* belongs?'

'Well, it is a *lady's* wedding-ring, after all . . . your wife's?'

Hawkins nodded awkwardly. It was clear that he had not anticipated such an interrogation when retrieving the ring.

'Watson, be so good as to pour our visitor a sherry, and you, sir,
take a seat by the fire while you tell us your tale.'

I did as I was bidden while Hawkins, with a shambling reluctance, sat where Holmes had indicated. Holmes passed the sherry to
him, which he gulped down in one go.

'Now, sir, how did you come by your loss?'

'I don't rightly know. I'd been drinking in the White Hart last
night, and probably had too much for my own good, and I reckon as
I was making my way home it must have fallen out of my pocket.'

'But why were you carrying your wife's wedding-ring in the first
place?' I asked, as Holmes manoeuvred his way behind our visitor's
chair.

Hawkins stared distractedly for a moment and then, heaving a
sigh, he began to present his explanation.

'It is a keepsake, gentlemen. My wife is dead this many a year,
and that ring is all I have to remind me of her.'

'Very good, very good!' crowed Holmes sarcastically. 'Close to the
truth – but I am afraid, not close enough.'

Hawkins began to rise from the chair, but Holmes came up
behind him and clapped the pistol to the side of his head.

'Sit down, sir,' he said. 'Now, let's do away with all these fairy-
stories, shall we? Watson, let me introduce you to Mr Jefferson
Hope, the murderer of Enoch Drebber.'

Chapter Sixteen

From the journal of John Walker

'Who the devil are you?' Hope's face was suffused with anger, but he remained seated, his hands grasping the edge of the chair until his knuckles shone white.

'My name is Sherlock Holmes. It will mean nothing to you.'

'Are you the police?'

'No. I am an unofficial consulting detective. In this instance I am working for the police, but above all I am interested in justice.'

'Justice! Pah! There ain't no justice in this world. If there was, I wouldn't have had the need to come after Drebber and Stangerson.'

'You admit, then, that you murdered Enoch Drebber?' I asked.

'I admit nothing. Fate saw to it that he died instead of me. That was a kind of justice, I suppose.'

'Be so good as to tell us what happened last night,' said Holmes, moving around to face Hope, his gun still trained on him.

A strange smile lit upon our visitor's face. There was no merriment in it, just a dark sardonic bitterness which unnerved me.

'It will be a pleasure,' he said. 'I've kept so much pain bottled up inside me, gentlemen, it will do me good to spill some now. I've nothing to lose by it. I have been trailing Drebber and his associate, Stangerson, around this globe for many a year. They were rich, I was poor, so it was no easy matter for me to follow them. They always managed to keep one step ahead of me until they landed in London.'

'Why were you following them?' asked Holmes.

'I sought revenge, of course. It won't matter much to you why I hated these men; it's enough to say that they were guilty of the death of two fine human beings – a father and a daughter. She was the woman I loved and who loved me back. We were to be married, but they took her from me and forced her into a sham of a marriage; forced her to marry Drebber. *Mormons!*'

He spat the single word out as though that alone would explain the cause of his pain and grievance. After a pause, he continued. 'This broke poor Lucy's heart, and she died. I took the marriage-ring from her dead finger and I vowed that Drebber's dying eyes should rest upon that very ring, and that his last thoughts should be of the crime for which he was being punished. I had no redress in the law, so I determined that *I* should be judge, jury and executioner, all rolled into one. If you have any drop of humanity in your souls, gentlemen, you would have done the same, if you'd been in my place.'

Holmes, his face an impenetrable mask, remained silent. I wondered if my companion sympathized with the plight of this wretch, as I did. My heart went out to him.

'When I got to London, my funds were almost exhausted and I had to take on work to survive. Driving and riding are as natural to me as walking, so I applied at a cab-owner's office, and got some employment. I was to bring a certain sum to the owner each week, and whatever was over I might keep for myself. There was seldom any excess, but I managed to scrape along somehow. The hardest job was to learn my way about, for I reckon of all the mazes that ever were contrived, this city is the most confusing. But I stuck at it with the help of a map, and I reckon I got on pretty well.

'I won't bore you with how I came to trace my two gentlemen, or how I bided my time, because I know you are eager to learn about last night.' The strange dark grin came again. 'They had got wind of me, knew I was close behind them, and so were about to leave London, but they missed their train. Stangerson beached up at Halliday's Private Hotel, near Euston, while Drebber was entertaining himself. I managed to pick him up as my fare. He was drunk. He had a craze for drink – and women. In the end, they were his downfall. I took him to the empty house in Lauriston Gardens. I'd managed to get a key for the place after one of my clients dropped it in my cab.'

'How did you poison him?' I asked.

Hope shook his head. 'Don't imagine I killed him in cold blood. That would be a bleak kind of justice indeed. Oh, no, I had long determined that he should have a chance in the matter, limited though it might be. Among the many billets that I have filled in America during my wandering life, I was once a janitor and sweeper-out of a laboratory at York College. One day the professor was lecturing on poisons, and he showed his students an alkaloid, as he called it, which he had extracted from a certain South American arrow poison. According to him, it was so powerful that a mere grain of the stuff meant death. I spotted the bottle in which this preparation was kept, and when they were all gone, I helped myself to a little of it. I was a fairly good dispenser, so I worked this alkaloid into little soluble pills. Each of the deadly pills I placed in a small box. I also had an identical box containing similar pills made without the poison. I determined that at the time when I had my chance my gentlemen should each have a draw out of one of the boxes, while I took a pill from the other. As I did not know which box contained the poisoned pills, our fates were in the lap of the gods. From that day I always had my pill-boxes with me, and last night the time had finally arrived when I could use them.

'If either of you two gentlemen has longed and pined for something to come about, so much so that your insides ache with the need of it, you will have some idea of how I felt when I took Enoch Drebber into that empty house. Twenty years I had waited, and now . . .' Hope leaned forward in the chair, his eyes glazing over as he slipped back in time to that fateful evening. 'I lit a candle to give us light, but my hands were trembling and my temples throbbing with excitement. In that terrible gloom I sensed the presence of my sweet Lucy and her father. They were with me there, with me at the end. I held the candle close to my face. "Now, Enoch Drebber," I said. "Who am I?"

'He gazed at me for a moment with bleared drunken eyes, and then I saw horror spring up in them, convulsing his whole face. He knew me all right. I was the dreaded demon from his past. He staggered back with livid features, and I saw perspiration break out on his brow. I could not help but laugh, and I did, loud and long. He must have thought he was trapped with a madman.

' "What do you want with me?" he asked, in a pathethic, child-like voice.

' "You dog!" I cried. "I have hunted you from Salt Lake City to St Petersburg, and you have always escaped me. Now, at last, your wanderings have come to an end, for either you or I shall never see tomorrow's sun rise." He shrunk further back as I spoke, and I could see on his face that he thought I was in some sort of mad fit. I reckon that I *was* for a time. The pulses in my temples pounded like sledgehammers, and I believe I would have had a fit of some kind if the blood had not gushed from my nose and relieved me.

' "I come to take revenge on my dear Lucy. Lucy Ferrier, the woman you killed." I cried, locking the door and shaking the key in his face. "Punishment has been slow in coming, but it has overtaken you at last." I saw his coward's lip tremble as I spoke. He would have begged for his life, but he knew well that it was useless.

' "Would you murder me?" he whimpered.

' "There is no murder," I replied. "Who talks of murdering a diseased dog? What mercy had you upon my poor darling, when you dragged her from her slaughtered father and bore her away to your accursed and shameless harem?"

' "It was not I who killed her father. It was Stangerson. He's the one you want." he cried.

' "But it was you who broke her innocent heart," I roared, thrusting the box of pills before him. "Let the high God judge between us. Choose and eat. There is death in one and life in the other. I shall take what you leave. Let us see if there is justice upon earth, or if we are indeed ruled by cruel chance."

'He cowered away with wild cries and prayers for mercy, but I drew my knife and held it to his throat until he obeyed me. With trembling fingers he took one of the pills and swallowed it. I took the other and then we waited, facing each other in the dim light, to discover which one of us was to live and which one was to die. I shall never forget the look that came over his face when the first warning pangs told him that the poison was in his system. I smiled when I saw it. No, gentlemen, I *grinned*; grinned from ear to ear, and my heart sang. I held Lucy's wedding-ring before his eyes. But the action of the alkaloid is rapid. A spasm of pain contorted his features; he threw his hands out in front of him, staggered, his body rippling with fear, and then, with a hoarse cry, he fell heavily on the floor. I turned him over with my foot and placed my hand upon his heart. There was no movement. He was dead!

'The blood had been streaming down my nose, but I had taken no notice of it. I don't know what put it into my head to write upon the wall with it. Perhaps it was some mischievous idea of setting the police upon the wrong track, for I felt light-hearted and cheerful. And I needed to buy myself sufficient time to deal with Stangerson. I remembered a German being found dead in a hotel bedroom in New York, with the word RACHE scrawled on the wall. The police reckoned it was the work of some secret society, and the murderer was never caught. I reckoned what puzzled the New York cops would puzzle the London crew as well, so I dipped my finger in my own blood and scratched out the word. Then I left. It was still a wild night, but I didn't mind the wind and the rain; I was content. That was until I had driven some distance and I put my hand in my pocket and discovered that Lucy's ring was missing.

'I was thunderstruck. You must realize that the ring was the only memento that I had of her. Thinking that I had dropped it when I stooped over Drebber's body, I drove back and, leaving my cab in a side street, I went boldly up towards the house – for I was ready to dare anything rather than lose that ring. As Fate would have it, when I arrived there, I walked right into the arms of a police officer who was coming out, and only managed to disarm his suspicions by pretending to be hopelessly drunk.'

'And then you saw the advertisement in this evening's paper,' said Holmes.

Hope nodded. 'As I said, I was ready to dare anything to retrieve that ring, but I have to admit I never suspected a trap. The whole thing seemed innocent.'

'As I intended it to be.'

Suddenly Hope frowned as though some unpleasant thought had flashed across his mind. 'I hope it is not in your mind to detain me now, gentlemen. Not when half my task has yet to be completed.'

'At Halliday's Hotel?'

Hope nodded. 'Not murder, you see. Merely justice – but I have to carry it out myself.'

'I am afraid I cannot allow that to happen,' said Holmes softly. 'However much I may sympathize with your—'

That was as far as Holmes got before Hope leapt from his chair, his face ablaze with frustated anger, and snatched the large metal poker from the hearth. With a snarl, he brought it down on Holmes's wrist in an attempt at disarming him. Holmes gave a yelp of pain, but retained his grip on the revolver.

'Drop that poker, or I shoot,' I cried, aiming my pistol at Hope. He ignored my demand, and struck at Holmes again. This time my companion managed to dodge sideways in an effort to avoid the blow, but nevertheless the poker caught his arm, knocking it upwards. Holmes's gun went off, the sound reverberating loudly in our sitting-room. Hope froze for a moment, his eyes glazing with shock, and then slowly he crumpled to the floor. I rushed to his side, but it did not take any of my medical skills to tell me that the man was dead.

'I didn't mean to fire,' said Holmes breathlessly, as he knelt by my side, gazing at Hope's immobile face. 'The blow caused me to pull the trigger.'

'The bullet didn't kill him,' I said. 'See, it grazed his shoulder. I believe he died of a heart attack. From his complexion, I should say that such an event was merely a matter of time. The nosebleed was a warning.'

'The bullet may not have killed him, but *I* did, whichever way you look at it,' averred Holmes solemnly.

As I was about to respond, there came an urgent rapping at our door and I heard the raised voice of our landlady, Mrs Hudson.

'Mr Holmes? Doctor Watson? What is going on? Are you all right?'

Holmes grimaced. 'Get rid of her, Watson. Say a firearm went off accidentally.'

I nodded and, stepping to the door, I opened it sufficiently to be seen, whilst at the same time blocking Mrs Hudson's view of the room and of the dead body. With apologies for the disturbance, I explained away the gunshot as Holmes had directed. It was, I think, with some reluctance that she accepted my story, but at length she bade me good-night and left.

When I returned to Holmes, he was extracting two small tins from Hope's waistcoat. Slipping off the lids, he revealed the contents: two small white pills in each box.

'One is innocent, and one spells doom,' he said softly, closing the boxes and slipping them into his own waistcoat pocket.

'What now?' I asked.

'Well, we must inform Lestrade and Gregson that we have their murderer – or, at least, the dead body of their murderer. But I do not want to do that just yet.'

'Why wait?' I asked.

'Because,' he said, stepping to the coatrack and pulling on his overcoat, 'I have an important errand to carry out first.'

'Errand?' I asked, completely puzzled.

'Yes. At Halliday's Private Hotel.'

Chapter Seventeen

A single gas mantle burned low in Stangerson's room at Halliday's Hotel. The man himself lay face downwards on the bed, in an alcohol-induced slumber. On his bedside table there was a bottle of bourbon containing less than a third of its contents. He had taken to drinking in the mid-afternoon when he finally accepted that Drebber was not coming back. Something must have happened to him. Something dreadful. It was what he had feared all these years. Without his overbearing companion to dictate and organize, Stangerson was like a rudderless boat. He feared leaving the womb-like safety of the hotel room in case whatever terrible fate had overtaken Drebber might befall him also. And so he escaped into the fragile safety of alcohol.

He stirred in reaction to the shifting pattern of the gaslight, caused by the cool draught of air from the opening door. However, he did not hear anyone enter, or perceive the dark shape moving towards the bed, and only became aware that he was no longer alone in the room when the gas mantle was turned up full. The shabby chamber was suddenly thrown into bright relief.

Shaking his head to dislodge the bourbon woolliness from his brain, he pulled himself up into a sitting position and found himself facing a tall, thin man, whose features were veiled in shadow.

'Hope?' he croaked, but as soon as the word had left his mouth, he knew that this stranger was not Jefferson Hope. He was too tall, too slender, and from what he could see of him, he appeared more youthful.

The stranger affirmed this impression. 'No, I am not Jefferson Hope, merely his emissary.'

'Who are you?'

The stranger sat on the bed, his face now within the rim of light cast by the mantle. Stangerson observed gaunt, cadaverous features and bright piercing eyes peering from either side of a thin, hawk-like nose. The thin lips slid into a casual, mirthless smile.

'I am Sherlock Holmes.'

'I don't know you . . .'

'No. But I know you, Joseph Stangerson. Or, to be more precise — and precision is a passion with me — I know all about you and the part you played in the death of Lucy Ferrier and her father.'

What colour there was left in Stangerson's face drained away, and his mouth opened in a guttural gasp. Holmes could see that the man was too terrified to deny the accusation.

'I . . . I've got money,' Stangerson said at length, his voice trembling with fear.

'I am not interested in your money, Stangerson. What brings me here is justice. Mr Jefferson Hope, whom you wronged all those years ago, died tonight before he had a chance to administer the kind of justice you deserve. And so I have taken it upon myself to carry out his wishes.'

Stangerson's eyes widened in terror and his hand flew to his mouth to stifle another groan. 'You mean to kill me. To murder me!'

Holmes shook his head. 'I do not intend to kill you. We shall let Fate decide.' He withdrew a pill-box from his waistcoat pocket. 'You shall have your chance, just as your confederate had his chance.'

'Drebber? Where is he now?'

'On a slab in the police mortuary.'

'No!' Stangerson attempted to move, but Holmes pressed him back against the bedhead with one firm hand. 'You must stay and play the game. There is no escape.' He held the opened pill-box before Stangerson's face. 'One of these pills is poison; the other is harmless. The choice is yours.'

'I can't . . . It isn't right.'

'*It isn't right?*' Holmes's voice was like a guillotine, and his features darkened with anger. 'What do you know of right, you who shot a defenceless old man in the back? What claims can a cold-blooded murderer have to right? Take one of these pills – for, if you refuse, I swear I will kill you myself with my bare hands.'

Stangerson was mesmerized by the fury of this stranger whose eyes flamed with a wild, righteous madness.

'Take one,' came the injunction again.

Stangerson's trembling fingers hovered over the box, not daring to pick one pill in case it was the fatal one.

'*Take one!*'

Gingerly, he lifted one of the pills from the box.

'Now swallow it.'

Squeezing his eyes shut, Stangerson placed the pill on his tongue and gulped it down.

'We shall know within a few minutes,' said Holmes quietly, his anger now dissipated.

And so they waited in silence. Stangerson lay back on the bed, his face awash with perspiration and his eyes screwed tight shut.

It was just over a minute before he felt the stabbing pain in his stomach. With a cry, he fell from the bed on to the floor, curling up in a foetal position.

'No, God, no!' he moaned. 'For pity's sake, help me!'

'I have no pity for you. It has all been spent on Lucy and her father.'

Stangerson writhed for a further thirty seconds or so, his hands clutching his stomach, his utterances now faint and unintelligible, and then all movement ceased.

Sherlock Holmes knelt down and felt the man's pulse. His mission was complete. Joseph Stangerson was dead.

Chapter Eighteen

From the journal of John Walker

After Holmes had left, I covered the body of Jefferson Hope with a sheet and waited by the fire for my friend's return. I really had no idea what he intended to do at Halliday's Hotel, but I expected that he would drag Stangerson back to our rooms for the police to take charge of him. Although Stangerson had committed no crime in this country that we knew of, I felt sure there was a possibility of transporting him back to America in order to face trial for the murder of Lucy Ferrier's father. While I waited, the fire crackling in the grate and the wind rattling the windowpanes as though trying to gain entry, I scribbled down details of the evening's dramatic events.

Some two hours after Holmes's sudden exit, I heard his footstep upon the stair. The door opened and he stumbled into the room. Without removing his hat or coat, he sank into the empty chair opposite me. His face was ashen and the whites of his eyes were veined red as though he had been crying.

'The man is dead,' he said.

'Stangerson?'

'Stangerson.'

'But how. . . ?'

Holmes held Jefferson Hope's pill-box in the flat of his hand. 'The Higher Court decreed it.'

'You mean you administered poison to the man?'

Holmes shook his head. 'I gave him the same choice that Hope had given Drebber.'

I shook my head in puzzlement and ran my fingers through my hair. 'I don't understand. Why on earth did you go to such an extreme?'

'Because—' he snapped, and then broke off. His voice was strident and angry, but there was emotional turmoil mirrored in his moist eyes. He paused before starting again. 'Because I saw that it was the right thing to do. How was it fair or just that such a man should escape justice? He was a murderer and a coward. He was partly responsible for ruining three lives. I was wrong to stop Hope tonight. I should have allowed him to carry out the final part of his revenge. It was a righteous revenge.'

'But you yourself have now become party to murder.'

Holmes rattled the pill-box. 'I let him choose.'

'What would you have done if he'd chosen the harmless pill?'

Holmes gave me a look that chilled me. 'I only offered him the box containing the poisoned pills.'

'So it *was* murder.'

'Some would say so. And I am sure it will weigh on my conscience for a while – but not for long, for the man deserved to die.'

'It is not for you to make such a decision. You talked of a higher court. That was nonsense. *You* decided his fate. You intervened.'

'Yes, I did, in the name of true justice. While on earth we must strive for the best justice that this paltry existence can supply. There can be no doubt of the nature of guilt in the great crime of murder. The taking of another's life for purely selfish reasons is the most terrible offence a man can commit – and it must be punished.'

'An eye for an eye? Surely that is too barbaric and simplistic?'

'I agree. Such rhetoric needs to be tempered to the occasion. Each case must be judged on its own merits. But often an offence cannot be dealt with fairly by the ephemeral nature of institutionalized justice. Five hundred years ago, if I had been caught stealing a sheep, the lord of the manor would have been within his rights to have me killed. Not so today. He would have to answer to the local magistrate, and I would probably end up with a few months in some damp prison establishment. The crime is the same – but the law is different. That is because society's attitudes have changed. But what redress does the sheep-stealer from the Middle Ages have? Man's law is ephemeral and arbitrary. It shifts and alters on the tide of changing perceptions of society. Believe me, Watson, it is no measure by which to judge. True, refined, objective justice is time-less.'

'I still believe that you should have let the law deal with Joseph Stangerson.'

'The law had twenty years in which to deal with both Drebber and Stangerson, and it failed. Believe me, I am not easy within myself at what I did tonight. See, my hand is still shaking. My nerves are jangling. But up here, up here where it really counts,' he tapped his temple vigorously with his forefinger, 'I am calm. I am secure. The rational part of my being knows that I acted wisely, justly and in keeping with my moral beliefs. And soon its strength will subdue my errant emotions. I am a stronger man after what I have done tonight. My path is even clearer than it was before, and believe me, Doctor, the world is a better place without the likes of Enoch Drebber and Joseph Stangerson in it.'

'I see that you are passionate about the matter and have convinced yourself that you have done no wrong.'

'Yes, and I have to convince you also, if you are to be an associate of mine.'

I shook my head in some confusion. 'I'm not sure. In whatever way you dress up this business, you have taken a man's life tonight. In the eyes of the law, that is murder. The premise goes against all the teachings of my youth. I'm really not sure.'

Surprisingly, Sherlock Holmes smiled. 'Uncertainty will do for now. It is a large concept to swallow whole at the first encounter. I shall wear away at you. I know you are a good man, and that makes us brothers. You will see the light.'

'And in the mean time . . .'

'In the mean time, I must ask for your support. I must ask you to lie for me.'

'I thought as much.'

'Shrewdness is another of your sterling qualities. We must let the Yard know about poor Hope here, and lead them to believe he came here after he had sneaked into Halliday's Hotel and carried out his deed. It would be as the man wanted, I am sure: to be seen as the avenging angel visiting both of his tormentors.'

I thought for a while. At that moment, I believed that Sherlock Holmes had made a great mistake, a blunder. He had taken his role of detective beyond the pale. And yet I realized that if he had not had the ingenuity to lure Jefferson Hope to our lodgings, Stangerson would most likely have suffered the same fate. While I pondered these things, Holmes threw off his outer clothes and poured himself a brandy. The smell of the alcohol brought to my mind that night under the Afghan stars, leaning against the old tree and drinking brandy . . . How I had suffered for that action! Holmes was not a monster, was not *really* a murderer, and if he had transgressed it was for the best possible reasons. I could not now elevate myself to be his judge.

'Very well,' I said at length. 'I will corroborate your story and we shall not speak of this matter again. But do not at any time in the future put my loyalty to such a test again. This is the one and only time that I support such an action.'

How wrong I was.

Holmes struck my knee. 'Good man. I knew I could rely on you – otherwise I would not have told you the truth.' He smiled briefly and then drained his glass. 'Now, Watson, be a good fellow and arrange for a telegram to be sent to the Yard.'

Within the hour, both Lestrade and Gregson came round to Baker Street, along with a mortuary wagon. Holmes and I presented a doctored version of the night's events, which was swallowed completely by the gullible policemen.

'We'll get some men round to Halliday's Hotel right away,' said Gregson. 'A sad but tidy end to a baffling mystery.'

'Indeed,' agreed Lestrade. 'A nice bit of work on your part, Mr Holmes. But you were very lucky not to be more severely injured by this Hope fellow. You really should leave all that heroic stuff to us professionals. If you'd have told us about it in the first place, we could have nabbed him before he set foot in the room.'

'And spoil my night's entertainment?'

The policemen smiled, and each shook his head in bewilderment at my friend's definition of entertainment. They bade us goodnight and departed.

Holmes and I said nothing for a while, and then Holmes rose and stretched.

'I am for my bed,' he said. As he reached the door, he turned to face me. 'Thank you,' he said quietly, before leaving the room.

It was now my turn to pour a brandy nightcap. I cradled the glass in my hands as I leaned forward in my chair and stared into the dying embers of the fire. I knew that I could not reveal the truth of what happened that evening in my report to Moriarty. If I did so, I would be offering my new friend up as a sacrifice to the Professor. He would have a stranglehold on him for the rest of his life. No, Moriarty had to receive the official version of Hope and Stangerson's death, the one that we had relayed to the police. I sighed with weariness and sadness at the delicate layers of duplicity that were surrounding my life.

I was also aware that, from the point of a fictionalized account of my first case with Holmes, it was too simplistic and short. If I were to turn the Brixton Road affair into a popular piece of literature, I would have to weave further threads into the mystery, to embellish the plot, while retaining the essential details of the true story.

One thing I was sure of was the nature of my burgeoning friendship with Sherlock Holmes, that strange creature to whom I had been invisibly shackled. The form and course of our relationship had changed that night. We shared a dark secret which inevitably drew us closer together. The more I saw of Holmes and listened to him, the more I liked and admired the man. I knew there and then that I was going to protect him, protect him from Moriarty and, more importantly, protect him from himself.

Chapter Nineteen

Although Sherlock Holmes's involvement in the Brixton Road murder was mentioned only fleetingly in the press reports of the case, with Inspectors Lestrade and Gregson receiving the bulk of the credit for clearing up the mystery, somehow news of Holmes's detective brilliance began to circulate and be disseminated across the great city. A few more successes with private cases further enhanced the detective's reputation, and within six months there was a steady flow of clients calling at 221B Baker Street.

Holmes now relied upon Watson to accompany him on most of the investigations. He enjoyed the comforting presence of an intelligent man who not only had the great gift of silence at the appropriate moment, but also was an excellent sounding-board when he needed to discuss his ideas and theories. For his part, Watson – and now John Walker saw himself as such, his previous identity having been swallowed up by the mists of time and self-induced amnesia – was pleased with the arrangement. The experience he had shared with Holmes during the Hope investigation had in some mystical or spiritual way transmuted John Walker into John Watson. It was only his obligatory monthly reports to Professor Moriarty that reminded him of his duplicitous role. Otherwise, he enjoyed Holmes's company and thrilled to the excitement of the chase, the puzzle of the unsolved crime and those moments of danger which are an integral part of a consulting detective's career. He continued to keep a private record of the investigations, altering them in various degrees in order to make them entertaining mysteries for the reading public. He was determined that one day he would offer these to a publisher, but at present he realized that the time was not right.

And, of course, there was Professor Moriarty. Although it was indeed Moriarty who had originally suggested that Watson write about Holmes, he knew that he would have to obtain his permission before taking action. As time went on, the monthly reports to the Professor became slimmer and less detailed as Watson surmised that Moriarty was losing interest in the situation. Holmes now was fully occupied with private cases and never strayed into Moriarty's territory, and thus did not pose a threat to his organization's machinations. Holmes was no longer an irritant to him, but the Professor knew there was always a danger that one day . . .

And so the lives of Holmes and Watson seemed to be settled, and their relationship flourished, until one day a woman came into their lives and disturbed the placid waters.

From the journal of John H. Watson

I am in love with Mary Morstan. And I do not know what to do about it. I have no idea if she has any feelings for me – but even if she had, it would be an impossible match, for she is due to inherit a fortune.

Mary is a client of Sherlock Holmes's. She came seeking his help to unravel a mystery concerning her missing father, Captain Morstan, who had disappeared some ten years earlier. For the past six years, on the same annual date, she had been receiving through the post the anonymous gift of a single pearl. Accompanying the pearl on the most recent occasion was a note inviting her to meet her unknown benefactor, who pledged to do her a justice which she had been denied. She was concerned as to what action she should take, and so sought the advice of my companion.

As Mary told us her story in our sitting-room that dull September morning, I hardly heard a word she said, so captivated was I by the beauty of the woman. I say beauty, for to me she had that wondrous arrangement of features and a gentle but forthright manner which conjures up my ideal woman. And, if I accept it, she reminded me of my first love, Lauren, who was taken by influenza in her eighteenth year. Mary had the same large blue eyes and placid, spiritual expression when her features were in repose. As I was introduced to her, I felt a tingle as I shook her hand. She was blonde and dainty, with a quiet but precise way of speaking, and I can say that I have never looked upon a face that gave a clearer promise of a refined and sensitive nature. I admit that the objective observer might describe her features as being plain, but to me, who saw beyond the veil, she was beautiful.

During the course of the investigation, I felt us growing closer. She turned to me rather than Holmes for reassurance. On one occasion, I escorted her home. She was living with a friend, Mrs Forrester, who had been an early client of Holmes's. It was in the early hours of the morning, and Mary and I sat close together in the cab. Her hands sought mine, and I whispered some words of comfort concerning the case. She could not know of the violent struggle within my breast, or the effort of self-restraint which held me back from taking her in my arms and kissing her. Yet there were two thoughts prominent in my mind which sealed the words of affection on my lips and held back my arms from embracing her. She was weak and helpless, shaken in mind and spirit. It would be callous and calculated to take advantage of her by professing my love at this time. Worse still, she was rich. If Holmes's investigations were successful – and I had every reason to believe that they would be – she would inherit a fortune. It was unthinkable that a fellow like myself should aspire to such a match, and indeed any approach I made would seem like the vulgar attentions of a fortune-seeker.

Of course there was one other reason which barred me from declaring my feelings for Mary: Professor Moriarty. I was his slave. His puppet. What would he say if I told him that I was in love and intended to marry? Such an act would inevitably take me away from Baker Street and away from Sherlock Holmes. Such an act would be seen as treachery.

My heart weighed like lead when we reached our destination. The servants had retired hours ago, but Mrs Forrester had sat up awaiting Mary's return. She opened the door herself, a middle-aged, graceful woman with a caring nature, and it gave me joy to see how tenderly her arm stole round the other's waist, and how motherly was the tone of the voice with which she greeted Mary.

I was introduced, and Mrs Forrester earnestly implored me to step in and tell her our adventures. I knew Holmes was waiting for me to start the next stage of our investigation, and so reluctantly I had to refuse the offer.

As my cab drove away, I stole a glance back, and as I write this I can still see in my mind's eye the two ladies on the step, two graceful clinging figures, and the half-opened door, the hall light shining through the stained glass, the barometer and the bright stair-rods. It was soothing to catch even that passing glimpse of a tranquil English home in the midst of the dark business which had absorbed us. It was like a mirage to me, the essence of quiet domestic bliss, which I believed at the time would elude me forever.

However, perhaps I more than most should not be surprised at the unpredictable and fickle way in which Fate plays with our lives. It is as the poet has it – our fate is 'Lock't up from the mortal eye/In shady leaves of destiny.' It was my destiny to be with Mary. I see that now, but then, as the carriage rumbled through the darkened streets and the little tableau of Mary with Mrs Forrester slipped from sight, I felt sick at heart.

Sherlock Holmes, ignorant of the emotional strains I was experiencing, carried on the investigation with relentless vigour. He was in search of the great Agra Treasure, which had been stolen some ten years before by Mary's father and his co-conspirators, Colonel John Sholto and Jonathan Small. Small, the only survivor of the thieves, had recently arrived in London after escaping from imprisonment on the Andaman Islands, in search of what he considered to be his rightful inheritance. If the truth be known, many of the details of this case escaped me, as most of my thoughts were full of Mary. The published version of this investigation, the novella called *The Sign of the Four*, had perhaps more inaccurate passages and invented moments than nearly any other bearing my name. I know how my heart soared when we discovered that the treasure was lost and that Mary would not become an heiress after all. However, in my naïvety, I never considered two important things: that in law, the treasure was not Mary's to keep anyway, and that she was of such a noble character that she would not contemplate calling any part of it her own.

I had arrived at Mrs Forrester's with the treasure chest to find Mary waiting for me in the sitting-room. With the aid of the poker, I wrenched open the chest – to discover that it was empty.

'Thank God!' I cried out loud, my heart soaring, when I realized that the treasure was now no longer a barrier to our union. How could it be? There was no treasure.

Mary looked at me with a quick, questioning smile.

'Why do you say that?' she asked, but from her tone and expression I was aware that she knew the answer already.

'Because now you are within my reach,' I said, taking her hand. She did not withdraw it. 'Because I love you, Mary, as truly as ever a man loved a woman. And the treasure, the possible wealth that it would bestow on you, sealed my lips. I could not as much as give you a hint of my true feelings while there was a possibility that you would become a rich woman. Now there is no threat. That stumbling-block has gone and I can confess that I love you.'

She drew close and smiled. 'And that is why you said, "Thank God!" '

I nodded.

She kissed my cheek. 'And then I say thank God, too.'

For a moment we stared into each other's eyes, and then I pulled her to me and we kissed.

The elation I felt as I left Mary Morstan on the step of Mrs Forrester's that night soon dissipated when I remembered that I still faced a greater and more insurmountable hurdle, in the dark shape of Professor Moriarty.

How could I marry Mary and stay true to my accursed bargain

with him? But I was not about to give up my romantic dream without a fight. At the earliest opportunity, I wrote to the Professor requesting an interview, and then I waited. Once again, this creature of the underworld held my life and happiness in his hands.

Chapter Twenty

From the journal of John H. Watson

It was two nights after the denouement of the Agra Treasure affair. I had dined with Mary, and we had talked at great length about our feelings and our possible future together. Of course, I had said nothing about my role in the life of Sherlock Holmes or even breathed the name of Professor James Moriarty. It pained me to begin our close relationship while still concealing those important elements of my existence, but I knew that I could never share those truths with her. However, the sheer joy of being able to be with this wonderful woman blotted out most of my concerns. After seeing her home, I called at The Butcher's Arms, an inn on Marylebone High Street, for a brandy nightcap. I assumed that Holmes would be waiting up at Baker Street, and I wanted to savour a quiet drink on my own and enjoy the happiness I felt in loving and being loved by that darling girl.

As I sat in a private compartment, smoking a cigar, watching in quiet contentment the floating tendrils of smoke ease their way towards the ceiling, a rough-looking fellow with rosy cheeks and dark beady eyes put his head round the corner and grinned at me.

'Beggin' your pardon, but it is Doctor John H. Watson whom I have the pleasure of addressin,' ain't it?'

'Why, yes,' I said, with some surprise.

'That's good,' continued the fellow, sidling up to my table, ' 'cause I got a personal note for you here.'

He pulled out a long cream envelope with my name scrawled on the front.

'I was told to pass this on to you, Doctor Watson.' He handed me the envelope. 'My pleasure.' He grinned once more, exposing a row of irregular and yellowing teeth, raised an imaginary hat in a parting gesture, and disappeared from view.

A chill ran down my spine. I recognized the type of envelope and the handwriting. What unnerved me was not the message from Moriarty, but the nature by which it had come to me. Until fifteen minutes earlier, I had no notion myself that I would be taking a drink at this particular inn – and yet one of the Professor's minions had found me here. How closely was I being watched? Was there *any* privacy in my life?

With nervous fingers, I tore open the envelope and read the message within:

Dear me, Watson, I knew you had a romantic imagination – but this! It smacks to me of breaking your contract. That will never do. However, I am not an unreasonable man. I shall give this matter some thought and make certain enquiries. I shall contact you in due course. M.

So he knew. Without my telling him, he knew of my affections for Mary Morstan. There was nothing I could do without my actions being reported back to Moriarty. Some nervous instinct made me swing round in my seat, expecting to see the fellow there. I downed the brandy quickly and left, feeling far from the relaxed romantic fellow I had been a short time before.

As I walked back to my Baker Street lodgings, the full implications of Moriarty's message sank in. 'Certain enquiries' could mean only one thing. I cursed myself for ever entertaining the possibility of a happy future with Mary. Through my stupidity, I had drawn this innocent girl into the thrall of Moriarty's web. However, despite my dark dismay at the way things were turning out, I knew that there was nothing I could do now but wait, hope and pray.

When I returned, Holmes was still up. He was sitting by the fire, poring over a thick volume that had arrived in the afternoon post. It was in French and pertained to the work of Alphonse Bertillon, a French criminologist who had developed a system for the identification of criminals which consisted of a series of anthropometrical measurements of the body, especially the bones. As I took a seat opposite him, he closed the book with a noisy thud.

'It is interesting, and Monsieur Bertillon has been most thorough in his cataloguing of criminal types, but overall I fear he is too prescriptive and makes no allowances for deviations and anomalies. This is a weakness which, in the end, will undermine his system.' He broke off and stared at me. It was clear to me that I had been unable to disguise my troubled emotions with a stoical expression.

'You understand what I refer to?' he said, holding up the book.

'Yes, yes, of course.'

He smiled a smile one might give to a naughty child who has just apologized for his misdemeanours. 'I thought as much, but hoped against it.'

I frowned. 'Hoped against what?'

'Romance. Love. Affections of the heart. Whatever trite description you wish to use. You have fallen under the spell of Miss Mary Morstan and are in the process of taking on the characteristics of a sentimental mooncalf.'

I was momentarily stunned by the cruelty of Holmes's outburst.

'I can see it in your eyes, in your manner and in your voice,' he continued. 'Saccharine emotions are eating away at your reason.'

'How dare you talk to me like that?' I cried, trembling with anger.

He responded with a wry, condescending smile.

Something snapped within me. I jumped up and grabbed Sherlock Holmes by the lapels of his dressing-gown and shook him.

'Whatever I do or do not feel for Miss Morstan, it is not a topic for you to sneer at, or about which to denigrate my feelings and emotions.'

Holmes was genuinely shocked by the vehemence of my attack. His features paled and he tried to pull away from me.

'I apologize, my dear Watson. Unreservedly. I had no idea that you would be so sensitive upon the subject. Please forgive my light-hearted remarks.'

'Light-hearted? Your remarks were unfeeling and pompous and intended to wound,' I snapped, releasing my grip on him. I realized that my ill temper was only partly fuelled by Holmes's comments. The untenable situation in which I found myself was causing frustrated anger to build up inside me.

'I may be thoughtless and I may at times be pompous,' said Holmes evenly, 'but I never say things intended to wound you, my dear Watson. I hold you in too high a regard for that.'

'I apologize also. I behaved like a schoolyard bully,' I responded, sinking back in my chair.

'Let's mend fences with a nightcap. Allow me.'

He poured us a brandy and soda apiece, and we clinked glasses, each of us bearing a wary smile.

'I have sublimated all such emotions as love in order to pursue my detective career, and I forget how powerful and overwhelming an emotion it can be. I assume that I was right and that you are in love with Miss Mary Morstan?'

'Yes, I am.'

'I feared as much. Now, Watson, before you grab me by the throat again, hear me out. The inevitable result of love is matrimony, which would in turn mean that I would lose a most companionable lodger, my investigating associate and the keeper of my casebook. I have never taken it upon myself to make friends. Indeed, our relationship fell out so easily that I cannot say I made any effort with you, either. It just came about naturally. And now you are going to up sticks and leave me for domestic bliss in the suburbs. Is it any wonder I said I feared as much?'

'Put like that . . .'

'If the truth be known, Watson, I do not really approve of love. It is an emotional thing, and whatever is emotional is opposed to that true cold reason which I place above all things. I should never marry myself, lest I bias my judgement.'

'I trust my judgement may survive the ordeal.'

Holmes chuckled. 'I fear it will.'

'But you pre-empt issues. Miss Morstan and I have only just started walking out. As yet she does not know the depth of my passion for her,' I lied. 'And I have no notion how she will react when I pluck up the courage to tell her.'

'Ah, so I will have you around for a few months yet.'

I thought of Moriarty. 'A few months at least.'

'Ah, well, that is some comfort.'

I looked across at my friend, his lean features dappled by the fire-light. He looked content and at peace with himself. How I envied him.

'Have you never loved?' I found myself asking him.

'What is the definition of love, I wonder? A palpitating heart and the sense of total self-sacrifice to another party? If so, no, I don't think I have. I loved my parents. And I loved the rough little terrier we had when I was a lad, but that's not the sort of thing you refer to, is it? Romantic love: closeness, passion, sex.'

I was shocked by this base definition.

Sherlock Holmes read my expression and his eyes twinkled. 'What? You don't think sex is part of love?'

'It's not that ... but you use the word as though it were a commodity to be added to the list.'

'Well, to a person like me, it is. I tried sex once, as an experiment. I needed to know what it was like. The scientist in me overcame my reticence.' He shrugged his shoulders and extracted his pipe from his dressing-gown pocket. 'It wasn't for me. It encourages you to expose more of your inner feelings than is appropriate, to give too much of your own self away. I am too private a person to feel comfortable with that.'

'But sexual congress must be arrived at through a loving rela-tionship.'

'I'm sorry to say, Watson, old chap, that I find that sentiment a nonsense. Ask the prostitutes down in the East End if they agree. It is a bodily function that is quite separate from the feelings of the heart. Man and woman can perform and enjoy this human activity, if it is to their taste, without any reparation to love.'

'That sentiment is crude and despicable.'

'Possibly, but true. As soon as I had experienced the full horrors of sexual intercourse, I determined to channel all my energies, subvert the sexual ones, into my work. How much more satisfying it is to realize that my mind is capable of governing my body and deterring any unwanted appetites.'

I stamped my drink down on the table by my chair, appalled at my companion's assertions. 'You spurn all the finer feelings of the human heart in this so-called aesthetic rejection of human love.'

'The words of a writer and a romanticist. There are thousands of poor wretches in this city of ours who do not have the luxury to indulge in these "finer feelings", as you call them. They react to the animal instinct of procreation and satisfaction. Love is abstract and ethereal. A heady potion, no doubt, but give me cocaine every time.'

I rose, lost for words and more angry than I could express. I made my way to the door, but was halted by Holmes's cry.

'Oh, Watson,' he said, rising from his chair, 'do not take what I say to heart. My words are no reflection on the nobility of your feelings or the genuine nature of your affection. They are the thoughts of a very odd and repressed individual who is so entrenched in his views of the world that he often forgets the hurt he may administer by expressing them. You are the normal, hearty and well-adjusted fellow in this partnership; I am the cold, calculating ... and damaged other half. Forgive me if I have upset you.'

I glared at that pale, cadaverous face with contempt.

'Good-night,' I said, closing the door with some force.

I slept little that night. My mind was a whirlpool of thoughts. At first I was angry with Holmes for the contemptuous way he had dismissed the importance and quality of love; and I was also angry with myself for being goaded by his icy observations. I should have acknowledged that such was the nature of this man that his ideas and beliefs were ingrained and had nothing to do with my particular circumstances, and I cursed myself for not realizing this at the time. Of course, I was also plagued by worry regarding Moriarty's hold on me. After surviving the hurdle of the Agra Treasure and its threat to keep Mary from me, I was aware that that problem was a mere bagatelle compared to the danger that *he* posed to our relationship. With a snap of his fingers he could, if he so wished, have Mary eliminated. And it was all my fault.

I tossed and turned for most of the night as my brain sought a solution to my dilemmas. The grey light of dawn was creeping into the room before exhaustion allowed a shallow sleep to overtake me, my problems still intact and apparently insurmountable.

Chapter Twenty-One

The same evening that John Watson had discussed his romance with Sherlock Holmes, Professor Moriarty was entertaining a guest to dinner in his sanctum. The occasion was a business one, concerning forged documents and Bank of England plates. The matter was dealt with successfully. After the meal, the two men retired to the library to smoke, take port and relax.

'How is the business with Sherlock progressing?' asked the portly guest casually, as he prepared to take a pinch of snuff, delicately balanced on the back of his hand.

'I am rather bored with it now. It is true that your brother has developed into a crime-fighter without pareil, as we both suspected, and that with a little nudging from our man Watson he now follows the paths of crime which lie in a different direction from my endeavours. Paradoxically, that is part of my dilemma: the plan has been successful, and so there is no excitement in the case.'

Mycroft Holmes brushed away the errant grains of snuff from his waistcoat and peered over his pince-nez.

'Ah, well, the lion may only be sleeping. There may come a time when Sherlock will pose a serious threat to you,' he said.

'I would almost welcome the challenge. However, I suspect that now Holmes has a successful detective practice, the broad strokes of my crimes will no longer interest him. He is a connoisseur, and prefers rather bizarre miniatures to the simple, clean masterpieces that I create.'

'He always had a love of the unusual and the recherché.'

'There you are, then,' said Moriarty, leaning forward and pouring more port into Mycroft's empty glass. 'And now Watson is wanting to leave.'

'What on earth for?'

Moriarty curled his lip. 'He has fallen in love.'

'Ah, he has, has he? Man of the world, this Watson, eh? No doubt it is with that young woman involved in the Agra Treasure investigation.'

'The same. He wants to marry her and most likely carry her off to suburban bliss away from Baker Street.'

'And you will allow him to go?'

'I don't know. Maybe it is time to let the fellow slip his leash. He hasn't put a foot wrong since he moved in with your brother, and now perhaps he is not needed any more. I would welcome your thoughts on the matter.'

Mycroft beamed and relaxed, his body slipping down comfortably into the depths of the chair, while his legs stretched forward until they almost touched the hearth.

'Well, it would leave you a little exposed again, although you have Mrs Hudson on hand. It might spice up the game.'

'It might,' agreed the Professor.

'I've never met this Watson, but from his reports to you and what you have told me about him, I gain the impression that he is a reliable fellow and that if he left he would remain true to you, or rather to his unwritten contract with you, especially if some threat were placed over his head to ensure his loyalty.'

'The girl . . .'

Mycroft beamed again. 'Indeed. Love makes a man very malleable. Moreover, is it not likely that once having tasted the exciting fruits of detective work, Watson will never be able to keep away from the tree? After a few months enduring the monotony of domestic life, he'll be banging on the door of Baker Street, begging for Sherlock to allow him to accompany him on some case or another.'

'I like the scenario. To facilitate this arrangement, it would mean moving pieces on the board in a radical fashion, but they have been static too long.' Moriarty drained his glass. 'I appreciate your counsel, Mycroft. Wise words.'

'Informed words to some extent, at least. The man is my brother, after all.'

Moriarty chuckled. 'That has always fascinated me. Two men from the same stable as it were, but both so different.'

'Not as different as all that. Oh, I know physically I would make two of Sherlock – that is my love of good food, good wine, good living.' He raised his glass and took a drink to illustrate his point before continuing. 'But our brains are of a similar intellectual quality. It is just that we use them for different purposes. We both enjoy the thrill of intrigue, legerdemain on a grand scale . . . It's just that we have taken diverse paths.'

Moriarty looked at the large man opposite him. His face was massive, but there was a keenness about the features that clearly denoted the man's intellectual brilliance. His eyes, partly shielded by the golden rims of his pince-nez, were as sharp as knives. Despite the smooth words of explanation, Moriarty did not understand Mycroft Holmes, and this worried him. Of all the individuals who worked closely with him in his organization, Mycroft remained the only dark horse. The Professor knew that in the world of crime one could not afford the luxury of close attachments – he himself had none – and yet Sherlock Holmes was this man's brother, a dissoluble blood-tie. Mycroft had a shining intellect and therefore would be acutely aware that if his brother became a real threat to the organization, Moriarty would have no compunction in sweeping him away, crushing him like a fly; and yet Mycroft revealed no concern or real interest in this possibility.

'The old adage is wrong. Chemically, blood is thicker than water, but in the metaphorical sense the idea is nonsense. I do not hate my brother, but on the other hand I have no special affection for him, either. We are two individuals making our own way in a cruel world. We each must face our own destiny.' Mycroft's face creased into a smile. 'Sorry, Professor, I've been reading your mind again.'

'In certain circumstances, that could be a dangerous occupation.'

'Then, sir, I shall have to ensure that those circumstances do not arise.'

There was a moment's silence, when the air crackled with intensity between the two men, and then they exchanged knowing smiles.

'This Watson business intrigues me,' said Mycroft Holmes some moments later, when they had lit their cigars. 'I have until now kept out of your dealings with Sherlock, but I do think it is time I introduced myself to his friend Watson. I'm sure you'd welcome my views on him and this marriage business.'

'Well, I don't suppose it would do any harm,' observed Moriarty, non-committally. 'I know that I can rely on your *discretion*.'

'Implicitly. Now, as it happens I have a little business I can put Sherlock's way. A fellow called Melas, a Greek interpreter, who lodges on the floor above me, has become involved in some intrigue and came to me for help. I think I see the matter clearly, but playing detectives is not a game in which I'm interested. I could throw this morsel Sherlock's way and thus create an opportunity to meet Watson.'

Moriarty chuckled. 'Oh, my dear Mycroft, you had it all worked out before you arrived this evening: a *fait accompli*.'

Mycroft returned the chuckle. '*Touché*, Professor. Now you are reading *my* mind.'

From the journal of John H. Watson

After a virtually sleepless night, I came down to breakfast the following morning somewhat bleary-eyed. There was no sign from the friendly demeanour of Sherlock Holmes that we had exchanged heated words the night before. He had an enviable facility for isolating moods and arguments, invoking a kind of emotional amnesia that forbade him the need to dwell on past upsets and allowed him to get on with his life.

'I heard you stirring, so I've sent down to Mrs Hudson for your breakfast. It should be here in a trice.'

'Thank you,' I said, and sat opposite Holmes at the breakfast table, most of which was covered with the pages of various newspapers. From this mess, he extracted a note and waved it aloft.

'We have a case, unless I'm very much mistaken,' he declared.

'Oh?'

'This is a note from my brother, asking—'

'Your brother?' I cried, shaking my tired head. 'Did you say your *brother*?'

'I did.'

'You never told me that you had a brother.'

'The occasion never arose. His name is Mycroft, and he is my senior by seven years. We rarely see each other, except when business brings us together. He helped me with funds when I first came to London.'

'But what does he do?'

'Ah, well, all that is a bit vague. He has an extraordinary faculty for figures, and officially he audits the books in various government departments, but I believe his responsibilities go somewhat further than that. I well believe he has the ear of the Prime Minister when certain situations arise.'

'Why have I never heard of him?'

'The powers behind the Government are never well known, Watson. Don't be naïve. However, he is well known in his own circle. At the Diogenes Club, for example.'

At this point, our conversation was interrupted by a discreet knock at our door and the entrance of our landlady, bearing my breakfast and a fresh pot of coffee.

'There you are, Doctor,' she said, placing the dish before me, 'and make sure you eat it all up. You're looking decidedly peaky this morning.'

'The Diogenes Club?' I remarked, after Mrs Hudson had left us. 'What on earth's that?'

Holmes laughed. 'It is the queerest club in London, and Mycroft one of the queerest men. When he's not working in some government building somewhere, he can be found in the club.'

'But what sort of club is it?'

'There are many men in London who, some through shyness, some from misanthropy, have no wish for the company of their fellow man. Yet they are not averse to comfortable chairs and the latest periodicals. It is for the convenience of these individuals that the Diogenes Club was started, and it now contains the most unsociable and unclubbable men in town. No member is permitted to take the least notice of any other. Save in the Strangers' Room, no talking is allowed under any circumstances. My brother was one of the founding members.'

'And for what reason does he frequent the club? Shyness, or misanthropy?'

'We talked last night of my wariness regarding emotions and forming any kind of attachments. Apart from yourself, I have no other friends. Mycroft shares this belief to a much greater degree than I. He was born to be solitary. He alone satisfies his own needs for company and stimulation.'

'Pardon me for saying so, but he sounds most odd.'

Holmes laughed. 'Not at all. He is not really odd. You will find him the most amiable fellow when you meet him.'

'I am to meet him?'

'This morning at eleven. He has a case for us, and he specifically asked me to bring you along.'

'Really?'

'See for yourself.' He threw the note to my side of the table, where it narrowly missed landing on my fried egg and bacon.

The notepaper was headed: *The Diogenes Club, Pall Mall*. The note, written in neat copperplate, read simply:

Sherlock,
    Call around at eleven today. I will see you in the Strangers' Room. Bring your associate Watson with you. There is a matter which may interest you.
                              Mycroft.

It was just striking the hour of eleven when Holmes and I entered the Diogenes Club. Holmes cautioned me not to utter a word as he led me into the hall. Through the glass panelling I caught a glimpse of a large and luxurious room in which a considerable number of men were sitting about in cavernous chairs, reading newspapers. Holmes showed me into a small chamber which looked out on to Pall Mall, and then, leaving me for a while, returned with a companion whom I surmised must be his brother.

Mycroft Holmes was a much larger and stouter man than Sherlock. In fact, his body was absolutely corpulent, and he moved with the elegant slowness that fat people are forced to adopt because of their weight. However, there was something about his concentrated expression that was remarkably similar to that of his brother. Mycroft's eyes, bright behind a pair of pince-nez, seemed to retain that faraway, introspective look which I had only observed in my companion when he was exerting his full powers.

'I am glad to meet you, sir,' said he, extending a broad flat hand, like the flipper of a seal. 'I gather you accompany my brother on his investigations.'

I nodded. 'It is a pleasure to meet you also.'

'Now that the pleasantries are over, let us get down to business. You have a case for me, Mycroft,' remarked Holmes, in a cold brusque manner.'

Mycroft glanced across at me and smiled. He took snuff from a tortoiseshell snuffbox and inhaled it noisily. 'Not a man to stand on ceremony, my brother, Doctor Watson. A case, Sherlock? Well, I suppose we might call it a case. Certainly, it is a singular matter.'

It was entertaining to me to see how this giant of a man treated his brother with a kind of light-hearted tolerance, as though he were a hungry schoolboy anxious for his tea. I saw that in Mycroft I had another colourful character to add to my Baker Street world, which was forming very nicely, ready to be fictionalized.

'Well?' said Holmes, slapping down his gloves impatiently on the table. 'Let me hear the facts.'

In reply, Mycroft scribbled a note upon a leaf of his pocketbook and, ringing the bell, he handed it to the waiter.

'I have asked Mr Melas to step across,' said he. 'He lodges on the floor above me, and I have some slight acquaintance with him, which led him to come to me in his perplexity.'

In the end, the affair was a slight one and required little detective work on behalf of my friend. Indeed, it was rather a clumsy matter, which I may very well delete from any collection of Holmes cases that I create. As it turned out, the main culprits escaped the grasp of both Holmes and the law.

Returning from our abortive expedition to apprehend them, my friend was in a foul temper.

'A very unsatisfactory matter,' grumbled Holmes in the cab on our way back to Baker Street. 'It had all the elements of a fine case. If only I had been called in earlier.'

I could only nod in agreement. Indeed, the case had promised much and contained suitably dramatic elements for a fine story, but it lacked a satisfying denouement.

When we arrived back at our rooms, we found Mycroft waiting for us there with a bottle of champagne on ice. One look at his brother's face informed him of the disappointing outcome of the evening.

'Never mind, Sherlock,' he grinned, uncorking the champagne with a discreet pop. 'You tried your best. You cannot always be assured of success in your detective endeavours.'

'It appears not,' replied Holmes sullenly, and, flinging his coat upon the rack, he retired to his room.

'He was always a petulant boy,' observed Mycroft, handing me a glass of champagne, unabashed by Holmes's rudeness. 'It looks like we'll have to share the bottle between us.'

I thanked him and we took seats either side of the fire, Mycroft automatically taking the chair that his brother usually occupied.

'In the absence of Sherlock, allow me to raise a toast on his behalf. To crime – bigger and better crime.' He chuckled and I joined him.

'You seem very comfortable here, Watson.' Mycroft eyed his surroundings.

'I am,' I replied.

'And yet, Sherlock tells me that you have plans to leave. Romance is in the air.'

'He told you that?' I was most surprised. I had assumed that

Holmes would treat my private life with the utmost discretion.

'We are brothers, after all.' Mycroft filled my empty glass. 'I am not the man on the omnibus, or a chap in a music hall bar. I am sure he meant no harm by it. I gather from his tone and demeanour that he was concerned about losing your company.'

'Well, that is not certain at present.'

'Ah.'

'There are . . . It is still very much in the early stages.'

'Forgive me, Watson, if I trespass too much into your personal territory, but are you sure of your feelings towards the young lady?'

'I am.'

'And hers towards you?'

'Yes.'

'Well, then, the rest is trivial. I wish you well. But promise me one thing, old boy. When you do take the bridal path, as it were, you won't desert Sherlock altogether, will you?'

I shook my head. How could I? I thought. Little did Mycroft know of the chains that bound me to his brother. But at the same time, my natural instinct was to remain faithful to my friend. He was the only man I could call by such a name.

'Good man. More champagne, Watson?' He filled my glass again. 'Now I must be off. I have another appointment in the city.'

With some effort he lifted himself out of the chair and placed his glass on the table. It was then that I noticed he had hardly touched the champagne, and that it was still his first glass.

'You finish off the bottle, Watson,' Mycroft beamed, pulling on his coat. 'A nice little nightcap. I hope we meet again. Give my regards to my brother. I'm sure he'll be over his sulk in the morning.'

With that he swept out of the room, slamming the door behind him.

Chapter Twenty-Two

From the journal of John H. Watson

For the next week or so, I lived in a kind of limbo. Not knowing what my future held – or that of my beloved Mary. She brought me the only glimmer of sunshine in those dark days. We met regularly, for lunch or for a walk in the park, and on one occasion to visit the theatre, and our relationship deepened and strengthened. I was in no doubt that she was the woman with whom I wanted to spend the rest of my life, and I was certain that Mary felt the same about me. Although I was always happy and relaxed in her company, occasionally in unguarded moments my expression must have told her that there was a shadow hanging over our happiness.

'There is something troubling you, isn't there, John?' she asked me one evening as we were travelling back to Mrs Forrester's in a cab.

I smiled and shook my head. 'Of course not,' I answered lamely.

She leaned forward and kissed my cheek. 'I think I know my John by now. I look at you from time to time when you're not aware, and I see such . . . such sadness in your eyes. There *is* something, I know. If you are unsure of your feelings—'

'My God, Mary, no! Please never think such a thing. I love you so very, very much.'

She smiled. 'I'm so glad . . . because I love you so very, very much also.'

We embraced. The closeness and the fragrance of her sent my senses spinning.

'So, what is the matter then?' she asked softly, as we drew apart.

In my intoxicated state – intoxicated by the nearness of her – I felt, for a moment, as though I would like to tell her the truth. Thankfully, my saner nature intruded. Oh, how wonderful it would be to tell Mary everything – everything from my discharge from the army, to my meeting with Moriarty and my career as his spy. To unburden myself to someone who loved me would be the most wonderful release; however, not only would that be incredibly selfish, but also it would be very dangerous. In possession of such knowledge, Mary would be perceived as a threat to Moriarty, and her life would not be worth a pin's fee. And on learning of the *real* Watson, of John Walker, Mary might well reject me for my subterfuge and my failings. No, I had to continue my career of dissembling.

'It's Sherlock Holmes,' I said.

'Holmes?' Mary's pretty brow furrowed in puzzlement.

'Despite his cool assured behaviour, he has rather come to rely on me in many ways – as a companion, a sounding-board and a friend. He has no other.' I could have added that neither had I.

'I see, or rather, I *think* I see,' said Mary.

'He has taken the notion of my leaving Baker Street rather badly. He does not relish the idea of being left alone and there being no one to accompany him when he is investigating a case. He uses me to test out theories.'

'Uses you . . . Indeed,' said Mary, her features hardening.

I gave a wry grin. 'Well, yes, he does use me. That is his way. However, I am sure that he respects me and cares about me in his own way.'

'And this is what is troubling you, John? Leaving Mr Holmes to his own devices?'

'Well . . . yes.'

Suddenly her gentle, serious face broke into a broad smile and she laughed. 'Oh, John, only you could be so caring, so sensitive to such a matter. Sherlock Holmes is a grown man, and I am sure he is perfectly capable of looking after himself and working his theories alone. And anyway, you are not leaving the country. Vacating your Baker Street rooms does not mean that you'll never see him again or never accompany him on one of his investigations; it only means that in the evening you will come home to your loving wife.' She laughed again.

'Do you mean that you wouldn't mind me keeping in touch with Holmes, and helping him out now and then?'

'Of course not, silly. I am not one of those women who want to mould their husbands into something they're not. I fell in love with you as you are; it would be wrong and foolish to attempt to change you.'

Without further words we embraced and kissed again, thus closing the matter for the time being.

It was only a few days later that I received a note from Moriarty instructing me to rendezvous with Colonel Moran. With a fluttering heart I set out that morning for my appointment. Holmes had not risen when I left. He was in a malaise because there was no investigation on hand. I was too preoccupied with my own worries and concerns to attempt to stay his hand from reaching for the cocaine bottle. I was conscious that he was overdosing himself, but I believed that any words from me would have little effect on his determination to stimulate his mind artificially. One could only hope that some criminal puzzle would turn up soon to bring him back to sanity.

Moran's cab appeared at the appointed time and I climbed aboard.

'Good day, Watson. You are well, I trust?' came the familiar voice from the shadows of the cab. It was Moran's usual greeting.

'I am well.'

'Good. To business. You wish to break your contract with the Professor, leave your duties in Baker Street and marry.'

'I do not wish to break my contract, I wish to be released from it – or at least have the terms altered.'

'Nicely put, Watson, nicely put. And what do you intend to do, once you have married?'

'Set up home, of course, and, I hope, start in medical practice again.'

'And Mr Holmes? Within this new context, how do you see your relationship with him continuing?'

'I thought *you* would tell *me* that,' I said curtly. I was quickly growing tired of these games.

There was a sudden burst of light in the cab as Moran struck a match and lit a cheroot. I saw his chiselled features and the shaggy grey eyebrows briefly before they faded into the gloom once more as the match was extinguished.

'Very well, Doctor Watson. Your request has been granted.'

I gave a gasp of surprise.

'But,' snapped Moran, before I could say a word, 'there are conditions.'

I nodded. I knew there would be.

'First, you will keep in regular contact with Sherlock Holmes and at any time that he calls upon you for help, you will rush to his side immediately. Secondly, in a similar fashion, if you receive a message from the Professor instructing you to involve yourself with Holmes's current investigation, you will do so immediately. Understood, so far?'

'I understand.'

'Under no circumstances must you reveal these arrangements to your wife or, indeed, any living soul. Understood?'

'Yes.'

'Good. We will leave it up to you to plan the nuptials, but the Professor will organize your new dwelling and arrange the medical practice for you in Paddington.'

'Paddington?'

'A nice little place. A semi-detached property. Cosy, by all accounts, with the front parlour used as a consulting-room. It should suit you very well. It is not a thriving practice, but we don't want that, do we? You must have plenty of time on your hands to assist your detective colleague. If you grow bored, you could always practise your writing.'

Although, essentially, the news I was hearing was positive,

Moran's sneering tone confirmed that my shackles were neither being removed nor slackened; they were being replaced by another equally constrictive pair. But I was grateful that I now could ask Mary to marry me and to set a date.

'As you know,' continued Moran, 'in this organization we do not have written agreements. We take people at their word.'

An easy thing to do, I thought, when you do not give a man any alternatives. Moran paused, prompting me to respond.

'Yes,' I said.

'So, Watson, you agree to our arrangements and will abide by them?'

'In order to marry Mary, I will do all you ask.' As I spoke these words, I felt a leaden weight settle upon my heart.

'Good. Then it is decided,' said Moran.

Within the month, Mary and I were married. The ceremony took place at the Church of St Monica in the Edgware Road. It was a private ceremony, with only Mary and myself present. I had asked Holmes to be my best man, and with some grudging reluctance he had agreed. But on the appointed hour he failed to appear. We waited some ten minutes, hoping that he would turn up, but the clergyman who was performing the ceremony began to grow irritated at the delay and so in the end we were forced to engage the services of a loafer in the church as a witness. He was no doubt sheltering from the cold, and was most surprised when I bribed him with a sovereign in order to help us legalize the ceremony.

Despite the joy of the occasion, the fact that Holmes failed to turn up, that he had let me down, dampened my pleasure somewhat. I had hoped that he could have suppressed his own feelings about love and marriage for one brief occasion in order to please a friend. But, it seems, I was wrong.

Mary and I honeymooned in Brighton, and on arriving at our hotel there was a telegram waiting for me. It was from Sherlock Holmes. It read: 'Apologies for absence. On a case. Regards to Mrs Watson. SH.'

Chapter Twenty-Three

From the journal of John H. Watson

And so I slipped easily and contentedly into married life and my medical practice. I was so happy that for most of the time I was able to keep at bay the realization that I was still a controlled puppet in an artificial situation. My relationship with Mary and my love for her were real, and they, along with ministering to my patients, formed the true anchor in my life. The medical practice had been neglected by the previous incumbent, and I was aware that it would take time and a great deal of work to build it up to create a reasonable living. Gradually, more out of curiosity, it seemed, than any other reason, I began to attract a number of new patients, but I knew that this was a long road I had to travel. I suspected that the scarcity of patients was exactly why Moriarty had chosen this particular practice. He didn't want me to be too busy so that I would neglect my duties to him. But neglect them I did in the first three months or so.

I did not visit Holmes once during this time, and he did not communicate with me. Of course, I did not expect him to. It would only be in the hour of need that he would turn to me. I pictured him in his Baker Street lodgings – lodgings which he was now able to afford without the necessity of a fellow lodger – buried amongst his books and files, and alternating from week to week between cocaine and ambition, the drowsiness of the drug and the fierce energy of his own keen nature. However, his fame as a detective continued to spread. Occasionally, I read of some of his activities in the newspapers, particularly his summons to Odessa in the case of the Trepoff murders, and it seemed clear to me that he had completely recovered from the idea of not having a colleague to accompany him on his sleuthing quests.

I did feel a little guilty about not visiting him, not for Moriarty's part, but because I regarded Sherlock Holmes as my friend. However, I suppressed this guilt until one evening nearly four months after my marriage, when I was returning from a journey to a patient and my way led me through Baker Street. As I passed that well-remembered door, I was seized with a keen desire to see my friend again. On the instant, I rang the bell and Mrs Hudson admitted me. She was effusive in her greeting and gave me a welcoming hug.

'It's grand to see you back in the old place,' she said. 'Things haven't been the same since you left. At least you could keep him in order.'

'Has he been difficult?' I asked, nodding my head towards the staircase that led to Holmes's quarters.

'You could say that. Moods! I've never met a man who has such moods. And how can I plan my housekeeping when I never know when he'll be in? Sometimes he disappears for three days at a time without a word or warning – or explanation, when he finally turns up, demanding ham and eggs because he's starving.'

I couldn't help but chuckle at Mrs Hudson's dilemma.

In response, she chuckled too. 'What a man, eh?'

I nodded.

'Can't you come back and put some routine and sense into his life, Doctor Watson?'

'I'm a married man now, Mrs Hudson. My main responsibilities lie elsewhere.'

'Of course you are. What can I have been thinking? And you look well on it. I can see your good lady is looking after you well.'

'Almost as well as you,' I said.

Mrs Hudson patted my arm and smiled.

'Is he in?'

'Yes, Doctor, and I'm sure he'll be happy to see you.'

I was not quite so sure. On opening the door, Sherlock Holmes gave me a brief smile and bid me enter. The room looked as though a whirlwind had rampaged through the chamber minutes earlier. There were papers strewn everywhere.

Holmes cast aside a sheaf from my old chair and bade me sit down.

'You catch me in mid-search,' he said casually, indicating the papers. 'There's a particular piece of information I need, and I am having trouble locating it.'

'Your filing system used to be so accurate.'

'So it seemed. I cannot understand it.' His eyes had that dreamy, faraway look that told me that he was under the influence of drugs. He lit his pipe, the hand wavering unsteadily as he applied the match to the bowl.

'You don't look well, Holmes. You are ill-using yourself.'

'Probably,' he nodded. 'I get down in the dumps now and then, especially when there are no cases on hand, but that is my way.'

I caught the hard, cold inflection of that last comment, which was telling me to mind my own business. I knew it was useless to pursue the subject. There was an awkward silence while I struggled and failed to find something to say.

'Wedlock obviously suits you,' he remarked at last. 'I think that you have put on seven and a half pounds since I saw you.'

'Seven,' I answered.

Holmes raised his brow in dispute. 'Really? I should have said a little more. Just a trifle more, I fancy, marital contentment is to blame, no doubt. And in practice again, I observe. You did not tell me that you intended to go back into harness.'

'Then how can you be so sure?'

'Because I am Sherlock Holmes. Have you forgotten, Watson? I *see*. I *deduce*. You used to know that.' He sighed with irritation. 'If a gentleman walks into my room smelling of iodoform, with a black mark of nitrate upon his right forefinger, and a bulge on the side of his top hat where he has secreted his stethoscope, I would be dull indeed if I could not pronounce him to be an active member of the medical profession. Satisfied?'

I nodded and smiled weakly. 'Sharp as ever.'

'You are too kind. And now, Doctor, what reason do you have for calling upon me this evening, having dragged yourself away from your cosy hearth and adoring wife?'

There was no mistaking the disdain in his voice and my hackles began to rise at the rude and insulting way in which my friend – or my former friend, as I was now beginning to see him – was treating me.

'I came out of friendship to see how you were.'

'And here was I thinking that you were just passing and acted upon a whim. After all these months I would have thought you harboured scant concern for my welfare.'

Holmes's words wounded me, not only because they were harsh, but also because they contained within them a germ of the truth.

I rose stiffly. 'I can see that you are busy and that I am intruding. I merely wished to . . . to—'

'Wished to. . . ?' Holmes echoed my words. 'I don't think, Watson, you really know *what* you wished. Yes, I am busy, and no doubt Mary has arranged a hot meal for your return.'

A flame of anger flared within me, and at that moment I could have struck Holmes down, but I contained myself. My reason told me that it was partly the drugs talking and partly the bitterness Holmes felt towards me for deserting him for over three months.

I hurried to the door and bade him good-night.

When I reached the foot of the stairs, I could hear the strident melancholy strains of Holmes's violin piercing the silence.

As I stepped into the night, my eyes were moist with frustrated anger. I was angry with Holmes and I was angry with myself. I had neglected my friend, I knew, but most men would have understood. Of course, Holmes was not most men, and his own selfish streak blinded him to the feelings and sensitivities of others. He was being unreasonable, but I had behaved badly. If only I had gone to see him after my marriage – just to renew contact. But in cutting myself off from him for nearly four months, I had carelessly severed the link between myself and the only man whom I regarded as a good and close friend.

It was with a heavy heart that I returned to my new home. A lamp was burning in the sitting-room. A decanter of brandy and a glass were placed in the centre of the table by the fire, which still glowed with life. A note was propped up against the decanter: 'Enjoy a nightcap, my darling, after your heavy day. You deserve it. Come to bed quietly. Mary.'

I could not help but smile at this loving gesture, and my heart warmed in appreciation and gratitude. I might have lost Holmes, but I had my beloved Mary, and she was worth all the male friendships in the world. For a moment, my hand hovered over the brandy decanter, and then, with a sigh, I put it to one side. Whatever discomforts I felt in the world, brandy would not help them. This I knew from experience.

A week later, Professor Moriarty was having a meeting with his chief of staff concerning a matter of great importance. Moran leaned over the plans laid out on Moriarty's desk and scrutinized them carefully. Flakes of ash dropped from the end of his cigar and he wafted them away.

'I really think it could work,' he said at length.

'It *will* work,' came the sharp response from the Professor, who was some feet away from him, staring out at the river below, which was dark and turbulent in the purple dusk. He turned suddenly and joined Moran by his desk. 'I do not allow for margins of doubt or error, Moran. I would have thought you would have known that by now.'

'Of course,' Moran replied softly.

'In some ways the project is a double-edged sword. I shall have the pleasure of committing the most fabulous crime and benefiting richly from it; while on the other hand my genius and daring will go unrecognized, unnoticed because no one will know that a crime has been committed.'

'Now, that is the brilliance of the scheme.'

Moriarty nodded gently. 'Yes.' He paused, lost in thought for a moment, and then rubbed his hands in a business-like manner. 'But we get ahead of ourselves; there are certain procedures, certain contingents to set into place first, and time is running out. The stone is due here in another ten days. After our signal failure with Mellors and Bentham, we shall have to make a move on to Graves.'

'That is being attended to as we speak, Professor. By morning, he should be at the warehouse.'

'*Should*?' Moriarty raised his brow.

'Will,' affirmed Moran.

'Let us hope so . . . for all our sakes.'

Sherlock Holmes crouched in the shrubbery, waiting. He had seen his man return home alone an hour earlier. He had glimpsed him through the net curtains of the sitting-room, reading the daily paper and then writing some letters before retiring upstairs. Now the house was in darkness, apart from a dull glow emanating from the front bedroom. The detective glanced at his watch. It was difficult to see in the darkness, but he could make out that it was now past eleven o'clock. It would not be long before they would strike. There was nothing he could do until they put in their appearance. His conversation with Harry Drysdale, his friendly nark in The Lord Nelson, had led him to believe that there would possibly be three men involved, but he could not be certain.

'They're keepin' this one tight to their chests, they are, an' all,' Drysdale had said, grinning, before downing his pint of ale.

Two or three -- not good odds. That is why Holmes had brought his pistol with him. He had been tempted to contact Watson to see if he would be free for an evening's adventure, but Holmes felt guilty at the rough and antagonistic way he had treated his friend on their last meeting, and he reasoned that it was unfair to put such pressure on him. There was certainly danger in this nocturnal endeavour, which he felt he had no right to ask Watson to share.

As Big Ben struck midnight, the light went out in the bedroom. The occupant was at last seeking the refuge of sleep. Not, surmised Holmes, that he would get much that night. After a five-minute interval, he saw two shadowy figures steal up the pathway to the porch. There was a brief flash of a lantern as one of the men dealt with the lock. They were professionals all right, thought Holmes, for with the minimum of time, effort and noise, they had gained entry to the house, closing the door behind them.

Now he had to make a decision. Did he go into the house and catch the intruders red-handed, or wait until they emerged with their trophy? Both strategies had their drawbacks. Entering the darkened house, he was placing himself at risk, especially with two men moving in the shadows. But they might quite easily leave by a back entrance while he was left waiting at the front.

Taking a firm hold of his pistol, he approached the front door. As yet, there were no sounds emanating from the house. He entered, and holding his breath he listened intently. Suddenly, he saw a flash of light on the landing and heard a man cry out.

Without hesitation, Holmes rushed up the stairs. The front bedroom door was ajar, and he could see inside the room clearly. A bedside lamp had been lit, providing harsh illumination which projected the figures of the two men into giant dancing shadows on the wall. One of the intruders was holding a cloth over the face of the man in bed. It was obviously doused in chloroform to subdue the victim. His arms were flailing in protest, but gradually as the chloroform took its effect, his body grew limp and his arms dropped to his side.

'That's it,' said one of the men, with a rasping guffaw. 'Time for a big nap.'

'Right, let's get Rip Van Winkle out of here,' said the other.

'I don't think you are going anywhere,' announced Sherlock Holmes, striding into the room, pistol in hand.

The two men froze at the sight of the gun.

'Who the hell are you?' asked one of the men.

'I am Sherlock Holmes.'

There was something in the expression on the man's face that alerted Holmes to his danger. Instinctively he turned round, while stepping to the side, but he was not quick enough. He received a savage blow to the side of his head, and for a moment an explosion of bright light filled his vision. He staggered backwards, his gun going off, the bullet embedding itself in the ceiling. His attacker, the third man, who had come up behind him, kicked the weapon from the detective's hands.

Sherlock Holmes knew he was now in serious trouble. His only hope of survival was to escape. As the three men advanced on him, he scuttled like a crab towards the window. Snatching up a chair, he jabbed it at the pane, creating a jagged aperture large enough for him to clamber through. By now, one of the men had retrieved the gun and fired at Holmes, but the bullet whistled past the detective's head. Holmes knew the next shot would be more accurate. Without hesitation he launched himself through the window, catching his jacket on the jagged glass as he did so. He felt a sharp stab of pain as the glass pierced his skin. He was now more than half way out of the window, and he spied a rhododendron bush in the garden below which he hoped would break his fall. Just as he scrambled out on to the ledge, one of his attackers launched himself forward and stabbed Holmes in the leg. The detective gave a fierce gasp of pain, but he would not be stopped now. With a Herculean effort, he wrenched himself free of his attacker and then suddenly found himself spiralling through darkened space.

Chapter Twenty-Four

From the journal of John H. Watson

A few days after my visit to see Holmes, I received the urgent message that set in motion a series of events that led to the most dramatic conclusion. The message came from Professor Moriarty. It was terse and to the point: 'You have neglected your duties, Doctor! Holmes is interfering in my affairs. You must stop him. Act immediately!'

How was I to act? I had no idea what the Professor expected me to do. But I was aware that if I did not do something, my life, and those of Mary and Sherlock Holmes, would not be worth a pin's fee.

Without delay, I engaged myself in a series of subterfuges. By now, through necessity, I had become adept at such activities. I informed Mary that Holmes was in dire need of my assistance and that I could not deny his plea for help. Without so much as a frown or a pursed lip, she said that she understood and that I had to follow my feelings in the matter. Hurriedly, I engaged a locum to look after my patients for a few days, spinning some yarn about attending to an elderly aunt in the North who was close to death. I then hailed a cab and sped to Baker Street, not knowing what I would find there, what reception I would receive or how I would explain my arrival.

On entering the sitting-room, I found an old man asleep on the *chaise-longue*. He was heavily whiskered and had the reddish complexion that one finds in heavy drinkers. His old tweed suit had seen better days, as had his shabby boots, and his hands and nails were thickly begrimed. Despite my appearance, he continued to snore quietly, his chest rising and falling in a regular rhythm.

I looked in vain for my friend. I peered into his bedroom, but the smooth lay of the eiderdown indicated that he had not slept there that night. When I returned to the sitting-room, the old man had awakened and was on his feet. He eyed me with some amusement, and then, just as I was about to challenge him as to his identity, I caught a familiar gleam in the grey eyes. It was Holmes.

'Morning, Watson!' he cried, pulling off his side whiskers with a theatrical gesture. 'How good to see you.'

I could not help myself: I burst out laughing.

Holmes grinned and bowed. 'Septimus Hitchcock at your service, sir,' he said in a rich Cockney accent.

I shook my head is wonderment. 'What on earth. . . ?'

'A long story – one which I will have pleasure in recounting over a late breakfast. I do hope you can stay.'

I nodded.

'Good man,' he said, in buoyant humour, his demeanour bearing none of the irascible bitterness I experienced during our last encounter. 'Call down to Mrs Hudson and order coffee, toast and boiled eggs for two, there's a good fellow. If I know her, she will already be about the task. By the time I've shed my ancient persona, and had a wash and shave, our feast will be ready for us and then I will provide you with the details of my latest escapade.'

With a gentle pat on my shoulder, he disappeared into his bedroom. I couldn't be sure at the time, but I thought that he was limping.

Fifteen minutes later, I was sitting opposite the spruce, clean-shaven and familiar version of Sherlock Holmes. He was encased in one of his dressing-gowns, and he was smoking his old clay pipe. The coffee, toast and eggs lay before him, untouched.

'Have you heard of the Elephant's Egg?'

The phrase echoed down the corridors of my memory. Unusual and amusingly preposterous as it seemed, I *had* heard of it before –

but I could not place it in context. I shook my head in denial.

'It is one of the biggest – if not *the* biggest – rubies that the world has ever seen. Hence its fantastical sobriquet. It is the property of the Raja of Kalipaur.'

'Ah, yes,' I said, the phrase now slotting into place. 'He is sending the stone as a gift to the Queen.'

'Indeed. A tribute to Victoria, Empress of India. The stone is estimated to be worth somewhere in the region of two million pounds.'

I whistled softly. 'A very nice gift indeed.'

'It has come to my attention that someone intends to steal the Elephant's Egg as soon as it reaches these shores.'

At these words I froze. I knew that there could be only one criminal daring and audacious enough to attempt such a robbery: Professor Moriarty. And only Sherlock Holmes was clever and resourceful enough to stop him. So this is why I had been sent: to interfere with Holmes's investigation, to lead him off the scent.

To say that I suffered from mixed emotions on hearing Sherlock Holmes, his face wreathed in a beatific smile, refer to the proposed threat of the precious ruby would be a gross understatement. I was delighted that the challenge of such a case had stimulated my friend to such a degree that he was indeed himself again. The Holmes of old, capricious and mischievous – the eager foxhound once more. On the other hand, I realized that in this particular case he was about to challenge the greatest – and more importantly – the most dangerous criminal genius of the age. And I was the creature bound to his will while my true loyalties lay elsewhere. I saw myself as the medieval heretic who is tied to four horses in order to be torn asunder for his treachery. It was at that moment that I knew, whatever the consequences might be, that I had to choose, for my own sanity, for the love of Mary and for the only true friendship I could call my own. Up until now, my loyalty to Holmes had never been tested. True, I had reported back on his detective work but I had never attempted to interfere with it for any reason. Now I knew I couldn't, and – more importantly – I *wouldn't*.

'How do you know all this?' I said quietly, trying desperately not to reveal my agitation.

Holmes waved his arms like errant butterflies. 'I have my methods,' he replied, leaning backwards, allowing puffs of smoke to spiral to the ceiling. 'It is the job of the detective to know many things and to keep abreast with items of current information in the criminal world. Within the last fortnight, two jewellers have met rather sudden ends. A suspicious death and a suicide, which in itself is always a suspicious death.'

'Two jewellers?'

'Experts in their field. Not only for judging the quality and price of sparkling stones – but also in the cutting and shaping of such gewgaws.'

'What has this got to do with the Elephant's Egg?'

'Everything! I believe these two men to have been murdered.'

'Why?'

'You were always good with the questions. That piercing inquisitiveness is one of your more accomplished qualities. Why indeed? The two men – their names are incidental – were experts at cutting up large stones – jewels, agates, rubies – into a series of smaller items. If you were to steal a red blob as large as the Raja's ruby, you would want it to be cut up into several slivers, glittering babies which collectively would fetch as much as the mother egg. It would be almost impossible to sell the original – but smaller treasures would be an easy sale.'

The logic was clear, and I was certain Holmes was right.

'The deaths were clumsy and hurried. The coincidence is too great to ignore. A large precious stone is due to arrive in this country and be placed on display – bait enough for the greediest and sharpest of thieves – and two men who would be capable of . . . *adapting* the stone for easy disposal are themselves disposed of.'

'But why murder, when, if what you say is true, these two jewellers would be useful to the supposed thief?'

'*If* they agreed to his demands. There are still some upstanding fellows in our community who would resist the temptation to break the law, whatever the consequences. However, once they had been approached and once they had refused, our master thief could hardly let them go.' Holmes drew his forefinger along the line of his neck.

I shuddered, not solely because of the graphic image he had presented, but also because I knew he was right. Moriarty would have no compunction in disposing of these recalcitrant jewellers. Moriarty was a man of ice, without warmth or consideration for others. We were all just pawns on his great chessboard, and we could be taken at any time to enhance his game.

'I investigated these murders. Scotland Yard, blinkered as usual, saw nothing suspicious in the men's demise, but I collected sufficient evidence to convince myself that I was correct. My next move was to find out how many other jewellers in the city were expert enough to carry out this specialized operation. Surprisingly there are not many – but one name stuck out from the rest: Patrick Graves.'

The name meant nothing to me.

'He was involved in a counterfeiting scandal some years ago. A matter concerning a diamond necklace. Not every stone was a fake, and so it was easier to convince the unsuspecting buyers that they were all genuine. He could sell three necklaces for the price of one set of stones. A tidy profit when you are dealing with items of fifty thousand pounds a time. He had aristocratic connections and a good lawyer: he was found not guilty. So much for British justice.'

'If, as I think you are saying, this Graves fellow has a natural criminal bent, why wasn't he approached first by . . . by the. . . ?'

'Master thief,' added Holmes, as I stumbled over my words.

I nodded.

'I'm not sure. Perhaps a thief should not employ a thief. There is no honour among thieves. But after two failures with upright gentlemen, it seemed to me that Graves was the next likely candidate. Two nights ago, I visited his house in Chiswick and I was just in time to witness his abduction – or, to be more precise, I was just in time to prevent his abduction, but I failed. There was only one of me and there were three of them . . . brawny fellows, too.'

'I should have been with you!' I blurted the words without thinking, and regretted my utterance instantly.

Holmes gave me a wry grin. 'Perhaps you should. You might have prevented me from receiving a blow to the back of my neck and a nasty stab wound to my leg.'

'Great heavens! Let me see the wound. How severe is it?'

'The wound is fairly deep, but it has not severed any arteries. I have stitched it myself in an amateur but acceptable fashion. It will heal in time.'

'Why didn't you come to me for treatment?'

Ignoring my question, Holmes rose and crossed to the window and looked out. 'These are dangerous times, Watson. I know I am being watched. That's why you saw me in disguise just now. I never leave the house without assuming some other persona than my own. More than ever I feel that my life is in danger.'

'In what way?'

'Well, I think you know, my friend,' he said slowly.

I shook my head. 'I don't know what you mean.'

With a wave of his hand, he beckoned me to the window.

'See that fellow down there? The one in the brown bowler and grey overcoat?'

'Yes.'

'Another of Moriarty's men. On guard to watch over me.'

'Moriarty's men. . . ?' I found myself repeating the phrase dumbly as my stomach began to tighten with fear.

Holmes gave me a sour grin. 'Professor James Moriarty, the greatest criminal in London Town. He's very adept at employing fellows to spy on people, as you well know.'

The words had hardly left his lips before I saw his fist coming towards me. The action was so sudden and so surprising that I remained rooted to the spot. His knuckles smashed against my chin with great force, and my head exploded with sharp pain and bright dazzling lights. Staggering backwards, my knees gave way and I found myself sinking to the floor.

When my vision cleared, I observed Holmes standing over me with a strange expression on his face. He gave a wry chuckle and then, leaning forward, he held out his hand to pull me to my feet.

'That was very satisfying. I have been wanting to do that for a long time,' he declared.

Dazed by the blow and bewildered by Holmes's behaviour, I dropped into the chair by the fire, rubbing my chin. It was then that the full significance of his actions sank in.

'My God,' I said. 'You know!'

'Yes, Watson, I know. I probably know everything. I know that your real name is Walker. I know that you were drummed out of the army for drunkenness, and I know that you have been a paid employee of Professor James Moriarty since arriving back into this country. My dear fellow, I certainly wasn't going to set up home with someone about whom I knew absolutely nothing. I did a little digging, and soon discovered your real identity. That wasn't very difficult. I have been building up a dossier on Moriarty for some time, as, no doubt, he has on me. When I discovered that you had been in his company just before we were introduced, it was a simple deduction. Obviously, you were to be his spy in the camp.'

I shook my head in disbelief. 'And yet you still went ahead with the arrangement?'

'I was flattered that I warranted so much attention.' He chuckled. 'And I liked you. You seemed a decent enough fellow, and I thought it would be fun playing cat and mouse with the two of you.'

'So, you've known all this time.'

'Of course I have. What sort of detective would I be if I could not detect that the man with whom I shared lodgings was in the employ of the most powerful criminal in the city?'

'Then you must know that I had no choice in the matter.'

'Very few have, where the Professor is concerned. Yes, I knew. I could not have tolerated your existence if I thought you had entered into the contract willingly.'

'Why are you telling me all this now?'

'Because we have come to the final chapter of our saga, Watson. It is time to destroy Professor James Moriarty and his organization, once and for all.'

'He is too powerful. It's not possible.'

'All things are possible, with careful plotting and planning. I am offering you the opportunity to join forces with me now to end this man's grip on London – and, indeed, upon your own life.'

My heart pounded at the prospect that Holmes described. It was like a mirage, a fantastic illusion that would fade if one reached out to touch it. To be free, really free, of the dark threat that had hung over me since that fateful meeting in Reed's club seemed like a happy dream beyond the grasp of daytime reality.

'How could you trust me?'

'All I would need is your word.'

I grinned. 'I don't need time to think. I will help you. You have my word. But I believe that we shall lose the battle. As I said, Moriarty is very powerful, and he has eyes and ears everywhere.'

'I am fully aware of that, and that is why we must trust no one – and I mean *no one*. Not even Scotland Yarders like Lestrade and Gregson; not even your Mary. We cannot be sure who is free from the taint of Moriarty.'

'But Mary . . .'

'No doubt she would protest the same about you, and she would be wrong, wouldn't she?'

I nodded dumbly. It was a hateful thought, but I realized that it was a possibility.

'When we have our case, there is one fellow at the Yard who will help to bring the matter to a head, but for the moment we can only trust each other. Is that understood?'

'Yes,' I mumbled, my mind in a frantic whirl.

'Don't fret, Watson; I would not engage upon this very dangerous game unless I was sure of a safe outcome. You must trust me, and your actions must not waver – or we are all lost.'

I nodded and managed a half-smile.

'Good man,' he said, lighting his pipe and sitting opposite me. 'Now, I think I'd better put you fully in the picture. Let me start by telling you how I managed to escape from the bruisers who were abducting Patrick Graves.'

Chapter Twenty-Five

Just as Sherlock Holmes scrambled free out on to the ledge, one of his attackers launched himself forward and struck him in the leg. The detective gave a fierce gasp of pain as he wrenched himself free, and then suddenly he found himself falling through darkened space.

Blotting the pain of the wound from his mind, Holmes twisted his body, aiming it at the large rhododendron bush below him. He landed spread-eagled atop its leafy branches. It broke his fall, but it was only a temporary resting-place, for the weight of his body was too great to be supported by the bush and he tumbled in an ungainly fashion on to the lawn. At moments like this, Holmes's ability to think and act quickly was remarkable. He knew that if he stayed where he was, he would be captured or more likely killed by the assailants. If he fled, all his efforts that evening would come to nought. There had to be some centre ground. He scrambled awkwardly to his feet, gritting his teeth as the wound in his leg screamed with pain. He ran as fast as he could to the garden wall, and vaulted over on to the pavement. He crouched low against the bole of a large oak tree by the kerb. On the other side of the street he spied a carriage. The driver appeared to be peering at the house in anticipation.

Two of the assailants appeared in the garden, one swinging a bull's-eye lantern around wildly.

'He's scarpered!' cried one fellow.

'Yeah,' replied the other. 'Never mind him, let's get this bleeder away before the whole neighbourhood wakes up.'

The third man appeared at the door with a large burden over his shoulder, wrapped in a grey blanket. The burden was Patrick Graves. The man blew on a silver whistle and the driver brought the carriage to the gate. Graves was bundled inside, followed by two of the men; the other, obviously the leader, jumped up alongside the driver.

'Let's go,' he croaked, and the carriage set off.

Holmes slipped from his hiding-place and ran after the carriage. With iron determination he blotted from his mind the stabbing pain in his leg, and, clutching hold of one of the metal bars running parallel across the back of the coach, he pulled himself forward and managed to secure a foothold on the back of the vehicle. With amazing dexterity for an injured man, he was able to settle himself into a crouching position to the back of the carriage, hanging on in a precarious fashion as the vehicle gained speed. In this manner, he travelled with the abductors through the dark and winding streets of London.

Despite his limited vision, Holmes's encyclopedic knowledge of London allowed him to deduce the direction in which they were travelling. All signs told him they were headed towards Rotherhithe. The detective clung on for dear life as the carriage swayed and rattled its way east.

After some twenty minutes, the roads narrowed and darkened – the frequency of gas lamps diminishing. They were now in the vicinity of the West India Docks – an area of warehouses, giant wharves and silent, uninhabited streets. And then the carriage slowed down as it approached the gates of some huge warehouse. He heard one of the men blow hard on a whistle four times, and, peering around the edge of the carriage, Holmes saw the gates begin to open. Now he had to think fast. Decisions had to be made. Should he drop from the vehicle before he became trapped in the warehouse, or should he risk going inside to face the unknown? Once inside the warehouse, he felt certain that he would be able to discover much more concerning Moriarty's plot to steal the Elephant's Egg. The danger was, of course, that he would be trapped there, thus rendering the knowledge useless. In such situations as this, with his heart racing and his adrenalin pumping, Sherlock Holmes gave way to the emotional rather than the rational response. He stayed with the carriage.

It rumbled into the vast and apparently empty warehouse, a great industrial cathedral with a high vaulted ceiling which echoed with the rattle of the carriage. In the distance, Holmes spied a group of men, some of whom were carrying lanterns. The welcoming committee. Nimbly, Holmes jumped from his perch and, keeping to the shadows, he scrambled to a stack of discarded packing-cases by the wall, and hid there. And waited. He was inside and safe for the moment. And then the doors of the warehouse closed with an echoing clang. He was inside, but trapped.

Graves was unceremoniously unloaded from the carriage as the group of men, three in all, approached. Holmes recognized one of them – Scoular, one of Moriarty's lieutenants. He seemed to be in charge.

'You have our prize?' he asked, pointing at Graves.

'We've got him. He's groggy now, but he's only had a few drops of the old chlory. He'll be right as rain shortly,' said the leader of the abductors, the one who had hit Holmes from behind.

'Was there any trouble?' asked Scoular, his face a cold mask.

'A little. Some geezer tried to interfere.'

'Yeah,' said another. 'Called himself Sherlock Holmes.'

Scoular's eyes narrowed. 'What happened?'

'We gave him what for, and he scarpered.'

'You fools! He should have been silenced.'

'He was a very slippery customer.'

'There were three of you.'

Scoular's observation hushed the men for a moment, and then the leader piped up again: 'But we had Graves to deal with as well, and we got him for you.'

Scoular nodded, and turned to his confederates. 'Maxwell, you take care of Mr Graves; and Jenson, pay our friends here and make sure they leave the premises with some speed.' He looked up at the driver of the carriage. 'Take them back to the city and drop them somewhere quiet.'

The bigger of the two men took Graves's limp body and hoisted it over his shoulder, like a roll of carpet. The abductors were paid off, and within minutes the carriage had departed, taking its three passengers with it.

Holding his lantern aloft, Scoular made his way back down towards the far end of the warehouse, accompanied by his two accomplices, one of whom bore the limp frame of Patrick Graves.

Sherlock Holmes followed them at a distance, keeping to the sides of the building and beyond the feeble rays of the lantern.

The men halted, and suddenly a bright shaft of yellow light shot up from the floor of the warehouse, sending a golden glow up into the rafters. Silently, Holmes dropped to the ground. He saw that Scoular had opened a trap-door, and it was from here that the light was emanating. Without a word, the men disappeared from sight and then with the same suddenness of its arrival, the bright beam of illumination vanished as the trap-door slammed shut. The detective was left alone in the Stygian gloom and silence. It was as though he had been witness to a strange shadow-play, and now the show was over. But the show was not over, he determined. This was merely an interval. He had come this far; it would be futile to give up now. He knew that this was the closest he'd ever been to Professor Moriarty, and he intended to get even closer. Somewhere above him a bat, disturbed by the sudden shaft of light, fluttered briefly from one rafter to another and then settled again.

After five minutes, when his eyes had fully acclimatized to the darkness, which was softened only by the moonlight that struggled through the grime on the row of windows placed up the wall near the roof, Sherlock Holmes rose to his feet. His leg still ached and he could feel the wetness of the warm blood seeping through his trouser leg, but he ignored it. He *had* to ignore it. There were greater concerns at issue here. Slowly he approached the trap-door, and with his heart in his mouth, he gently tugged at the rope-ring which raised it. Again, yellow light escaped into the warehouse. He saw that there was a staircase which led downwards to what appeared to be a narrow corridor. Holmes noted with surprise that this was expensively panelled and carpeted.

Like a man operating underwater, he slipped through the aperture and gently replaced the trap-door. *Trap-door*, he thought. How appropriate. He was now trapped within the lair of London's greatest criminal. And he had walked into this trap himself. With a wry grin, he made his way down the staircase.

At the bottom, he listened, straining his ears for any sound. Remarkably, there was none – just a hissing silence. He moved along the corridor and soon came upon two doors: one straight ahead of him and the other to his right, which was twice the size of the first. Gingerly pulling the large door ajar, he discovered that it led to to a lift. A metal cage was in readiness to propel the occupant downwards to who knew where. Reckless as he might have been to come this far, he certainly was not going to risk taking a ride in a lift, especially in Moriarty's domain.

He tried the other door, which led to another short passage – almost an anteroom – and a further door. As soon as he began to open this, he heard voices. He stopped and peered through the crack that he had created. He gazed down upon a magnificent high chamber, wonderfully furnished and illuminated by electricity. As far as he could determine, the door was situated on a minstrel gallery above the chamber. The gallery ran round the four walls, made up of shelves which housed a vast quantity of books. Down below, two men were in quiet conversation. Crouching low, Holmes slipped through the door and lay on the floor, edging forward enough to survey the scene below him.

From his vantage-point, Holmes had an excellent view of the room and its occupants. He recognized one of the men straightaway. It was Colonel Sebastian Moran, Moriarty's second in command. Holmes observed the other man closely. He was a tall fellow, with finely chiselled, sardonic features and a hard cruel mouth and a mop of dark unruly hair. He had about him an air of power and authority. It was clear to Sherlock Holmes that this was Professor James Moriarty, the Napoleon of Crime. He was in his presence at last. A thrill of excitement rippled through his body. Here was his dark *doppelgänger*, a man as passionate about committing crime as Holmes was about solving it. Excitement transmuted to nervousness and uncertainty. It was as though he had only just realized the precariousness of his position. Oh, he had been clever to trace the devil to his lair, but he would have to be much cleverer to leave without being discovered. He pushed these thoughts from his mind; bridges to be crossed later. Moving even further to the edge of the gallery, he strained his ears to catch what the two men were saying.

Moriarty leaned in a nonchalant fashion on the edge of the mantelpiece while Moran paced up and down in front of him.

'I'm not at all happy about Holmes's appearance tonight,' Moran was saying.

'Neither am I,' replied the Professor, in silky tones. 'But I will take steps to prevent his further involvement in my plans. We must utilize Watson again, and if that fails, I shall simply have to rid myself of this nuisance once and for all.'

'Wouldn't it be better to do that straightaway?'

'Possibly, but my mind is filled with the Elephant's Egg operation at present, and I'd rather not be distracted by having to devise a suitable finale for Mr Sherlock Holmes.'

Moran nodded. He knew better than to attempt to persuade his master otherwise.

'Everything is in place at the Indian end,' continued Moriarty, as though he were speaking his thoughts aloud. 'Our man is ready to take the place of the Maharaja's envoy on the sea voyage. It is a substitution which has been worked out with the greatest precision. Reed is overseeing this. So when the ship docks in England, not only will the envoy be a fake but the ruby also. No one will dare to examine it that closely. It would be most impolite to scrutinize such a gift. No one will realize that it is merely a very convincing piece of red glass. It will be presented to the Queen in a special ceremony at Windsor Castle, after which it will be lodged in the vaults there, with all the other trinkets she has acquired during her reign. It is unlikely that it will be seen again – or at least for some time. Meanwhile, we shall have the pleasure of profiting from this most bountiful of eggs.' Moriarty allowed himself a brief smile.

'That's if Graves is prepared to co-operate.'

'He will, Moran, he will. We have wasted too much time on these reluctant jewellers. He'll do as I ask . . . even if I have to use force.'

As though on cue, a door opened and Scoular entered, accompanied by a groggy-looking Patrick Graves. Scoular shepherded the jeweller to the sofa by the fire.

'Our man is coming round,' he declared.

Moriarty grinned. 'Good. Moran, be so kind as to give our visitor a reviving brandy.'

Moran did as he was ordered. Graves took the brandy glass and greedily downed the drink in one gulp, which brought on a coughing fit. The other three men waited patiently like statues until he had finished.

'Mr Graves,' said Moriarty, approaching the sofa, 'I have something for you, an offer that can make you a substantial amount of money or one that could result in you losing at least one of your limbs.'

Graves, who was already pale, blanched at the harshness of these words.

'Do I have a choice?' he asked at length, in a halting fashion, his voice no more than a dry whisper.

'Indeed you do.'

Graves grinned slyly. 'Then I'd rather take the money option.'

Moriarty chuckled in a theatrical manner while his two companions gazed on Graves with stony stares. 'A man after my own heart.'

'Another brandy, perhaps?' Graves held out his glass like a beggar.

'Give our friend another snifter, Moran, and Scoular, you see he gets a good night's rest. We can discuss details in the morning. I don't think we have any need to worry. I'm sure Mr Graves will be as co-operative as we wish.'

'Certainly will, gentlemen,' agreed Graves, before taking another gulp of brandy from his refreshed glass.

Sherlock Holmes, positioned high above this drama, concluded that he had learned as much as he needed for the time being, and that it would be prudent to make his escape. With infinite care he retraced his steps back through the two doors and along the panelled passage and up the wooden staircase. Below the trap-door, he paused and strained his ears for any noise, any sound of movement. He could hear none. He pushed up the trap-door sufficiently for him to survey the warehouse. It appeared as empty and deserted as when he had left it. His heart pounding with pleasure, he scrambled through.

As soon as he was on his feet, he felt an arm grasp him around the neck. A gruff voice snarled in his ear, 'And what the hell do you think you're doing?'

Holmes swivelled his head to catch a glimpse of his assailant. It was the coach-driver, back from his travels. With great speed and dexterity, Holmes grabbed the man's arms and, placing all his weight on his good leg, he heaved him over his shoulder. It was a practised Baritsu move. The man rose as though he were a rag-doll, and landed with an unhealthy thud on his back some three feet away from the detective. He gave a cry of pain, and before he was able to lift himself from the ground, Holmes straddled his body and administered a powerful right hook to his chin. The driver's head fell backwards, his eyes tight shut and his mouth agape. Holmes could not help but smile with pleasure at his own strength and ability. He then carried out a search of the man's clothing until he found what he was looking for: the keys to the warehouse door.

Within five minutes, Sherlock Holmes, limping badly now, was three streets away from Moriarty's warehouse. After half an hour, he was in a cab on his way back to Baker Street.

Chapter Twenty-Six

From the journal of John H. Watson

I listened with increasing horror to Holmes's narrative. I knew that he cared little for the danger in which he placed himself by continuing with his plan to outsmart Moriarty and to bring him and his organization down, but I wondered how much he realized that, in doing so, he was placing me and my wife in great danger also.

My fears must have been mirrored in my glum expression, for Holmes leaned over and patted me on the shoulder.

'Have no fear,' he said, with a steely glint in his eye. 'Moriarty will not win; you have my word on that.'

It was meant as a comforting gesture, but it did not comfort. I knew at first hand the power and extent of Moriarty's vast organization – how far his tendrils extended over this great city. There was no dark corner or crevice to which his agents did not have access. He was the puppet-master supreme; he controlled many who were at his beck and call at every hour of the day or night. Holmes had no such organization. Essentially, he was one man – a David challenging this terrible Goliath. No matter how brilliant my friend was, the odds were heavily stacked against him.

'What do you intend to do now?' I asked.

'There's a fellow at the Yard with whom I've been working on the Moriarty case – Inspector Patterson. He's the only one I can trust, and even then I have kept certain details from him. However, I shall inform him of Moriarty's scheme to switch both the Maharaja's envoy and the stone itself. The envoy is due here at the end of next week. He must be protected. With the co-operation of the Indian police, it should be easy to pick up your louche friend Reed, now that we know of his intentions. Moriarty's scheme will be scuppered before the boat docks in England. If it is not too late, I will suggest that the stone be transported secretly to this country by another route, to ensure its safety. It is more than likely that the Professor has contingency plans up his sleeve. We cannot be too careful.'

'And then what?'

'I shall disappear. Baker Street is too hot for me now. I'll not disclose my whereabouts to anyone, including your good self, and so you can say with all honesty that you don't know where I am. And I suggest that you arrange for your wife to take a trip out of town for a few weeks. Is there some relative or friend who lives in the country?'

'I suppose so . . .' I hated the idea of sending Mary away, but I knew it was for the best.

'Good. Things will be a little tricky for the next week or so, but after that London will be a healthier and safer place to live in.'

'And what do you want me to do in the mean time?'

'Nothing. Nothing yet. Nothing until I contact you – which I will, in due course. For now, we need to add some touches to give authenticity to the story of my disappearance.'

Some five minutes later, I stood on the threshold of my old room, ready to leave. Sherlock Holmes and I shook hands.

'Do take care, old friend,' he said.

'I fear less for my safety than your own.'

He grinned and closed the door.

I decided to walk back to Paddington. It was a bright spring day and I felt in need of fresh air. I wanted to sort things out in my mind, to try and gain a clearer perspective on matters. As I was passing the gates by Hyde Park Corner, lost in thought, I suddenly became aware that a tall figure had fallen into step with me and was walking by my side. It was Scoular.

'How are you, Doctor? Well, I trust,' he said. The words were pleasant enough, but they were delivered without warmth or friendliness.

'I am well,' I responded in kind.

'And Mr Sherlock Holmes, is he well? How is his leg? You visited him this morning.'

I nodded. 'I went to Baker Street to see him. He wasn't there.'

Scoular's eyes narrowed as he repeated my words. 'He wasn't there?'

'He's gone away.'

'Where to?'

'I don't know. There was this note waiting for me.' I handed him an envelope that Holmes had given me.

Scoular took it roughly and extracted a note, which he read out loud: 'Watson: matters are too hot for me in London at present, so I've decided to move away for an indefinite period. You shall not see me for some time. Regards to Mrs Watson. I remain yours, Sherlock Holmes.'

Scoular emitted a cry of disgust and almost screwed the note up. 'This is some kind of trick,' he said.

I shook my head in ignorance. 'Ever since my marriage, Holmes has confided in me less and less. I can only take this message at face value. I have no idea where he is or what his plans are.'

'Very well. I will keep this note. The Professor will no doubt find the contents most interesting. Remember, Watson, where your allegiance lies and on whom your life depends. If Sherlock Holmes gets in touch with you for any reason, you must contact us immediately. Is that understood?'

'Of course.'

'Good,' he said softly, and then stepped back, merging with the crowd of pedestrians on the pavement. Within seconds, he was lost from sight.

I removed my hat and with my handkerchief mopped my brow. Moriarty was clever enough to know that the note was a blind. He knew that Holmes would not desert the city at this crucial time. The Professor would set his hounds on my friend. Never had Sherlock

Holmes been more vulnerable.

'You'll take tea with me, Mr Scoular, won't you?' Mrs Hudson placed the kettle on the gas ring in readiness, but her visitor shook his head.

'On some other occasion, maybe,' he said politely, but without warmth. 'I just need to know – the *Professor* needs to know where Sherlock Holmes is.'

Mrs Hudson, wiping her hands on her apron, sat down in her favourite chair by the hearth and smiled. 'I don't know. As you know, he rarely confided in me in the old days, but just recently I reckon he could give a clam a few lessons or two.' She chuckled at her own conceit, but Scoular's disapproving glance cut her merriment short.

'When did you last see him?'

'I can't be sure, and that's the truth. He's taken to wearing an assortment of wigs, false noses and all kinds of costumes, so I'm never sure whether it's him in disguise or one of his visitors. I haven't served him any meals now for over a week.'

Scoular gave a sigh of impatience.

'Doctor Watson came round this morning,' she continued, 'so I assumed he was home then, but Watson popped in to see me on his way out and said that he'd waited for his friend in vain. There was a note saying he'd gone away for a few weeks – but it didn't say where to.'

'I've seen the note,' said Scoular. 'Rather too convenient to be real, and most probably a dupe to make us think he has run away.'

Mrs Hudson shook her head. She didn't know what Scoular meant. 'You're welcome to go up and look in his rooms, if you want.'

'I know that,' he rasped with impatience. 'And I shall do so presently. In the mean time, if you see any trace of Holmes or anyone who might be Holmes, you must inform the Professor imme-diately. *Immediately*, is that clear?'

Mrs Hudson nodded. She knew this was an order, and it dismayed her. She had grown very fond of her eccentric and unpre-dictable lodger, and she didn't want any harm to come to him. But she had no choice in the matter: he didn't pay her wages.

'Good,' said Scoular, pulling on his gloves. 'I will visit you again this evening after dark and search Holmes's quarters, and then I'm afraid I shall be forced to start a little fire.'

'Oh, mercy me, no! You're not going to burn down my lovely home?'

'Nothing as extravagant as that, I assure you. Merely a small conflagration in Holmes's rooms which will destroy his files and records and render the place uninhabitable. Your quarters will be safe.'

'How can you be sure of that?' Mrs Hudson asked with asperity.

Scoular smiled for the first time since he had arrived. 'I can't.'

From the journal of John H. Watson

It took a great deal of persistence to persuade Mary to make a surprise visit to her aunt in Exeter. Instinctively, she knew something was wrong and that the matter was connected with Sherlock Holmes.

'Are you in any danger?' she asked, fixing me with her blue eyes.

After years of dissembling, lies came easily to me – but not when dealing with Mary. I hated telling her an untruth – but I had to. I don't think she believed me when I told her there was nothing to worry about, but at the same time I felt she knew that what I had asked her to do was in her best interests.

That evening she packed, and I sent a telegram to Exeter to give Mary's aunt notice of her arrival. Very early the following morning, I saw Mary off at Paddington Station. Not since my stay in the stinking cell in Candahar had I felt as miserable and alone as when the train chugged its noisy way out of the station, with Mary leaning out of a carriage window, waving goodbye. With Holmes in hiding and Mary gone, I had no one to turn to.

As I made my way back up the platform, a voice whispered in my ear. 'Going on a trip then, is she, the good lady wife?'

I turned to see a thin, rat-faced fellow in a loud brown-checked suit grinning back at me. With mock politeness, he raised his brown bowler.

'The Professor sends his compliments. No news of Mr Holmes, I presume?'

I shook my head. 'No news,' is all I could find to say.

'And the wife?'

'Mary has gone to visit her aunt, who has not been well.'

'Left you all alone, has she? Well, never mind, Doctor Watson. We're never far from your side. Do keep in touch.'

With an infuriating smirk, he raised his hat again and walked away. I stood rooted to the spot. I gazed unnervingly at the throng that passed by me. How many of them were the Professor's men? What could I do? How could I act if I were under that fiend's microscope all the time? Rather dejectedly, I continued on my way up the platform, brooding on what I considered to be a very dismal future.

It was then that I saw the newspaper billboard by the news kiosk. The headline ran: FIRE AT SHERLOCK HOLMES'S ROOMS.

Chapter Twenty-Seven

With practised ease, Sherlock Holmes shinned up the drainpipe at the rear of 221B Baker Street, as he had done many times in the last month. Despite his wounded leg, he was still very agile, and without any trouble he was soon level with the window of his bedroom. Slipping up the sash, he managed to scramble inside. Immediately, acrid fumes assailed his nostrils and caught the back of his throat, causing him to stifle a cough.

The walls of the room, scorched by flames, were blackened by smoke, and the bed and mattress had been reduced to a heap of sooty debris. The floor was damp and slimy. Holmes had read in the papers how the fire brigade had arrived in time to arrest the spread of the fire and that there had only been 'internal damage to the upper floor.' However, whatever the flames had failed to destroy, the water had completed the task.

Slowly Holmes moved into the sitting-room, and the sight before him made him gasp. This darkened shell was barely recognizable as his cosy old quarters. The furniture had been reduced to charred flakes, and no doubt his books, files and case-notes were those piles of damp ashes swept to the side of the room. Sherlock Holmes was a stranger to sentiment, but at this moment he felt an overpowering wave of sadness sweep over him. It wasn't just the loss of the material things – his files and notes – that upset him; it was the destruction of what had been his own closeted world, and, if he was honest with himself, the warm memories created here, particularly those he shared with Watson.

An errant breeze, finding entry through the smashed windows, stirred up a swarm of minuscule charred remnants which permeated the atmosphere like a cloud of tiny insects, and once again Holmes found himself holding his handkerchief to his mouth in order to prevent a fit of coughing. And then, suddenly, his nerves tingled and his senses quickened. Without proof, without deduction, he knew that he was not alone. There was some other presence in the room with him. Instinctively he reached inside his coat for his revolver, but before his fingers could take hold of the butt, a voice spoke to him from the shadows by the door.

'Leave your gun where it is, Sherlock Holmes.'

Holmes did not move.

'I am not playing games,' came the voice again. 'Take your hand away from your gun and put your arms by your side, or I will blow your head off.'

Holmes had met many villains in his time, and he knew when they were bluffing or not. This man was deadly serious. He retrieved his hand from his coat pocket, leaving the revolver *in situ*, and did as he was told.

The figure stepped from the shadows. A shaft of morning light from the window fell across his face. The detective recognized the man immediately. He was Scoular, one of the Professor's more ruthless lieutenants. He was grinning, his gun trained on Holmes.

'I knew that you would come,' Scoular said, the grin broadening. 'I knew that you couldn't resist coming back here to check the damage and see what you could salvage from your records. And you didn't disappoint me.'

'So this is *your* handiwork, is it?'

'It is. And I am quite proud of my efforts. I can assure you that there is not one sheet of paper left in a legible form in the whole place. I searched thoroughly before setting fire to it. Any documents referring to the Professor were taken away and destroyed separately.'

'How very thorough.'

'Oh, we are, Mr Holmes. We are. You should know that.' The smile faded. 'For a man of your intelligence and skills, you have been rather stupid. Headstrong. You should have known that if you intended to meddle in the affairs of the Professor, you would get more than your fingers burned. You should have known that you would lose your life.'

'I was aware of that possibility, but nothing ventured, nothing gained,' said Holmes urbanely, but his eyes were focused on Scoular's revolver, which was aimed at his heart.

'You should have been dealt with a long time ago. I urged it, but the Professor preferred to play his little game of cat and mouse with you. But that is over now. This time, you have gone too far.'

'Ah, you mean the affair of the Elephant's Egg? Reed has been captured and the ruby is safe, eh?'

'You should have dropped it, Mr Holmes, you really should.'

'It is not in my nature to give up. It has been a long crusade, but one which will have a successful conclusion.'

Scoular took a step forwards and cocked the pistol. 'Not for you, Mr Holmes.'

'Killing me will not alter the outcome now, I'm afraid. Assured as I am of the eventual destruction of Moriarty's organization, and the capture of its leading figures, including yourself and the Professor, of course, I am happy to sacrifice my life. I am pleased to think that I have been able to free society from any further effects of his presence. In any case, with this matter my career has reached a crisis, and I realized from the start that it might end with my death.'

'Then you are more foolish than I first thought. To throw away your life in the feeble belief that you could beat the Professor.'

'You do not understand, Scoular. You are so warped with your own criminal machinations that you cannot see the dark shadow that you and your kind throw over this city. How corrupt and filthy you are. How your evil doings destroy the goodness and the hope in the teeming masses that fill our streets, attempting to live good and simple lives. Your robberies, your forgeries, your murders, your greed – they diminish us all. Injustice tarnishes everything it touches. You, Moriarty and his kind are carriers of a disease, a

203

plague of evil. How could I rest, how could I care one jot about my own life, while this plague remains unchecked?'

'Well, you are correct about one thing; I do *not* understand your point of view. But I do know that you will never beat the Professor.'

'Oh, how tired I am of this conversation, Scoular. If you have a task to perform, pray carry it out now before I die of boredom.'

Scoular frowned. He could not believe how resigned Holmes seemed, considering that he was moments away from death. He was either very brave or very foolish. The fact that he could not tell which unnerved him.

In truth, Holmes was relaxed because he saw no way out of his dilemma. What he had said to Scoular was the truth. He was prepared to sacrifice his own life to secure the destruction of Moriarty's empire. One did not fear the inevitable, one accepted it. He had taken the main incriminating documents from Baker Street the previous day and left them in a safe place that only Inspector Patterson knew about. Once these were safely in the hands of Scotland Yard, the operation would be set up to arrest Moriarty and dismantle his organization. Holmes knew that he might not have many minutes to live, but Moriarty had but a few days before his game was up also.

'I hear that you are not a religious man, Mr Holmes. You have no prayers?'

'I have no prayers.'

Scoular shrugged and held the gun at arm's length. 'Goodbye then, Mr Holmes.'

A gunshot thundered and reverberated in the burned-out chamber.

Chapter Twenty-Eight

From the journal of John H. Watson

With horror, I read the report in the newspaper of the fire at Baker Street. It appeared that our old rooms had been gutted, but the fire had not spread to Mrs Hudson's quarters. Thank goodness the report indicated that 'the celebrated private detective, Mr Sherlock Holmes, was absent from the premises when the conflagration took hold.' However, it was clear from the report that all his precious files would have been consumed by the flames. I prayed that there was nothing essential regarding Moriarty in the room when the fire was started. Surely they would be with Holmes – wherever he was. He would not have left them there, in such a vulnerable location. However, the truth was that I could not be sure. If his evidence *had* gone up in smoke, we were lost. As I contemplated this prospect, I felt an awful gnawing feeling growing in the pit of my stomach.

I was in no doubt that the fire had been instigated by Professor Moriarty. For all I knew, he might have been the one to light the match. All niceties had been put to one side now. He was out to get Sherlock Holmes – out to destroy him. And it would not be long before he came after me – my usefulness was over. Within twenty-four hours the landscape of my life had changed, and as such I realized that I had been released from my shackles. The contract had been torn up and my puppet-master had cut the strings.

Strangely, I felt elated. Despite the very real threat of death now hanging over me, once again I was my own man. I was free to act independently, and free to be myself.

I was suddenly reminded of that dark, skeletal tree in Afghanistan where I had crouched down and, in a weak moment, with the aid of a brandy bottle, surrendered my liberty to an unforgiving future. That was in the dream-world of yesterday, part of another life. Now, in a strange twist of Fate, I had recovered my freedom, my individuality, once again. There was a difference though, for I was no longer John Walker. He had faded away in the cold desert night. Now I was the creature I had been fashioned into: John H. Watson. I had *become* the fiction. I was the Watson of my stories – and, more importantly, I was the friend, the biographer and champion of Mr Sherlock Holmes.

This realization brought a smile to my face, and the gnawing pain in my stomach evaporated. I flung down the paper and hurried from the station. Within minutes I had hailed a cab and was on my way.

A gunshot thundered and reverberated in the burned-out chamber.

Sherlock Holmes braced himself for the pain of a bullet ripping through his flesh. None came. Then he realized that Scoular had not fired his pistol; the shot had come from elsewhere.

With an inarticulate grunt, Scoular took a few paces forward, the expression on his face a mixture of surprise and amusement. He aimed his pistol at Holmes once more, but before he was able to pull the trigger, his knees gave way and he slumped silently to the floor, falling on his face amongst the wet debris. Holmes observed a patch of blood in the centre of his back.

A figure stepped out of the shadows, a smoking gun in his hand. It was Watson.

'For preference, I would not have shot the fellow in the back, but I really had no alternative,' he said matter-of-factly.

'Watson, by all that's wonderful!' cried Holmes, hardly able to take in the situation.

'It struck me that the fire was a ruse by Moriarty to lure you back to Baker Street, and that therefore he would have someone waiting for you – waiting to kill you. I got here as quickly as I could. Luckily, I was just in time.'

Holmes was lost for words. Not only did he always find it difficult to express his gratitude, but also there was something different about Watson's behaviour that inhibited him. He seemed more assured, more confident, and somehow a little colder, as though a touch of humanity had seeped out of his soul.

At length, Holmes stepped forward and clasped his friend's hand warmly. Watson responded in kind.

'I . . . I cannot thank you enough. You saved my life, you really did,' said Holmes.

'I hope you would have done the same for me,' replied Watson simply.

'So I would.'

For a brief moment the two men stood, still clasping hands, and smiled at each other.

'Well,' said Watson, eventually breaking away and kneeling down by Scoular's body, 'we have certainly burnt our bridges now. I'm not sure what the penalty for killing one of the Professor's trusted servants is, but I am sure that it is not very pleasant and that he will want to exact it to the full as soon as possible.' He turned the body over and gazed at Scoular's face, which looked back at him with an unnerving glassy stare. 'Poor devil,' he said quietly.

'Save your sympathies for us, Watson,' observed Holmes, reverting to his business-like self. 'London is now far too dangerous for us. We must get away until Patterson's force has carried out its work. Within a week, Moriarty's gang will be no more.'

'What do you suggest?'

'Would you come to the Continent with me? A week in foreign climes will do our health the world of good. There is a train leaving Victoria this evening which will take us to Dover. What do you say?'

'I say yes.'

'Good man. I have already taken the liberty of booking two first class tickets for a private compartment in Carriage B. Spend the rest of the day collecting a piece of luggage and some clothes for the trip. Do not go home on any account.'

Watson nodded.

'We'll leave by the back entrance. Not a salubrious exit – down the drainpipe and over the garden wall – but far safer than the front door. Then we shall separate. I will see you in the appointed carriage at six o'clock this evening. Do not be late.'

'I will not.'

Holmes paused, and once more he clasped Watson's hand. 'Thank you again for all your help, Watson. You are the finest fellow one could wish to have with you when in a tight spot. The drama is almost over. The last act is about to commence. We must not lose our nerve now or slacken our vigilance. We both have come a long way. We must not fail at the last.'

Chapter Twenty-Nine

From the journal of John H. Watson

Carrying my new suitcase filled with freshly purchased clothes that I hoped would be sufficient for our sojourn to the Continent, I made my way down Platform Three of Victoria Station, heading for Carriage B of the Dover train, as I had been instructed by Sherlock Holmes. My heart sank when I observed that the carriage was already occupied by a venerable Italian priest. He gave me a brief greeting as I entered, and then returned to his contemplation of a book of prayer.

Stowing my luggage in the overhead rack, I stepped back out on to the platform, eager to catch a glimpse of my friend. In vain I searched among the group of travellers for the lithe figure of Sherlock Holmes. There was no sign of him. A chill of fear came over me, as I perceived that his absence could mean only one thing: some blow had befallen him during the day; Moriarty had caught up with him.

The porters were slamming all the doors in readiness for departure and the guard was ready with his whistle to send the engine on its way. Reluctantly, I clambered inside the carriage and slumped down in my seat.

'Don't look so glum, Watson. Everything is going according to plan.'

I turned in uncontrollable astonishment. The aged ecclesiastic had turned his face towards me. For an instant the wrinkles disappeared, the nose drew away from the chin, the lower lip ceased to protrude, and the mouth to mumble, the dull eyes regained their fire, and the drooping figure expanded. The next moment, the whole frame collapsed again and Holmes was gone as quickly as he had come.

'Great heavens!' I cried. 'How you startled me!'

Holmes grinned. 'Every precaution is still necessary. I have reason to believe they are hot upon our trail.' He rose from his seat and peered from the window. 'As I thought. See, Watson, see?'

There, some way down the platform, were two men running in a vain attempt to catch the moving train. I recognized them both: Colonel Sebastian Moran and Professor James Moriarty. Reaching the end of the platform, reluctantly they accepted the futility of their pursuit. They came to a halt and stood stern-faced, watching the train as it sped away.

'By the skin of our teeth, Watson. By the skin of our teeth. Despite all our precautions, you see we have cut it fine,' said Holmes, laughing. Throwing off the black cassock and hat which had formed his disguise, he packed them away in his luggage.

'But we made it,' I replied, my heart lightening at the thought. 'And as this is an express train, and the boat runs in conjunction with it, I should think we have shaken them off very effectively.'

Holmes lit his pipe before responding. 'My dear Watson, you do not imagine that if I were the pursuer I should allow myself to be beaten by such a slight obstacle as this?'

I shook my head.

'And neither will the Professor. This man is on the same intellectual plane as myself and has as much dogged determination in his pursuits as I have in mine.'

'What will he do?'

'Exactly what *I* should do.'

'Which is. . . ?'

'Engage a Special.'

'But that would take time.'

'Not too much time, with Moriarty's contacts, money and powers of persuasion. And our train stops for a while at Canterbury, and there is always a delay at the boat. I am sure he will catch up with us there.'

'What can we do?'

'We shall get out at Canterbury.'

'And then?'

'Well, we must make a cross-country journey to Newhaven, and so over to Dieppe. Moriarty will again do what I should do. He will travel on to Paris, track down our luggage and wait two days at the depot. In the mean time, we shall treat ourselves to a couple of carpet-bags and make our way at leisure to Switzerland, via Luxemburg and Basle.'

'You had this contingency all planned,' I smiled.

'Of course,' he said, sending a cloud of smoke spiralling to the luggage rack.

At Canterbury we alighted, only to find we had to wait an hour before we could get a train to Newhaven.

I was still gazing ruefully at the rapidly disappearing luggage van containing my brand new leather valise containing my brand new wardrobe, purchased earlier that day, when Holmes tugged at my sleeve and pointed up the line.

'Already, you see?' said he.

Far away, from among the Kentish woods, there rose a thin spray of smoke. A minute later, a carriage and an engine could be seen flying along the open curve which led to the station. We had hardly time to hide behind a pile of luggage abandoned on the platform before the Special passed with a rattle and a roar, beating a blast of hot air in our faces.

'There he goes,' said Holmes, as we watched the carriage swing and rock over the points. 'It seems that the Professor has underestimated me. It would have been a fine *coup-de-maître* if he had deduced how I would act once I was aware that he was on my track. But he didn't. It reveals a very satisfying weakness in his strategy. However, the vital question now is whether we take our dinner in the buffet here, or run the chance of starving before we reach Newhaven.'

We made our way to Brussels that night, and spent two days there, moving on our third day as far as Strasburg. On the Monday morning, Holmes telegraphed Inspector Patterson, and in the evening we found a reply waiting for us in our hotel. On opening it, Holmes swore vehemently, tore up the telegram and hurled it into the grate.

'I might have known it. Damned incompetence!'

I had rarely seen Holmes this angry. His normally pale features were suffused with the glow of anger.

'What is it?' I asked.

'He has escaped!'

'Moriarty?'

'They have secured the whole gang, with exception of its leader. He has given them the slip. Of course, when I left the country, there was no one intellectually competent to deal with him. But I did think I had put the whole game in Patterson's hands. That certainly alters cases. I think it best if you return to England now.'

'What on earth for?'

'Because you will find me an extremely dangerous companion now. The Professor's occupation is gone. He is extremely vulnerable if he returns to London. If I read his character right, he will devote the whole of his considerable energies to revenging himself on me. My demise will be his *raison d'être*. I certainly recommend you return to your wife and your practice at once.'

We sat in a Strasburg *salle-à-manger*, arguing the question for half an hour. I was hardly going to desert my friend now. Indirectly he had been responsible for cutting the bonds that bound me to Moriarty and granting me freedom. I also realized that, while the villain lived, isolated though he might be now, he still posed a threat to both Holmes and me. If Holmes was correct – as I believe he was – that Moriarty's sole desire now was to destroy Holmes, then it would not be too long before their paths crossed. I wanted to be there when that happened. Eventually, I convinced Holmes that I was going to stay to the bitter end.

That same night we resumed our journey, heading for Geneva. For a charming week, we wandered up the Valley of the Rhône, and then branching off at Leuk, we made our way over the Gemmi Pass, still deep in snow, and so by way of Interlaken, to Meiringen. It was a lovely trip, the dainty green of the spring below, the smooth virgin white of winter above; but it was clear to me that never for one instant did Holmes forget the shadow which lay across him. In the homely Alpine villages or in the lonely mountain passes, I could still tell by his quick glancing eyes and his sharp scrutiny of every face that passed us, that he was convinced that, walk where we would, we were never clear of the danger that dogged our footsteps.

Once, as we passed over the border of the melancholy Daubenese, a large rock which had dislodged from a ridge clattered down and roared into the lake behind us. In an instant, Holmes raced up to the ridge and, standing on the pinnacle, he craned his neck in every direction. It was in vain that our guide assured us that such a fall of rock was a common occurrence in the springtime. Holmes said nothing, but smiled sardonically with an air of a man who sees the fulfilment of that which he had expected.

And yet for all his watchfulness, he was never depressed. On the contrary, I can never recollect having seen him in such exuberant spirits. As we walked we conversed on many subjects, and Holmes both amused and amazed me by his knowledge and insight and also his ignorance. Any topic which bore no connection – however tenuous – with the detection of crime held no interest to him, and so he remained ignorant of it. How I smiled when he protested that he couldn't care a fig if the earth went around the moon or the other way around.

'Whichever is correct, it makes not a jot of difference to me or my work,' he said with warmth. 'It is of the greatest importance to store only the important facts, facts that can be of use to you, in the brain attic, otherwise you would have the useless facts elbowing out the useful ones.'

On arriving at the little village of Meiringen, we put up at the Englischer Hof kept by Peter Steiler the elder. That evening, we dined in the little restaurant. At first we spoke little, as though we

had talked out all conversation that was possible without referring to Moriarty. At one point, Holmes raised his wineglass in a
toast.

'To you, my dear Watson,' he said solemnly. 'Without you and your
support in these last days, I doubt if I would have achieved the
success in bringing down Moriarty's organization.'

I was too moved to respond in words. I just raised my glass in
acknowledgement of the sentiment, and took a drink.

'With this case,' Holmes continued, reflectively, 'I feel I have
reached the climax of my detective career. I think I may go so far as
to say that I have not lived in vain. If my record were closed tonight,
I could still survey it with equanimity. The air of London is the
sweeter for my presence. In the many cases in which I have been
actively involved, I do not believe I have ever used my powers on the
wrong side. I would certainly crown my career with the extinction of
the most dangerous and capable criminal in Europe.'

The word 'extinction' was voiced with a dark relish.

Our landlord spoke excellent English, having served for three
years as a waiter at the Grosvenor Hotel in London, and he came to
talk with us after we had finished our meal. I was very tired, so I
excused myself and headed for bed. Holmes seemed happy to stay
and chat with Herr Steiler, who was no doubt pleased to have the
opportunity to practise his English conversation.

We left the next day with the intention of crossing the hills and
spending the night at the hamlet of Rosenlaui. However, on Herr
Steiler's strict injunction, we were told that we should not on any
account fail to take a small detour in order to pass by the magnificent falls at Reichenbach.

It is indeed a fearful place. The torrent, swollen by the melting
snow, plunges into a terrible abyss, from which the spray rolls up
like the smoke from a burning house. The shaft into which the river
hurls itself is an immense chasm, lined by glistening coal-black
rocks, and narrowing down into a creaming, boiling pit of incalcula-
ble depth, which brims over and shoots the stream onward over its
jagged lip. The long sweep of green water roaring forever down, and
the thick flickering curtain of spray hissing forever upwards, turn a

man giddy with their constant whirl and clamour.

Holmes and I stood near the edge in rapt silence, peering down at the gleam of the breaking water far below us against the black rocks, and listening to the half-human shout which came booming up with the spray out of the abyss.

The path had been cut half-way round the falls to afford a complete view, but it ended abruptly, so that the tourist had to return the way he came. We had turned to do so when we saw a Swiss lad running along the path towards us. He clutched a letter in his hand.

'Doctor Watson!' he cried, above the roar of the falls, his eyes darting from Holmes to me and then back again.

'I am Watson,' I said, and he handed me the letter. It bore the mark of the Englischer Hof and was addressed to me by the landlord. It appeared that within a very few minutes of our leaving, an English lady had arrived who was in the last stages of consumption. She had wintered at Davos Platz and was journeying now to join her friends at Lucerne, when a sudden haemorrhage had overtaken her. It was thought she could hardly live a few hours, but it would be a great consolation to her to see an English doctor. Could I possibly return? Herr Steiler assured me in a postscript that he would look upon my compliance as a very great favour, since the lady absolutely refused to see a Swiss physician, and he could not but feel that he was incurring a great responsibility.

Holmes read the letter over my shoulder. 'You must go, old fellow. You cannot refuse the request of a fellow countrywoman dying in a strange land.'

I felt he was right, but I was reluctant to leave Holmes's side. He dismissed my concern with the wave of his hand.

'I will stay here a while longer, admiring the falls, and then make my way to Rosenlaui, where you can join me this evening at The Golden Cock.'

I agreed and sent the lad ahead of me to inform Steiler that I was on my way.

Holmes and I shook hands and parted. As I turned away, I saw my friend with his back against a rock and his arms folded, gazing down at the rush of water. There was something infinitely sad about his features.

As I made my way back down the path, doubt and suspicion clouded my mind. How did Steiler know I was a doctor? I had never communicated this fact to him. In fact, I had hardly spoken directly to him. Holmes, of course, might have told him – but for what purpose? Unless . . . unless it was in the creation of a ploy to call me away.

When I neared the bottom of the descent, I looked back. It was impossible from that position to see the falls, but I could see the curving path which wound over the hill and led to it. Along this path I observed a man walking rapidly. I could see his black figure clearly outlined against the green behind. I stopped in my tracks. There was no doubt in my mind that this man was Professor James Moriarty.

Suddenly it all became clear to me. The errand of mercy was a nonsense, a clever ruse created by Holmes and carried out with the collusion of Peter Steiler. It was meant to lure me away from Holmes, away from danger, so that my friend could face his foe, Professor James Moriarty, alone. He must have known that the hour was near when Moriarty would finally track us down. Perhaps he had already made enquiries at the Englischer Hof. Certainly Steiler could have confirmed that. I now saw that Sherlock Holmes was prepared to sacrifice his own life in meeting Moriarty and deter-mined to save mine. A rendezvous between two determined men on the edge of the terrible Reichenbach Falls could only end in one way.

With a beating heart, I raced back up the path towards the falls.

Chapter Thirty

A sense of calm had settled upon Sherlock Holmes as he leaned against the rock, gazing meditatively at the frenzied waters of the Reichenbach Falls. For the last few weeks, his mind and emotions had been as furious and disturbing as the powerful tide of water that roared down past him into the terrible chasm below, but now, suddenly, the tension and the worry had evaporated. He felt at peace with himself and his fate. The end of the affair was very near, and he was prepared for it. He was ready to sacrifice his own life to ensure the destruction of his mortal enemy. Once he had accepted that, all the inner turmoil, worry and anxiety seemed to disappear, and he was at peace with himself. After all, he was living on borrowed time. If it had not been for Watson, he would be a corpse already, shot by Scoular in his Baker Street rooms. On that occasion he had been caught unawares, with no contingency plans. This time it would be different.

He consulted his watch. He knew that he would not have long to wait. Once Moriarty observed Watson returning to Meiringen, he would put in an appearance.

Almost in accordance with his thoughts, a figure appeared some-way down the path. A tall man in a dark cloak walking vigorously. As he advanced and his face became visible, Holmes's heart skipped a beat. It was as he had deduced. It was the man he was expecting. It was Professor James Moriarty.

He was a handsome man, thought Holmes, although his features, now damp with the spray of the falls, were cold and cruel. His dark eyes glittered in triumph as he approached the detective.

'So, we meet at last, Mr Sherlock Holmes,' said the Professor.

Holmes smiled. 'Indeed we do. "Journeys end in lovers meeting."'

Moriarty gazed down at the swirling torrent and smiled. 'You have chosen a propitious location for this historic encounter. You realize, of course, there can be only one outcome.'

'You are the mathematician, but I had calculated that it could end in one of three possible ways – although I assure you my choice is narrowed down to one of two.'

'It was such a pity that you were so tenacious, Mr Holmes. You should have let it drop, you know. It would have been more sensible for yourself and kinder to your friends. Nevertheless, it has been an intellectual treat for me to see the way you have conducted the whole business. I do not think I could have handled the matter better myself.'

'I take that as a compliment. But it is the case that in certain situations one has little choice over one's actions. I could no more give up my pursuit of you than fly to the moon. It is an innate part of my nature to seek out and destroy the wrongdoer, the criminal in civilized society. I am driven, as no doubt you are driven, to fulfil a destiny.'

Moriarty's face turned into a sneer. 'Speeches. Well, let me respond simply by stating that it has been a fascinating duel between us, Mr Holmes. A stimulating game, but now the game is over and you must pay the forfeit.'

Holmes had been observing the Professor's movements very closely, and before Moriarty could pull his revolver from the folds of his cloak, Holmes leapt forward and grabbed his hand. For a moment the two men grappled, Moriarty holding the gun high in the air while Holmes secured an iron grip on his arm so that he could not bring it down. As they fought, they slithered on the mud nearer to the edge of the pathway. With Herculean effort, Holmes shook Moriarty's arm so fiercely that he was forced to relinquish his hold of the revolver and it flew into the air in an arc, far out across the chasm, and disappeared down into the smoky foam.

Moriarty retaliated by clasping his hands around the detective's neck, squeezing hard to crush his windpipe, while at the same time pushing him nearer and nearer to the edge. Holmes's feet slipped on the wet mud and he found his strength failing. Despite his efforts to dislodge Moriarty, the villain maintained his ferocious grip. Briefly wrenching his head sideways, Holmes glimpsed the cauldron of water boiling below him. He was now on the very edge of the precipice. Another foot and he would be over it, spinning into watery oblivion.

'Goodbye, Mr Sherlock Holmes,' cried Moriarty, his face contorted with hate, as he pushed harder. 'Goodbye.'

Chapter Thirty-One

From the journal of John H. Watson

When I reached the path which ran part of the way around the Reichenbach Falls, I saw that Holmes was in conversation with the dark stranger I had spied from afar, the stranger whom I was in no doubt was Professor Moriarty. The sense that both my friend and I had experienced throughout our sojourn, that our footsteps were being dogged, had proved to be true. And now at last Holmes's nemesis had caught up with him.

Slowly I crept forward, keeping close to the rock face so that Moriarty would not catch sight of me. Although I could not hear what was being said, because the roar of the falls drowned their words, both men appeared remarkably restrained in their attitude to each other. It was almost as though they were two old friends who had met by accident and were exchanging pleasantries, rather than an encounter between two implacable enemies. Only their strained faces betrayed the reality of the situation. And then suddenly, without warning, Holmes leaped forward and set upon Moriarty. I could see that the Professor had produced a gun, but thankfully Holmes managed to shake it from his grasp. As they grappled with each other, they moved inexorably nearer the edge of the path. Jerking my own revolver from my jacket pocket, I hurried up the path, but both men were so entwined in their struggle that I could not fire for fear of hitting Holmes. On reaching them, I saw that Moriarty was gaining the upper hand and was attempting to strangle Holmes while, at the same time, forcing him nearer the edge.

For a brief moment, I froze with indecision and fear, and then some innate instinct governed my actions. Without quite knowing what I was doing, I rushed forward and grabbed Moriarty from behind, pulling him back with me on to the path. So sudden and surprising was this action, that he automatically dragged Holmes back with him as well – back from the brink of oblivion. Both men collapsed on the ground. But it was not long before they were on their feet again. Taking stock of the situation, something approaching fear flashed into Moriarty's dark, malevolent eyes. Instinctively, Holmes and I acted in unison. Each grabbing hold of one of the Professor's arms, we dragged him backwards to the edge of the path. As he realized what was happening to him, what we were about to do, Moriarty's eyes widened in panic, an emotion alien to him, and he roared in terror, but his cry was swallowed by the thunder of the falls. He struggled violently, his body twisting and kicking in a desperate effort to wrench himself free of our firm grasp. But we did not flinch from our task.

At last we delivered him to the very brink. With a concerted effort, Sherlock Holmes and I flung the Professor over into the falls. Resembling a great bat-like creature, his cloak spreading like wings, he sailed out over the chasm, desperately clawing the air as if some miracle would allow him to clamber back on to terra firma. He seemed for a moment to be held in suspended animation, before slipping slowly from sight as the rising spray enveloped him as in a shroud. And then he was gone. Gone from sight; gone from our lives. Swallowed whole by the gushing torrent of the Reichenbach Falls.

Both Holmes and I staggered back from that dreadful chasm and gazed at the thrashing water for what seemed like ages. Then, strangely in unison once more, we burst out laughing. It was unstable, unnatural laughter – it was the laughter of release and guilt. Our bodies shook with hysterical mirth, and tears ran down our cheeks. In thinking back on that moment, I have tried to analyse my own feelings and why I should have responded in such a way at so dark a moment; but the experience was unique, and it is so very difficult to find a point of emotional reference. Certainly a burden had been lifted from my life and that of my dear friend, and together we had rid society of one of its most malevolent pariahs, but in doing so we had taken the law into our own hands. We had ourselves strayed from the path of righteousness. It must have been these conflicting emotions that helped to create our unnatural laughter; but I am sure there were other elements involved, which a more clever man than I could explain.

After a time we lapsed into silence, our eyes still locked on the gushing torrent of the Reichenbach Falls. It was Holmes who finally brought us back to some kind of normality.

'Now we must part,' he said, in a cold matter-of-fact fashion. 'We have achieved our goal, but at a cost to ourselves and our consciences. It would be better, for the time being at least, if the world believed that both Moriarty and I had perished in the falls. You can record the matter as such, thus absolving yourself of any part in the villain's demise . . .'

He held up his hand in a peremptory fashion as I attempted to interrupt.

'I need a rest from crime, Watson. There will be no real challenges now. After all, who could compare to Moriarty? I need to absent myself from the bleat of the distressed client for a while. I shall travel, study and learn. You will go back to London and report my death. And carry on with your own life. In time, when the dust has settled and I feel the urge to return to damp and foggy London and to Baker Street, I will return. Well, I *might* return. The future is uncertain, and I relish that.'

'You have planned this.'

'As much I was able to, yes. I knew that if I could destroy Moriarty and survive, I would feel free at last to follow some of my own desires, to extend my own education. When I am wiser and more fulfilled, it is quite probable that I shall take up my lens again and study the work of the criminal mind. Now go; go to the Englischer Hof and tell them the terrible news.'

'And you?'

'I shall disappear. Do not ask me where; I do not intend to lie to you.'

I felt a lump form in my throat. Here was a man I had deceived – or believed I had deceived – who still accepted me as a friend. And now that our friendship had been sealed irrevocably by the most terrible of acts, he was about to disappear from my life for ever. A deep sadness overwhelmed me.

Holmes smiled sympathetically. 'My dear Watson, do not look so crestfallen. We shall meet again, I feel sure. But for now, go. Go and do not look back.'

I did as he asked.

Extract from 'The Final Problem' by John H. Watson, first published in the *Strand Magazine*, 1893:

An examination by experts leaves little doubt that a personal contest between the two men ended, as it could hardly fail to end in such a situation, in their reeling over, locked in each other's arms. Any attempt at recovering the bodies was absolutely hopeless, and there, deep down in that dreadful cauldron of swirling foam, will lie for all time the most danger- ous criminal and the foremost champion of law of their generation.

The Swiss youth was never found again, and there can be no doubt that he was one of the numerous agents that Moriarty kept in his employ. As to the gang, it will be in the memory of the public how completely the evidence which Holmes had accumulated exposed their organization, and how heavily the hand of the dead man weighed upon them. Of their terrible chief, few details came out during the proceedings, and if I have now been compelled to make a clear statement of his career, it is due to those injudicious champions who have endeavoured to clear his memory by attacks upon him whom I shall ever regard as the best and wisest man whom I have ever known.

Epilogue

Watson did return to London, carrying with him the fiction that Sherlock Holmes had perished along with Professor James Moriarty at the base of the Reichenbach Falls. He was reunited with his beloved wife, Mary, and soon resumed his medical career. Although he slipped back into the domestic scene with comparative ease after his dark experiences, there was always an empty corner in his heart now that Holmes and detective work were no longer part of his life. He relived his adventures in the stories he published in the *Strand Magazine*, but it wasn't the same as the real thing.

Watson had hoped to hear from Holmes after a while, but there was no news from his friend. Mrs Hudson had disappeared, but Mycroft kept on his brother's rooms as a second bolthole for himself. Mycroft was secure in the knowledge that of all Moriarty's gang, he alone had escaped. No one, not even his detective brother, had known or even suspected his involvement with the Napoleon of Crime.

Watson's life darkened even further the following winter, when Mary succumbed to a bout of pneumonia and passed away two days after Christmas. Watson viewed this blow as a kind of divine punishment for his past deceptions and failings.

And then, one day, three years after the Reichenbach incident, an old bookseller walked into his consulting-room – an old bookseller who, removing his disguise, revealed himself as a familiar figure to Doctor John H. Watson.

Sherlock Holmes had returned.